What people are saying about …

taking tuscany

"*Taking Tuscany* is a lively ride through the Italian countryside. Life with A. J. and her Italian-American family in their inherited castle is all that an adventurous story should be. How can you go wrong with horseback-riding nuns, a mock Olympics, and a hint of amoré? Renée Riva's *Taking Tuscany* took me!"

Susanna Aughtmon, author of *All I Need Is Jesus and a Good Pair of Jeans*

"I've longed to spend more time with A. J. and the Degulio family since turning the last page of *Saving Sailor. Taking Tuscany,* the heartwarming and humorous sequel, was just what I needed. Bravo, Renée! Faith and family are everything."

Leslie Gould, award-winning author of four novels, including *Scrap Everything*

"Renée Riva creates moving multidimensional images of everyday people who are at their worst uproariously funny, and at their best, transcendent. In a beautifully textured setting, Riva weaves them into a jubilant coming-of-age tale about the true meaning of family. *Taking Tuscany* is a celebration of the ordinary that will leave you breathless with laughter and tears."

Sylvia Dorham, author, essayist, and voice-over artist whose credits include Riva's *Saving Sailor*

taking tuscany

taking tuscany

a novel

renée riva

David C Cook®
transforming lives together

TAKING TUSCANY
Published by David C. Cook
4050 Lee Vance View
Colorado Springs, CO 80918 U.S.A.

David C. Cook Distribution Canada
55 Woodslee Avenue, Paris, Ontario, Canada N3L 3E5

David C. Cook U.K., Kingsway Communications
Eastbourne, East Sussex BN23 6NT, England

David C. Cook and the graphic circle C logo
are registered trademarks of Cook Communications Ministries.

This story is a work of fiction. All characters and events are the product of the author's
imagination. Any resemblance to any person, living or dead, is coincidental.

LCCN 2009922187
ISBN 978-1-4347-6777-6

© 2009 Renée Riva
Published in association with the literary agency of
Alive Communications, Inc., 7680 Goddard Street, Suite 200,
Colorado Springs, CO 80920. www.alivecommunications.com

The Team: Don Pape, Jamie Chavez, Amy Kiechlin, and Jaci Schneider
Cover Design: The DesignWorks Group, Jason Gabbert
Cover Photo: Shutterstock and iStockphoto
Interior Design: Sarah Schultz

Printed in the United States of America
First Edition 2009

1 2 3 4 5 6 7 8 9 10

022709

Alla mia famiglia
con amore

Author's Note

Several years ago my Italian grandmother passed away and left our family an invaluable gift. Her last request was that my mom and dad and all five of us kids go visit the Old Country, her homeland. She also left us the means to do so. Being the obedient family that we were, we promptly granted her final wish: spring in Tuscany, a hilltop villa with a pool, and our family under one roof. There is something about visiting the origin of one's roots that is good for the soul. As man is made of dust, I got to see what kind of dust I was made of. Some of that dust is now sprinkled among these pages, setting the scene and breathing life into this story.

Somewhere between writing my first novel, *Saving Sailor,* and its sequel, *Taking Tuscany,* we lost our dad, Santo Benjamin. One day he was here, the next day, gone. I'm pretty sure God found him up there in heaven somewhere, but the rest of us down here are a little lost without him. You see, Santo was to my mom what Sonny was to Sophia in *Saving Sailor*—the love of her life. And my dad was to me and my four siblings what Daddy was to A. J. and her four siblings—our everything. To be perfectly honest, we are more than a little miffed that someone so full of life and love and laughter should be taken from us before what we considered "his time." As far as we knew, he was planning to go snow skiing the next day, not to heaven. But who are we to question God in such matters? He did, after all, come up with the idea of people, and families, and we must give credit that He knows what He's doing with us—and sometimes we don't.

My father had a motto in life that was passed down from his father. *La famiglia è tutto.* Family is everything. And so it is. My grandmother's last words to my mom were, "Keep the family together." And she and my father did.

From the time I was just a wee thing, toddling around the bocce ball court, the greatest blessing in my life has been belonging to our Italian family. Over the years it has been just one festive holiday after another … Grandma's homemade ravioli and polenta, bocce ball tournaments, Grandpa's Wrigley's Spearmint gum.

Sadly that first generation who came over on the boat has all passed on. But their legacy lives. *Taking Tuscany* is a tribute to those who knew what mattered in life and showed us the way. I am anticipating a great reunion up yonder (as A. J. would say) one day. For now, we have been left behind to carry the torch. May God help us. Until we meet again …

Acknowledgments

Apart from divine intervention there are two big reasons I was given the privilege of writing this book: Beth Jusino and Don Pape. You are my heroes and, in A. J.'s book, deserve to be sainted.

My literary angel and friend, Sandi Winn, you are worth your weight in *gnocchi* (Italian potato dumplings). Thank you for your help and friendship.

Molto grazie to my Italian wordsmiths: Immacolata Errico from Bella Italia; Conor Hogan, the Italian-speaking Irishman; and the world's best Italian chef, Nicola Calamari.

Mom, you already knew I couldn't spell, and now you know I can't type any better. Thank you for being my official proofreader, painful as it is.

My husband, Bear, um . . . I'd be a mess without you, as would be this book. *Sono innamorato pazza mente dite.* I'm crazy in love with you.

A *grandioso* thanks to my editors, Jamie Chavez and Jaci Schneider, for knowing what I meant to say … and more. And to everyone at David C. Cook who helped to bring *Taking Tuscany* to the people. Y'all are like family to me … or will be by the time we're done.

An *enormi* thanks to my faithful readers, especially my huge fan club: Alec Chunn and Logan Winn. *Grazie* … once again.

Starbucks. What can I say? You kept me awake.

Forever and foremost, Jesus, my Lord and Savior, thank You for letting me write stories. It is an honor and a privilege, and I am grateful. *Sia gloria a Dio.* To God be the glory.

From the shores of Indian Island...

(Excerpt from *Saving Sailor*)

Indian Lake, Idaho, July 1968

I'm sittin' in a rowboat in the middle of Indian Lake with my dog, Sailor. He's a collie-shepherd mix with one brown eye, and one that looks like a marble. He's wearin' a bright orange life jacket, as any seaworthy dog should when playing shipmate. Sometimes we pretend we're on the high seas awaitin' capture from handsome rogue pirates. But today we're just driftin'.

The oars lie on the floorboard of the wood dinghy; a slight breeze sweeps over us, rufflin' up Sailor's long fur. We're just soakin' up the sun, and floatin' by the island where our family spends our summers.

⁓⁓⁂⁓⁓

My mama is reclinin' on the dock in her new Hollywood sunglasses. She's got a paperback novel in one hand and a glass of iced tea in the other. My big sister, Adriana, is slathering on baby oil, singin' along to her transistor radio. My big brother, J. R., short for Sonny Jr., is gutting a fish over on the big rocks, while the younger twins, Benji and Dino, are still tryin' to catch their first fish of the day.

All of this is goin' on, while at the same time I'm in the middle of a conversation with God:

"... And so, Lord, if we get to pick what age we'll be in heaven, I choose nine years old, because I am havin' the best year of my life. I know I say that every year, but this time I mean it. And next year, if I change my mind, don't believe me. I promise it will always be nine."

⚜

I have this feelin' deep down inside that I will never change my mind. I just don't see how it can get any better than driftin' with my dog on a sunny afternoon, goin' wherever the wind takes us …

... to the Tuscan hills of Italy

Letters from Tuscany

May 10, 1972

Dear Dorie,

I'm sorry it's taken me so long to write. In response to your letter: Yes, I know I've only sent you picture postcards for the past three years. I was waiting until I had something good to say! What can I tell you? We are definitely not in Kansas anymore, Toto.

You asked how I like school ... I can hardly wait for summer. Changing schools two weeks before the school year ends ranks right up there with bashing my head against the rocks on Indian Lake. For starters, Annalisa Tartini, the queen bee of Macchiavelli, has already declared war on me for asking her friend Bianca where the art room is. She broke away from the group to show me, and has been snubbed by them ever since. Annalisa even came up with a special nickname for me. I'm so tired of being called a Yankee I could scream! As if I didn't stand out enough already. In cookie terms it's like being a vanilla wafer in a box of chocolate biscotti.

To add to the fun, I have to use my formal name at school, so when I'm not being called a Yankee, I'm Angelina—oh, joy. No one knows me as A. J. except for my family. In Italian that's "Aya Jaya." I don't know what's worse—Aya Jaya or Angelina. Just to clarify, this entire move has been a disaster.

I tried to warn everyone (*before* Mama talked Daddy into uprooting our happy American family and transplanting us onto foreign soil eighty million miles from home) that, according to the experts, these would be the most traumatic years of my entire life. In light of cultural differences alone, it was clearly not the best time to move a child like me halfway around the world—especially without my dog. Did anyone listen to me? All I got out of my sympathetic mother was, "A. J., cut the drama and get on the plane."

No one else in my family seems to have noticed we've moved. At least they look Italian—especially Adriana. She is the reason I had to go to a girls' school. She always drew so much attention from the male species, Daddy decided to send us both to Saint Dominique's. A lot of good that did. The boy's school was right across the campus from us, and the boys were forever sneaking over to spy on her. She was the campus goddess—an Italian-American beauty queen. They all went mad over her. And all the Italian girls hated her for it and wanted to run her out of town.

To help us both out of our misery, I secretly sent a box of her photographs off to a modeling agency, and the next thing we knew, an agent from Models of Milan showed up on our doorstep. Adriana moved to Milan as soon as she graduated. At least this way, she'll get paid to get gawked at.

As for me, they're not hiring blonde, freckle-faced midgets right now, so it looks like I'll just be hanging out all summer at our crumbling castle on the hill with the cracked swimming pool.

Wish you were here,

A. J.

May 15, 1972

Dear Danny,

How's Sailor? Here's what's new since my last letter—well, nothing's really new in this medieval town, but as of last week, I am no longer attending the Catholic girls' school. It has something to do with being accused of nearly burning down Saint Dominique's Academy of Perpetual Holiness. I now attend Scuola Media Superiore Macchiavelli—the Italian version of high school. I was already a year ahead of the Italian school system for starting Kindergarten a year earlier than they start in Italy. On top of that Daddy had me take the upper education exam when he pulled me out of Saint Dominique's. He was convinced I'd learned enough in private schooling to start the public high school early. I miraculously passed, hallelujah! For once in my life I'm ahead of my time! I plan to be out of here and back on the island the day I turn eighteen. Can't wait to see Sailor!

The sudden switch in schools was due to being in the wrong place at the wrong time. I was in the girls' loo last week when Daniela and Francesca were in the next stall over smoking a cigar. When the smoke hit Sister Giovanni's nostrils, I was the only one left in the restroom. By the time I convinced them it wasn't me, it was too late.

Daniela made up a big lie about Daddy sending me to school with a box of cigars to sell to kids so we could afford to attend private school. She said they only bought the cigar from me because they felt sorry for our family. Of course, they also said they lit it but didn't really smoke it—which is why it was still burning when it caught the trash can on fire.

Daddy decided it was a good time to pull us out when the head schoolmaster called and asked if the cigar story was true. He said if the faculty was really that dense, he had to question their teaching ability.

Little do parents realize the impact their actions have on the life of a child. Mine, in particular. Picture my life as a snow globe; inside you'll find a girl, a school, a few friends, enemies, teachers, and lunch tables—all moveable pieces.

After the shake-up of 1968, it took nearly two years to learn the Italian language, make a few friends, and establish my place in the lunchroom. Just when it seemed the blizzard was beginning to settle, that giant hand reached down again and shook that globe to Kingdom come. Now picture the girl swirling around, upside down; new school, new friends, new enemies, new lunchroom status ... round and round and round she goes, where she'll land, nobody knows. Just when I was getting used to being "the new weird kid" at St. Dominique's, now I'm "the new weird kid" all over again. I thought Daniela was stuck up ... you should meet Annalisa.

So how's life on the island?

Wish I was there,

A. J.

P.S. I've completely lost my Southern accent since moving here, but my Italian ain't half bad.

1

All Greek to me

"A. J., come over here and tell me something."

"What, Mama?" I make my way over to the big picture window in Mama's new guest villa.

"What is the first thing you notice when you look out this window?"

"A blue villa."

Mama grabs my arm and escorts me into the bedroom. "And this window?"

"A blue villa."

She grabs my arm again and pulls me into the bathroom. "And this window?"

"A blue villa."

"Exactly!" This time, instead of my arm, she grabs the peach guest towels off the rack and hurls them at the window. Then she runs into the bedroom and throws the new guest pillows at the bedroom window. Out on the horizon Uncle Nick's blue villa is basking in the sunset over Tuscany.

"How am I supposed to act gracious at Aunt Genevieve's birthday party, knowing the opening of my guest villa will be undermined by that blue monstrosity on the hill?"

"Oh, Mama, I wouldn't take it personally. Uncle Nick just likes the color blue."

Mama looks at me like I have lost my marbles. "Just likes the color blue? A. J., nobody in his right mind *paints* his villa blue. That is the charm of Italy—rustic, *natural* stone structures on hilltops. You don't take a beautiful historic monastery and paint it putrid blue."

"Maybe your guests won't notice it."

"Won't notice it? How could anyone *not* notice?"

I turn my gaze back out the window and cock my head in every angle possible. "Maybe they'll notice the poppies instead."

Mama gives me the exaggerated eye roll. "Poppies, schmoppies. Sorry, little Miss Pollyanna, but from my perspective, the only thing out there is one big ugly blue villa …"

Daddy walks into the room, looks at Mama, then glances at the pillows and towels lying on the floor. He looks back at Mama with a hopeful smile. "Does this mean we get to stay home?"

I'm sure Daddy would like nothing better than to skip the whole encounter with the relatives. Sometimes Uncle Nick is just too much for him. Unfortunately Uncle Nick is married to Mama's sister, Genevieve, who is turning forty-five tonight.

"No, it does not mean we get to skip the birthday party," Mama says. "I haven't had the chance to play Sofia Loren for the Greek relatives yet. The Italians sure fell for it at Adriana's photo shoot in Rome last month. *Miss Loren* was born in Rome, you know."

Daddy and I look at each other. *"We know,"* we say in unison. She's only told us that five hundred times since we moved here.

Mama marches out of her guest villa back to *Bel Castello*, our rustic, run-down *natural* stone castle, to get ready for the party. It's not a good sign that Mama is on her way to a party in her present frame of mind. The good news is Grandma Juliana—who insists we call her *Nonna* now that we're in Italy—won't be joining us tonight. She is still under the illusion that Uncle Nick is Italian, and would not be happy to discover the truth. She has something against marrying outside of "our rich Italian heritage." She also has a problem with Greeks. At the moment, she's not the only one. Mama thought Uncle Nick was joking when he mentioned his plans to paint his villa blue. But … apparently not.

After slipping into my mandated outfit and looking in the mirror, I head straight to Mama's room to try to talk her into letting me wear my denim overalls instead. As expected, the answer is no.

Mama is making her Miss Loren debut in a poppy red pantsuit and is sporting the latest Sofia Loren signature haircut. There's usually a movie-star buff in every crowd. We're all counting on one to notice Mama tonight so she can play her Sofia/Sophia autograph game. That's all it will take to shake her foul mood.

One thing Mama has going for her—she looks more like Sofia Loren than the real deal. People notice her almost everywhere she goes. And when they don't, she still looks great. Her sister, Genevieve, looks good *most* of the time but has these hips that won't quit. Sometimes they look like they need to quit growing.

"Mama, how is it that you and Aunt Genevieve are sisters, but she's always gaining and losing weight, and you just stay the same size?" She changes every time I see her.

"A. J., let me put it to you like this; inside every skinny woman, there is a chubby one fighting to come out. There's one main reason my sister battles weight. She likes to cook. Let that be a lesson to you. The more you can stay out of the kitchen, the better you'll look."

"But how do you find a husband who doesn't want someone who likes to cook?"

Mama smiles. "Watch this." She calls to Daddy in the bathroom, where he's getting dressed. "Hey, Sonny?"

"Yeah?"

"Would you rather have a great big wife who likes to cook for you all the time, or a slender bombshell who can't cook?"

"A slender bombshell who *can* cook."

"That's not an option. How about a slender bombshell who cooks occasionally?"

"That's you, baby. I'll take it."

Mama looks at me. "See that? He thinks he got a good deal—we both win. A good marriage is about making compromises you can both live with."

Daddy comes out of the bathroom wearing a Don Ho–style V-necked shirt and black slacks. He wanted to wear his old park-ranger pants from his days at Indian Lake State Park, so he could at least be comfortable. But Mama handed him the Don Ho outfit instead.

"So, Mama, where's the compromise on what Daddy's wearing tonight?"

Mama looks at the park-ranger outfit lying on the bed. "Some things are nonnegotiable."

We arrive on the marble staircase of the blue villa at sundown. Since Mama wouldn't let me wear my overalls to the party, I'm stuck in this gauzy getup that looks more like a gunnysack than a dress. Another nonnegotiable. If they decide to hold potato-sack races tonight, I'm all set. According to Adriana it's the latest fashion. Adriana is presently driving back from Milan and planning to make an appearance later tonight. That's one thing about Adriana; she never just shows up—she *makes an appearance.*

Ever since I turned thirteen last summer, Adriana and Mama have been running a conspiracy to turn me into a lady. I already have to wear a hideous blue and green plaid uniform three-fourths of the year, so with school finally out, I feel perfectly justified wearing nothing but overalls all summer long. Mama keeps threatening to burn them, but I have a backup pair just in case. One fashion model and a Hollywood-movie-star imposter is enough in one family. Someone needs to bring some normalcy into this picture.

Mama pulls her Hollywood sunglasses from her purse and slips them on. My Don Ho daddy ascends the marble staircase singing "Tiny Bubbles," with the twins singing backup. In case I didn't feel different enough as the only blonde amidst my *famiglia dei bronzo,* I can only imagine how I'll blend in with the Greek side of the family.

Daddy stops singing the minute he reaches the top step, which lands us directly in front of the white stone pillars lining the entrance to this Grecian palace. "Hmm, perhaps I should have worn my toga," Daddy says. We've been to Uncle Nick's villa a number of times before, but not since he turned it into a blue and white replica of Aphrodite's palace. You almost expect to be greeted by a set of palace guards, followed by Aphrodite herself.

"Well, look what the cat dragged in!" Uncle Nick bellows, with his thick booming accent. Uncle Nick is a hairy version of Hercules; a handsome Greek face on the body of a grizzly. He gives Daddy a hearty whack on the back, followed by his dreaded holy kiss on the cheek and a bear hug.

Mama skirts around Daddy and makes her way to her sister. I'm next in line for the traditional greeting. After having the air squeezed out of me by Uncle Nick, I get to endure Aunt Genevieve's Rigatoni Red lipstick all over my cheeks. *"Principessa,"* she says, squeezing my face between her hands until I resemble a clown fish rather than a princess.

"Come meet the rest of the family!" Uncle Nick slaps Daddy on the back again and herds us all inside.

Oh, whoa. Apparently they've imported a few more relatives since the last gathering. We may be the *only* Italian family here. Before I know what's happening, someone grabs my hand and pulls me into this circle of loud, dipping, kicking Greeks dancing the *kalamatianos.* I have watched my cousins dance the *kalamatianos* at holidays, but I have never joined in—and now I have no idea what I'm doing. At the moment, I'm just keeping my feet moving to avoid being dragged to death. As I'm pulled along, Dino grabs Daddy's camera. "A. J., smile!"

A flash goes off as I'm yelling, "I'm gonna ream ya!"

He laughs and takes another shot.

Just what I need—another means to further my already botched reputation in this town. *Round and round and round we go …*

My eyes catch a glimpse of Adriana as I whirl by the grand entrance. She is *making her appearance* in a shimmering silver and gold getup. All eyes are on her, as usual. This is one of those times I'm really happy to see her. "Adriana! Over here!"

The guy who's holding my hand looks at me.

"My sister!" I yell, wondering if he understands English. The next thing I know, every guy in the place is yelling, "Adriana! Over here!"

She finally spots me and cuts in line beside me. Not one to miss a beat, Adriana starts kicking her legs up, doing the cancan. "C'mon A. J., even you know this one."

We both start kicking our legs in sync with each other. Before you know it, the guy next to Adriana starts to join in, and so on down the line, until we have the entire circle dancing the cancan.

Finally the music comes to an end, and the feast is announced. I feel like a Gumby doll whose arms and legs have been stretched beyond normal limits. Wobbling my way out of the crowd to the patio, I'm faced with the horrific sight of a skinned lamb, rotating on a spit. *Oh, lovely.* I happen to be an avid animal lover—especially of *live* animals with their skins on. *Buon appetito!*

Someone in the crowd finally notices "Sofia." He yells something in Greek and I hear the words *Sofia Loren,* and suddenly all eyes shift to Mama. Me and Daddy and Adriana make our escape to one of the balcony tables—a good distance from the sizzling carcass. As soon as Dino and Benji show up, we send them around as scouts to bring us food. I make them recite the order back to me before sending them off.

"Little spinach-and-cheese triangles, baklava, and olives," Dino repeats.

"No lamb, no hummus, no mint jelly," Benji adds.

We've been through this before and have learned by experience what to eat and what not to eat at these functions.

Daddy asks Adriana how she liked her trip to Rome. She and Mama went together for Adriana's first photo shoot.

"Rome was great—right up until Mama went off on her Sofia Loren tangent. She insisted on signing her name for every autograph nut who came along. I must have heard 'I can't let my fans down' a hundred times."

Sounds like Mama.

Then Adriana says she loves the runway work, even though some of the designers are a little on the unusual side.

Speaking of unusual, Cousin Nicky stops by our table long enough to brag about his latest hot rod. "Hey, did you guys happen to notice the little red Lamborghini parked out front? That's my new baby." He rolls up his tailored shirtsleeves, most likely to reveal the glitzy gold watch on his scrawny arm.

"I thought you had an Alfa Romeo?" Heard all about it on his sixteenth birthday.

"Yeah, well, I totaled that baby. Just as well. My dad's going to let me start racing at the track with the 'Ghini."

Spiffy. Behind his tailored clothes and hot car, he's still your basic dweeb. But Cousin Stacy has lost a ton of weight and looks great. Says she won some awards for her poetry at L' Università di Firenze. I may be a tinge jealous—I'm pretty sure she's telling us the truth this time. She did go through a lying spell—for about ten years—but at age twenty, I think she may have finally outgrown the big fib phase.

The scout twins finally return with plates loaded up with food. Some of this stuff we've never seen before.

"Dare you to go first," Benji says to Dino.

"Double dare you," Dino shoots back.

As usual Benji falls for being the guinea pig. He dives right in ...

"*Ewww.*" He immediately leans over the balcony and spits it out.

Daddy's appalled and checks to make sure no one is sitting down below. "Who in the world raised you, boy?"

"It looked like it should taste good," Benji says.

We all like the baklava and send the boys back to fill up one more plate of that alone.

It doesn't take long before a couple of distant cousins of the male gender notice Adriana and make their way over to our table. They introduce themselves—Demetrios and Adonis—and try out some of their limited English on us. "Hello, how you are?"

"I am thank you, fine," I reply, and laugh—until Daddy gives me *the glare.*

Before long we're actually able to make some conversational headway with Demetrios and Adonis. We're even starting to enjoy their company when we're interrupted by escalating voices on the next balcony over. No need to look to know whose voice that is.

"All I am trying to say, Gen, is nobody in Italy *paints* a villa *cobalt blue*—apart from maybe a beach villa in Portofino. But this is Tuscany, and my guest hotel business depends on my ability to provide tourists with a pleasant view of the Tuscan landscape. Your color scheme does *not* go with the natural shade of the land."

The Italian hands begin to fly. "So whose business is it anyway what color we paint our villa?"

"Oh, for the love of Pete, only everybody who has to look at it. We're a hilltop over from you, and it stands out like a sore thumb."

"Is that so? What do you expect us to do, sandblast the whole thing just for you?"

"Sandblast it, whitewash it … whatever it takes."

Aunt Genevieve plants her hands on her big hips and says, "Well then, *little sister*, why don't you take that pretty little Sofia Loren face of yours on home if you can't be a gracious guest in *my* home on *my* birthday? And pull your fancy little lace curtains shut while you're at it."

"Well, I think I'll do just that."

Now that the main attraction of the party is my mama arguing with the birthday girl, Daddy seizes the moment and grabs Mama's hand. Before she can utter one more word, he hustles us all downstairs. "C'mon, kids, time to go." Not one to miss a good reason for leaving early, he herds us toward the door. But not before Uncle Nick notices. "Hey, you're not leaving, are you?"

"I'm sorry, Nick, but I'm afraid we are. Sophia's had an awfully long week trying to get the guesthouse ready for summer travelers," Daddy replies, without stopping.

"But we're just about to crack open a little *ouzo*."

"Another good reason to leave now," J. R. whispers. We've seen what "a little *ouzo*" can do at these gatherings.

"Oh, let them go," Aunt Genevieve remarks, coming down the stairs. "They don't care for our new color scheme anyway."

Uncle Nick looks at us as if someone just said we don't like chocolate. "You don't like blue?"

"Uh, we like blue," Daddy says. "Sophia's just concerned that it kind of stands out in the view from her new guesthouse."

Uncle Nick looks at Mama, then at Daddy. "Well, if that isn't the pot calling the kettle black …"

Daddy stops in his tracks and faces Uncle Nick. "How do you mean?"

"Well, Sonny, we've had to put up with looking at your old ruins for over three years now. We sit out here on our balcony night after night, wondering when you're going to put a little work into that place of yours."

Daddy's jaw begins to tighten. In a low, firm voice, he says, "For your information, Nick, the boys and I have been working our tails off on our property—as well as on a number of other properties. You might recall that's what I do for a living."

"Sure, I remember. So what's the holdup?"

Daddy takes a deep breath. "It takes time to restore dwellings that are centuries old. Most of the work takes place on the inside before it is evident on the outside. We've all worked very hard trying to get Sophie's place open for the summer season, and are concerned over her ability to draw guests—given the view."

"Sonny, you're my brother-in-law, and I love your family, but I think you're taking this whole thing a little too seriously. If you're really concerned about your customers objecting to our blue villa, your best bet is to advertise in a few Greek travel magazines. There's not a Greek I know of who wouldn't love to look out those windows and see a replica of a Grecian palace bathed in their national colors." Uncle Nick shakes his head. "I don't know, it almost feels to me like this may have more to do with a little jealousy than anything else."

The veins in Daddy's neck start to pound, which happens every time we spend too much time with Uncle Nick. Nudging him gently with my shoulder, I take hold of his hand. "Daddy," I whisper, "I think it's time to go."

Daddy squeezes my hand back. "I think you're right, A. J." Then he turns and leads our family out of the big blue monstrosity on the hill. *Arrivederci.*

2

Il mio Bel Castello
(My Beautiful Castle)

Bel Castello is the name of the villa Nonna inherited from her great-uncle, Bruno. He's the reason we are here. Because he died. The only glitch was Nonna failed to tell us the true condition of her "charming little castle" when she insisted we come to Tuscany to live with her. Daddy has come to realize that *charming* is just another word for *really old*. It has been nothing but *lavoro, lavoro, lavoro*—work, work, work—since we got here. Mama's guest villa has already taken three years to fix up. The castle was barely even livable before Daddy went to work on it. Now it's next in line for renovations, which, from the looks of it, should take the rest of our lives.

There is *one* thing that has worked in my favor since we moved here. I called dibs on the room in the top of the castle—the round tower room, three stories up. Uncle Bruno sold off nearly all of the land surrounding Bel Castello before he died, so Nonna inherited just the castle and a guest villa on a hilltop. Included in the deal were some nice cypress trees, fruit trees, a small olive grove, and one cracked Italian-tile swimming pool.

Once we agreed to move here, Nonna signed the whole estate over to Mama because she said she'd rather it all be Mama's headache to care for—as long as Mama feeds her until she dies. Mama does much more than feed her. I think Nonna got the easier end of the deal.

Bel Castello is rather small as far as castles go, but it's still a castle. Rumor has it the castle was built for the daughter of an emperor way back in the chariot days. In a sense I guess I could consider myself somewhat of a princess, if I wanted to stretch it a little. I'm keeping a princess journal for the times I feel like stretching it.

Princess journal entry: High spring on the crest of summer
spring + summer = spummer
*add "spummer" to dictionary

Spummer from My Castle Window

From my *bella vista* I see nothing but green hills that roll all the way down the valley. Spring is the best surprise of all. Scads of bright poppies burst into color from here to infinity. Like red birthday sprinkles on a green frosted cake, they bring the hills back to life after a long, barren winter.

With the coming of summer, hilltops will soon shine with sun-drenched villas the color of orange Creamsicles (with the exception of one blue villa in the not-far-enough distance).

My castle tower is where I indulge in my three favorite pastimes: reading, writing, and *philosopholizing. Another A. J.-ism for the dictionary. That's phil-o-soph-o-li-zing: being philosophical + analyzing = philosopholizing. In other words the world according to A. J. Sometimes there are just no good words to describe what it is I'm trying to say. I'm a word person and, I am sorry to say, Mr. Webster does not always

provide the word I'm trying to come up with, so I make it up,
right there on the spot.

I have my own dictionary started with about fifty of my
own words so far. Mama and Daddy call my words A. J.-isms.
It won't surprise me to see a few of them in a real dictionary
someday. Especially if the novel I'm working on becomes a best
seller. People will want to know what some of the words I made
up in my novel really mean. And I'll be able to say, "Look that
one up in your Funk & Wagnalls!"

My biggest fear about being so high up in this tower is the
unsettling knowledge of how old this castle really is. If someone
were to pull even one stone out from the wall down below, it
would probably go crashing down to the ground—with me
amongst the rubble. Apart from that, this wouldn't be such a
bad place to live—if I had Sailor here with me. And if I weren't
the only blue-eyed, blonde Amer-Italian, who will have no friends
for the summer, except for a dog and a horse up the road. And
if Francesca and Daniela didn't spread dumb rumors about
me that made me have to change schools two weeks before
summer break. And if I didn't have to be "the new weird girl"
twice in one lifetime. And if mail didn't take so long to go back
and forth from Indian Island to here.

—Reporting live from the castle, Princess Angelina

"*Ficucia!*" Daddy bellows up my tower stairwell. *Ficucia* is Daddy's
nickname for me—it means *little girl fig* in Italian. I think maybe that's
what I looked like as a baby. "There's a letter down here for you!"

Finally. Getting mail is the highlight of my life right now. I live for my mail—especially news from Indian Island. I pull a chicken feather from the back pocket of my overalls pocket to mark my place in my journal, and dash out the door. I fly down my spiral staircase and back up in less than a minute flat. There are very few things in life that get my blood moving that fast. News from home is one of them.

June 1, 1972
Dear A. J.,

Sailor is doing great and loves being back on the island. He liked the Oklahoma farm life, especially herding chickens, but he missed the lake as much as I did. He's barely been out of the water since we returned. I wish I could say my grandpa was doing as well, but his health is the reason my folks let me move back to the island. He still gets around, but needs help caring for the cabins and upkeep on the island. I'll be chopping wood all summer to store up for the fall and winter.

I've been keeping busy with the Baptist youth group and will be adjusting to a new school come fall— Squawkomish High. So you won't be the only "new weird kid" at school. Remember, people thought Jesus was a weird kid too. You're still the apple of God's eye.

> Hang in there,
> Sailor and Danny

The sun is a-shinin' and I'm headin' on out. Danny has a way of bringin' the Southern out in me. It took me a whole summer back on the island to get *fluent in Southern,* as I called it. Mama thought it was the craziest thing in the world to have an Italian daughter speaking with a Southern accent. But lo and behold, the Morgan family showed up from Oklahoma and had that entire island babbling in *Southern* from sunup to sundown. I was in heaven. Mama was not.

I fold my letter and stash it in my back pocket. I stash my mininotebook in my other back pocket in case I need to jot down random ideas for my novel. Then I stash *To Kill a Mockingbird* in the front bib pocket of my overalls, so I can read it for the hundredth time—but in Italian this time—while I'm out and about. Plenty of chicken-feather bookmarks in my side utility pocket. All systems go.

"Where are you off to, Angelina Juliana?" *Grandma Juliana.* She's the only one who calls me by my first and middle names. She likes to hear her own name, which came in second in the coin toss when my parents named me. Grandma Angelina came in first. It was all based on yet another Italian tradition: Give the grandkid your name—no matter what it is. That's another thing about Italy that bothers me; it's all about history and tradition, history and tradition … blah, blah, blah.

Adriana lucked out being named after our great-grandmother, Adriana Maria Degulio, who was still living at the time. It was her dying wish that her first great-granddaughter take her name. Who could say no to that? I tried to swap names with Adriana when I was eight years old, but couldn't afford her asking price. That's when I took things into my own hands and changed my name to Dorothy Jones at school—and was nearly disowned by both grandmothers.

"I'm just going for a walk, Nonna. Did you want to come?" She always says no, but she'll get mad if I don't ask.

"No. I think I'll just stay and talk to St. Francis."

"Okay. Say hello for me."

"Will do, but he rarely says hello back to anyone but me." She turns and shuffles back to the courtyard where her army of saint statues stands guard. She recently moved from the castle into the adjoining mother-in-law suite, along with her twenty-some statues. Daddy made it a priority to fix up her living quarters even before he finished Mama's guesthouse. He said he'd have her suite ready by this summer even if it killed him. According to Grandma, Daddy was never good enough for Mama, and she makes a point of reminding him of that every time she sees him. At least now it's a little less frequent.

When I reach the dirt road in front of our villa, I have a choice of going to the right or the left. If I choose left, I'll end up down by a small lake that I like to walk around when I feel like hearing frogs, crickets, and birds. If I go right, I'll end up visiting Caesar the horse and Napoleon the giant mastiff dog. Today feels like a Caesar-and-Napoleon kind of day. I pull my book out of my bib pocket and head to the right. I've done this same walk so many times with my head in a book, I could do it blindfolded if I had to. There aren't any cliffs I have to worry about walking off of, so it's a relatively safe reading zone. Well, once I bashed my head on a low-hanging tree branch. I was reading *A Tree Grows in Brooklyn*, so it was par for the course.

"Buon pomeriggio," Angelo calls to me from his front porch rocker. He's got a little bag of tobacco in one hand and his pipe in the other.

"Buon pomeriggio, Angelo."

Angelo is a nice old man—the first person I met when we moved here. I was so lonely that I went to visit Caesar and Napoleon every day, and Angelo would call out *buon pomeriggio* to me every time I walked by. He doesn't speak any English, so he had to wait for me to learn Italian before we could say anything besides *buon pomeriggio* to each other. He'd bring out Caesar's brushes for me whenever I came, then he'd sit and rock on his porch swing, smoking his pipe while watching me brush his old horse. One day he brought out his saddle and taught me to ride.

At first he would watch me ride around the corral, giving me pointers. Once I stopped falling off, he let me ride out in the vineyard. Now he lets me go wherever I want on my own. Sometimes I even go bareback. There is something about riding bareback through the Tuscan hills astride a big black horse that thrills my soul. Except for the time I fell off and had to walk all the way back. I still can't climb back on without stirrups.

Angelo points to the leather saddle hanging on the porch rail. I nod enthusiastically. He seems to enjoy having someone ride his old horse for him. I have a hunch he feels too old to ride anymore. He cinches up the saddle and adjusts my stirrups for me. I've learned to do this by myself, but Angelo insists on helping. Handing me the reins, he waves me off with a big toothless grin. I've noticed that people in the Old Country don't seem to care much about things like missing teeth or looking old. It's like, "Hey, we live in the Old Country and we expect to get old." That's just their way. It makes more sense than living in a young country like America and always trying to look younger than you are.

I'm kind of looking forward to the day when I don't have any teeth left in my head. Who likes to brush their teeth anyway? I think God figures we'll be tired of brushing our teeth by the time we hit eighty and takes care of the problem for us. So why push the issue with a set of fake teeth that you have to see floating in a glass of water first thing in the morning? *Ewww.*

Napoleon paces back and forth from the barn to the corral, never taking his eyes off me. He lives for having something to herd, and the bigger the better. With a slight nudge Caesar hits the dusty road at a snail's pace. Napoleon trots along behind, wagging his tail. I know most dogs don't trot, but Napoleon does. He's the size of small horse, and when he follows us, he trots.

We're all feeling a little lazy from the heat today, but I have an agenda to keep. There's something I need to investigate. I can see it just as we crest the hill. The big Franciscan convent next to the children's orphanage. Some of these nuns are teachers for the orphanage school. The sisters direct all of the Christmas and Easter plays and have the children perform at our cathedral on special holidays. But I'm not sure what those nuns do once school lets out for the day, and this is a good time to find out.

"C'mon, boys, let's go spy on the nuns." Napoleon wags his tail like he has had the same idea all along.

We meander our way up the stone-lined road that leads to the courtyard, where some of the sisters are hanging out the wash. Bringing Caesar to a halt near the wall, I have a bird's-eye view of the action. While I'm busy spying, Caesar covers as my alibi, posing as a horse that just happens to stop here to nibble on the lush weeds growing between the stones. Just beyond the courtyard, nuns are planting tomato starts. In the middle of the garden, a bright flower border encircles a statue of Mother Mary. Beside the statue I spy a small stone bench, which is exactly where I would find myself if I were in there. I'd just like to know what it feels like to be a nun. But I don't think that's an option they offer here. Nun for a day.

There's something so fascinating about these holy women who devote their entire lives to charity, children, and the sisterhood. And wear the same clothes every day. They're like a little family of their own the way they all work together so well; a circle of sisters who live and eat and sleep together. How could you not be a family when you spend that much time together? They probably don't fight as much as real sisters either—with God watching that close and all.

I never understood the difference between nuns and sisters until Sister Abigail, my catechism teacher back at Indian Lake, explained it to me. Nuns are the ones who take the lifelong vows and are usually cloistered—they have to stay cooped up inside the convent and pray for everyone out here. The sisters take temporary vows year by year and are allowed to go out and help people. But they are all sisters to each other. Since I can't tell the difference by looking at them, I call them both nuns and sisters—depending on what mood I'm in.

It's the cloistered nuns who really fascinate me—the ones devoted to praying for all of us sinners and staying secluded from the world. I'm glad someone is busy praying for the rest of us, but I would think they might start to feel like giant magpie birds in a cage after awhile. Magpies crack me up—the way they look exactly like little nuns wearing tiny little black-and-white habits.

Just when I'm thinking how reverent and holy these nuns look out in the garden, one of them lets out a shriek, "*Satana!*"

The other sisters come running.

"*Satana, Satana,*" she keeps screaming, over and over.

I'm thinking, *If Satan is in a place like this, I'm getting out of here*—then it crosses my mind that maybe she's talking about me!

Suddenly the other nuns burst into laughter. I notice they're all looking down, watching a small snake wriggle off into the garden.

"*Serpente,*" one of them giggles. They quickly settle down and get back to work.

I can certainly understand how a snake could remind a nun of Satan, seeing a serpent in a garden and all. Snakes give me the creeps too. That's probably the only animal I don't like, and I doubt pretty much that God will have any of them in heaven either. They'd just bring back bad memories for everyone—especially Adam and Eve.

One nun in particular has my full attention. The singing nun. And I don't mean the way most people sing. I mean, all out, from-the-heart-and-soul kind of singing. Beautiful songs. I hear them often when I ride through these hills. Her voice carries clear to the hilltops and probably all the way to heaven.

As though she can hear my thoughts, she glances over at me, stops singing, and comes toward me. I'm probably interrupting her holy time and will be asked to leave. "*Buon pomeriggio,*" I call out, so she knows I come in peace.

"Good afternoon," she says. "Do you speak English?"

My coloring is a dead giveaway. "Yes—I'm sorry if I interrupted your singing."

"No interruption at all. I'm glad you've come." Her eyes light up like little half-moons against her dark complexion—smiley eyes, I call them. She tucks a wisp of black and silver-streaked hair back beneath her wimple. She looks over at her sisters in the courtyard, then whispers, "I've been hoping you'd come."

"You have?"

"Yes. I have watched you ride over the hills before and I so hoped that one day you might stop by."

"Really?"

"Oh, yes. I have been wishing for someone to practice my English with, and gathered that perhaps you might speak English. And … I love horses. I used to ride…." Her voice trials off. "I'm Sister Maria Agastina. What is your name?"

"Angelina. A. J. for short."

"Angelina is such a beautiful name, do you mind if I call you that?"

"No." I wonder if nuns can tell a boldfaced lie when they hear one.

"What do you suppose my name would be in English?" she asks.

"Well …" *Hmmm, Agastina, Agastina …* "Maybe … Sister Aggie?"

"Sister Aggie," she repeats.

"Would you like me to call you Sister Aggie?" *It would sure be easier than Sister Maria Agastina.*

She smiles at the thought. "That would be fine."

I wonder if she's lying too.

Sister Aggie looks back at the courtyard again. "Angelina," she whispers, "do you think … would you perhaps take me for a ride sometime?"

I'm so stunned I practically fall out of my saddle. "You … you want to go horseback riding?"

"Yes, very much. I can't tell you how I've missed it."

"Well, um, sure then. Can nuns do that?"

She laughs. "Well, this nun will find a way." She thinks for a moment. "I have Friday evenings free. Do you think you could come by here Friday at dusk?"

"S-sure." I'm still a little shocked. "Wow, I didn't think they let nuns ride horses—I mean, I've never seen one ..."

"I can't imagine that the Lord would have anything against it. I don't think I'll announce it to the other sisters, though, or you may end up giving pony rides to the entire convent."

"Okay. I won't tell a soul."

Sister Aggie laughs. "Oh, I forgot to ask ... do you think we could ride bareback? I just love riding bareback."

"Um ... s-sure."

She turns and joins the others, who all look over and wave as I ride away.

Bareback? Holy moley! A nun who rides bareback ... what is the world coming to?

❧❧❧

When I return home, I retreat to my tower. I have to ponder this nun-on-horseback thing. From my window I can barely catch a glimpse of the old stone convent set upon the next hilltop over. I'm so fascinated that even nuns like to ride horses—and bareback, no less. I pull out my journal and make a new entry:

The Secret Lives of Nuns
Who would ever believe me if I said I was taking a nun
horseback riding? Bareback. Who would believe that nuns

would do such a thing? I thought they only cared about saving sinners and helping the poor. Do they really have secret desires like the rest of us? This would *be* a fascinating topic for a new novel ... once I finish the romance novel I've been working on since I got here. "Moon over Milan" is taking forever to write an ending for! Maybe because it's so close to my own life. So I'm afraid of botching up the ending for fear that it might predestine me to a lousy ending of my own, and I can't risk that happening.

Until I do finish "Moon over Milan," I think I'll keep some journal notes on this nun-on-horseback adventure, and one day, turn it into a fascinating novel. Who doesn't want to know what nuns do when no one's looking?

"... The gallant knight Damian appeared on his black charger at the window of her cell in the convent. 'Come away with me, Sister Aggie; you were destined for more than this.'

"'As much as I long to ride away with you, I cannot, for though you are my knight, God is my King, and it is He I am loyal to. But yea, upon each blue moon, return here to me, and take me for a ride in these dark Tuscan hills, and together we will dream of the life we shall never have ...'"

At dinner Mama says, "Well, A. J., since your birthday's coming up, how about celebrating on Friday night in San Gimignano?"

"Friday? This *Friday* is my birthday? But I was thinking it was on Saturday."

"It is on Saturday, but Friday is your birthday eve, so I thought we could all go out the night before to kick it off early."

"Oh, Mama, could we just stick to my real birthday instead?"

"Is there a problem with starting on Friday?" Mama asks.

"No … well, yes, actually … I kind of made plans for Friday night."

J. R. looks at me suspiciously. "Plans? What kind of plans?"

"Just … plans." This is one secret I plan to keep a secret. I can't risk people at school talking about things like this when they already think I'm weird enough.

"Oooh," Benji says. "If you ask me, it sounds like maybe it's a *date.*"

"Yeah, with *a boy,*" Dino chimes in.

"Well, I didn't ask you, and it's not a *date* with a *boy.*"

"Then who is it?" Benji jumps back in. "If it's not a boy, you shouldn't mind telling us."

This is the stuff that makes me wish I were an only child. "Mama, make them stop, would you?"

Mama looks at me. "I don't know—now you have me curious. What's the gig?"

"It's no gig. I have a date with Caesar, okay?"

Now Daddy gets in on it. "Caesar? You're giving up a night in San Gimignano for a night with Caesar?"

"Look, can we just celebrate my birthday on Saturday instead?"

"He must be *some* horse," J. R. says.

"May I please be excused, Daddy?"

"Yes, you may, but I'd like to have a talk with that horse before he takes my daughter out again."

Family!

Friday evening I arrive at the stable just as the sun is beginning to set. And following a sunset comes … *dusk*. That's what she said. Dusk. I hope I get dusk right. I wonder why Sister Aggie wants to wait until dusk. She must not want to be seen. I hope Sister Aggie was right about it not being a sin for nuns to ride horses, or we'll both end up in confession for this.

Caesar, Napoleon, and I arrive at the stone wall as close to dusk as I can guess. While watching Napoleon chase away a fly, I hear, "Angelina, over here."

I whip around and spot Sister Aggie's head poking over the top of the wall. "Sister." I'm relieved I got dusk right. Sister Aggie's wearing her full habit. "Is that what you plan to ride in?" I ask.

"I don't own anything else. Besides, I can't think of anything more exciting than galloping along with my habit flowing behind me, can you?"

"Well, actually, no, I can't." *I'm just glad no one else can see us.*

The next thing I know, Sister Aggie climbs the wall, then hoists herself to the top where she's level with me.

"Excuse me, Sister, but how on earth did you learn to climb like that?"

"Oh, I haven't spent my whole life inside a convent, you know. I've done a lot of climbing in my day. I'm not in bad shape for my age. Now, how about if you just line Caesar up along this wall and I'll hop on behind you."

I nudge Caesar as close to the wall as I can. Sure enough, Sister Aggie lifts her habit above her knees and slips right on behind me.

"Oh, Angelina, you have no idea how much this means to me."

Somehow I think I do.

Sister Aggie wraps her arms around my waist. "Let's run."

I give Caesar a quick nudge with my heels and he takes off. Normally I have to nudge him like crazy just to get him to trot for me, but tonight he seems to know we have special cargo on board, and he takes to the wind like a young stallion. We canter through the fields with a breeze on our faces, and Sister's long black habit billowing out behind us.

When we reach the top of the ridge, I turn to Sister Aggie. "Do you want to drive now?"

"I'd love to," she says.

We decide it might be easier to try to switch places while still on the horse, rather than climb off and on again—in case we can't get back up. Swinging both legs to one side, I attempt to scoot around Sister Aggie. She does the same. We get so tangled up, we nearly fall off, laughing. After much finagling, we manage to switch places. Sister Aggie takes the reins. She gives Caesar a swift kick *"Corriamo!"* Let's run!

And away we fly.

This will be one ride to remember. I was hoping something special would happen to help mark this day in history—my last day of being thirteen. But I never in my wildest dreams pictured doing anything like this. I feel like I'm back in medieval times playing Capture the Castle. Sister Aggie, Caesar, Napoleon, and I—together, in these dark rolling hills, we're taking Tuscany.

3

Buon Compleanno
(Happy Birthday)

Saturday morning, with no regard for my *Do Not Disturb the Princess* doorknob hanger, Mama bursts into my room tooting an obnoxious party horn. "Rise-n-shine, princess! Time for the birthday surprise!"

"What is it?" I mumble, from beneath my pillow.

"C'mon, your father and the boys have been working all summer for this moment." She pulls open my drapes so the sun is shining right in my face the second I come out from under my pillow.

"Come look. You'll love it."

Imagine my enthusiasm. I drag my body from bed and sleepwalk to the window. Once the sunshine jolts my eyeballs awake, I see Daddy and my brothers down by the pool. And there's water in it. Water … in the pool. They fixed the pool … "Mama, they fixed the pool!"

"Yes, they did—just in time for your birthday. C'mon, let's go take a look."

I fly down the winding staircase and out the door, letting everyone in Tuscany know how excited I am to have a pool for the rest of the blasted hot summer. "*La mia propria piscina!*" My own swimming pool!

"Happy birthday!" Daddy and the boys yell, as I skid to a stop on the pool patio.

Shiny blue and gold tiles—all whole—no chips or cracks. And water—it actually holds water. I knew they'd been working on it, but I thought it would take years—like everything else around here.

Mama makes it down the hill shortly after me. "Well, kiddo, we thought you might like to have a pool party for your big day."

My smile quickly fades. "A … pool … party?"

"Sure, invite some of your friends to come over to swim."

Friends? Let's see … a pool party with a horse, a dog, and a nun. "Mama, I don't … have … friends."

"Nonsense, A. J. What about all of your friends from school?"

"*All* my school friends? Like who?"

"Like … that little French doll, Bianca?"

"Mama, Bianca was the *only* friend I had, and she's spending her summer in the south of France." Has she not noticed I've been alone since school got out?

"Well, I'm sure there are other kids around here your age …"

"Okay, you find them and I'll invite them."

Daddy throws his arm around my shoulder. "How about we all go out to San Gimignano for the day? We can have lunch, do some shopping, then come back and go for a swim."

"Sure." Why not? That will help take the focus off of the fact that I have no friends.

"It's a plan!" Mama yells, like this is just the best idea to come down the pike in a good long time. "Everyone change into something decent and be ready to go in an hour. I'll get Nonna ready."

"*Nonna?*" Daddy and I say in unison.

"Yes, Nonna. This is a *family* celebration, is it not?"

An hour later all seven of us squeeze into a Fiat that was made to seat four. Apparently no one has heard of station wagons in this country. It's probably just as well that Adriana isn't here to join us or they'd have to strap one of us on the luggage rack. Actually I'm pretty sure it already crossed Daddy's mind when he tried to help Nonna into the front seat. She told him to get his cotton-pickin' hands off of her. Poor Daddy. He really tries, but Nonna won't give him an inch. He has to drive all the way to San Gimignano enduring Nonna's commentary on what a *scemo del villaggio* he is. Village idiot.

⤲⤲⤲

San Gimignano is a walled medieval city upon a hill. It's perched on one of the highest lookout points, partway between Siena and Florence. Daddy insists on parking at the bottom of the hill so we can all work up an appetite getting up there. I think he needs to air out a little after listening to Nonna all the way here. He's probably hoping it will wear her out so she'll have less to say for the rest of the afternoon.

It's a steep trek to the top, but once you get there, you feel like you're on the top of the world. There's an open marketplace where people sell their goods, artists paint pictures, and restaurants have a panoramic view as far as the eye can see. It's as good a place as any to turn fourteen.

"Okay, birthday girl, choose your bistro!" Another birthday tradition in this family—we either get to choose the meal we want Mama to cook for us, or the restaurant we want to eat at. We've all wised up over the years. Beyond macaroni and cheese, everyone's better off with plan B. Of course, I choose the restaurant at the summit. That works for everyone but Nonna, who complains the entire way up. It's all worth it once we reach the top, though. We're seated at an outdoor table with a knockout view. And a darn cute waiter to go with it.

Everything is white tablecloths and napkins here, the kind you don't want to spill anything on. The waiter comes by and asks for our drink order. I'm doing my best to explain in Italian what a Shirley Temple is. He keeps nodding, but I'm not sure he really gets what I'm saying. I tell him "7UP *con lo sciroppo rosso,*" 7UP with red syrup. Won't be the first time something I've ordered comes back wrong. It's become entertainment for the entire family to see what these Italians come up with when we try to order something American style.

Without warning Mama reaches into her humongous metallic red handbag and pulls out a big gold box. "Open it!" she says.

There is always cause for hesitation when Mama's excited about something she's picked out for me. I don't recall the last time I actually liked something she bought for me—I think it may have been a pink jumper when I was three years old.

I slowly untie the big gold bow, while trying to peek under the lid—just to know what to brace myself for. *Oh, good golly.* I've trained myself to smile no matter what … but … *this?* I lift out the most horrific one-piece, shimmery silver unit that looks like it's made from fish scales. "What is it?"

"It's a jumpsuit." Mama looks thrilled over her selection.

"A jumpsuit?" *As in something so incredibly ugly you want to jump off a cliff in it?*

"Adriana helped me pick it out on our shopping trip in Rome. Adriana says …"

I know, I know … it's the latest thing in fashion this year.

"… it's the latest thing in fashion this year."

Maybe for reptiles. "It's very … shiny. Thank you." *I'll be sure and wear it the first day of school so everyone can establish right from the get-go that I'm a total dork. Thank goodness for uniforms.*

"Go try it on while we're waiting for our drinks," Mama insists.

Are you joking? "Here?"

"Sure. Just slip it on in the ladies' loo—I'm dying to see it on you."

It's futile to fight Mama once she makes up her mind that she wants to see something on you. The last time she pulled this was in Florence, where she insisted I try on some black leather pants intended for Adriana's birthday present. She had to see them on me and try to envision them on Adriana. I tried to point out that, although we were the same size around, Adriana was a good foot taller than me. I ended up standing on a chair in the middle of the store, looking nearly as ridiculous as I look right now in this jumpsuit.

Trudging my way back from the loo to our table, I feel like something that should be shot and stuffed. *Hi, I'm A. J. the giant armadillo.*

"You look fantastic, kiddo!" Mama gushes. She has outdone herself once again.

Giving my brothers the don't-even-think-about-laughing glare, I slink into my seat just as our drinks arrive. The waiter plops something down in front of me that looks nothing like a

Shirley Temple. I think he got the 7UP right, but my red syrup somehow translated into tomato juice. With cherries on top.

"Nice-looking drink, A. J.," Dino quips.

"I dare you to drink it," I mumble.

"I dare Benji," Dino answers.

Benji falls for everything.

"You dare me? I'll take the dare."

The poor kid never learns. I slide my drink in front of him. Benji takes the plunge and starts to gulp the gagging concoction down. I'm getting a stomachache just watching him.

Nearing the bottom of the glass, Benji lifts his head with cheeks full of pop.

"Oh boy, he's gonna blow," J. R. warns.

Benji can't quite get the last swallow down and spews fizzy tomato juice all over himself and me. Now I look like armadillo roadkill.

The boys break into hysterics. "Smooth move, bro," Dino howls.

Mama looks aghast. "Oh, for the love of Pete! That tomato juice could just ruin that fabric. A. J., you should really try to run and wash it out before the stain sets."

"I'm okay." *It will be a great excuse to never have to wear it again.* Wiping myself off, I wonder what else can go wrong.

Nonna's been tinkering with an old wrinkled bow on a small box, completely oblivious to the spewing soda. She finally looks up and hands me the little square box wrapped in used tissue paper. "This is something I've been saving for years, Angelina Juliana. I wanted to wait until you were old enough to appreciate it."

Daddy looks over at me with raised eyebrows like he can hardly wait to see what it is.

I cautiously untie the wrinkled bow, peel off the crinkled paper, and open the tattered box. I'm staring at two tarnished cuff links sitting on a square sheet of cotton. "Cuff links. How nice." I have no blouses that use cuff links. I glance over at Daddy. He's grinning from ear to ear.

"Thanks, Nonna."

I start to put the lid back on the box.

"Wait, honey, you didn't look under the cotton."

"Oh." I set the cuff links aside on the table, then carefully lift up the square cotton pad. Lo and behold, it's a gigantic pewter cross as big as my fist with bright red fake rubies embedded in it, strung on a heavy metal necklace.

"It's just like the one the Pope wears. Go ahead, honey, put it on," Nonna insists. "Besides, I need that box back."

Lifting the heavy icon, I place it around my neck for all to admire. *Holy mackerel. I'll have to remember to take this thing off before I go swimming or I'm sunk.* While trying to straighten my neck back up, I hear Daddy's muffled laughter seeping out from behind his water glass, strategically placed in front of his mouth.

Mama gives Daddy *the look.* He clears his throat and does his best to shape up. It doesn't help much. Every time he looks at me he starts to snicker. To hide my utter embarrassment over this entire birthday ensemble, I excuse myself and meander over by the railing, where I try to appear fascinated with the view. I feel so ridiculous, I'm not sure whether to laugh, jump, or join the circus.

Daddy yells over to me, "Don't lean over that railing while you're wearing that, A. J. It's a long way down."

Now the boys all bust up laughing, which gets Daddy going again.

Mama elbows Daddy, but she starts to lose it too.

By the time our order is up, our waiter returns to find all six of us laughing hysterically, a severely stained table cloth and jumpsuit, and a grandmother who is so fixated on putting her little box back together, she is clueless of anything else going on. Oh, happy birthday to me! *Salute*!

Once the birthday feast is over, we hit the *Piazza della Cisterna*, the town square surrounding a big fountain. First stop: *gelato*—Italian ice cream. No matter how full you are, there's always room for *gelato*! It's not as creamy as ice cream, more like icy fruit or sherbet. And it is *delizioso*! Especially lemon gelato. While we're deciding where to go next, a pretty Italian girl walks past us, then turns around. "*Ciao*, J. R."

J. R. looks back, turns red, and says, "*Ciao*, Celeste."

Their smiles linger a little too long for "just friends." Everyone looks at J. R. with raised eyebrows.

"What?" he says, embarrassed as all get-out.

None of us have to say anything more—he knows we're on to him. You can't get away with anything in this family when it comes to love.

Nobody has anything in particular they want to look at, except Nonna. She's on the warpath for another saint statue. She's bound and determined to find a bigger version of one of the statues she already owns. After looking at every patron saint in the entire town, she finally finds it—a three-foot-tall statue of Saint Adelaide—and insists she must buy it. The only problem is the thing weighs a ton, and the car is parked at the bottom of the hill. Her solution is to have Daddy carry it for her.

Daddy reluctantly heaves the solid plaster statue onto his shoulder and begins his descent down the hill. Halfway down he turns to Nonna and asks, "So which saint is this, anyway?"

"Saint Adelaide."

"Saint Adelaide? Isn't that the saint for in-law problems—the one I always trip over?"

"That's the one."

"So why do you need a bigger one?" Daddy's clearly struggling under the weight of the thing.

"Because the other one didn't work."

We finally reach the car, and Daddy sets Saint Adelaide down while he pops open the trunk.

"Apparently this one doesn't work either," Nonna says, in a disappointed tone.

"What do you mean, it 'doesn't work?'" Daddy asks.

"You're still here. Take it back. I want a refund."

"Over my dead body," Daddy says, and heaves Saint Adelaide into the trunk, then slams it shut.

This has definitely been one of my more interesting birthdays.

Arriving home, we find Adriana waiting down by the pool. She came home to visit for a few days and to wish me a happy birthday. She even brought me something I can use—a new bathing suit. Mama had obviously let her in on the birthday pool surprise.

Mama tells us all to go change into our swimsuits and meet back at the pool for birthday cake and a swim. Nonna picks up my new bikini lying on the table in front of her. "Thank you for thinking of me, honey, but it's really not my color. I think I'd like to spend some time with Saint Adelaide instead of swimming anyway." She sets the bikini back down.

Somehow Nonna got the notion that the bikini was for her. Things like that have been happening a lot lately.

"If it's between talking to Saint Adelaide, or seeing Nonna in a bikini, I'd say she made the right choice," J. R. whispers to me.

The cool water feels refreshing after our long, hot day in town. Everyone is splashing and diving as if we've never seen water before. It's been nearly a year since we were on the Italian Riviera. But that was only for a week. We were so used to living on the water all summer long back at the island. *The island … the island …* Closing my eyes, floating on my back, I'm instantly there … drifting with Sailor in my dinghy … rescuing hundreds of drowning ants with a stick and delivering them to safety. I can still hear Mama's voice …

"A. J., what on earth are you up to with that stick?"

"I'm savin' drowning victims, Mama. There was an ant's nest on the bank over yonder, and the wind blew a bunch of 'em right into the lake. All the young 'uns is gonna drown if I cain't save 'em."

"A. J., if you don't cut that Southern babble right now, those won't be the only young 'uns that are going under."

Mama has always had a way with words.

Next, I think of the clear nights, star-gazing on Juniper Beach with Danny. Danny Morgan. I wonder if he ever thinks of me when he sees the stars come out at night, like I think about him. I wonder if he ever sings "I see the moon, the moon sees me, the moon sees the one I long to see …"

Mama interrupts my thoughts. "A. J., come and have some birthday cake." She gets everyone to sing "Happy Birthday" to me while I'm drying myself off. "Make yourself a wish—as long as it's not to have Sailor shipped over."

Mama has had it up to her eyeballs with me begging to have Sailor shipped here. I sit down to blow out my candles. "Okay … I wish that I will be shipped back to Sailor." I blow them all out with the help of a sudden gust of wind—I hope that's a sign from God that He's going to make sure that happens for me.

"Here you go, kiddo." Mama holds out a bundle of envelopes for me. "I saved these to give you on your birthday—I figured they were probably sent with your birthday in mind."

Taking the small pile of mail, I check the return addresses. A card from Grandma Angelina (most likely with cash inside). A card from my best friend, Dorie. A card from Aunt Genevieve and the Sophronias—I guess we're not back on speaking terms yet or they'd be over here for cake. And lastly, a letter … from Danny Morgan, Route 3 Box 10, Squawkomish, Idaho. I open everything but this one.

Mama removes the melted candles from my so-called cake. I'm staring at a round object, covered in blue blobs of frosting, with a few waffle wafers plopped here and there. "Wow. Who made the cake?"

"I did," Mama says. "Guess what it is?"

That's a good question. "Um, is it … the Sophronias' blue villa?"

Mama does not look humored. "No, it is not."

"I know what it is," Benji says. "It's the swimming pool."

"Well," Mama says, "I'm glad to see we have another creative genius in the family. Benji is absolutely right. The blue frosting is the waves, and the wafers are air mattresses."

"Oh, yeah, now I see it." *Kind of.* "I'd like a piece with an air mattress, please." *Anything but the big blue blobby waves.*

Mama can do a number of things well, but baking is not at the top of the list. There is something funny about this cake—apart from it being one part cake, two parts frosting. I've never tasted anything quite like it before … and will be fine if I never taste anything like it again.

It's the thought that counts.

Following cake, we swim until the moon comes up and everyone is shriveled like prunes. Reminds me of the good ol' days back at the lake. Dino announces that he's going to hightail his lizard skin off to bed. Following Dino, the rest of my party guests dwindle one by one. When it's down to just me, Mama, and Daddy, I take my cards and letter and head back up to my tower.

Sitting at my writing desk by my tower window, I slowly open the envelope and read the letter by moonlight.

> Dear A. J.,
>   I'm hoping this reaches you in time for your birthday because I know how much it will mean to you to hear from Sailor. I've enclosed a picture of him for you. He wants to

wish you a happy birthday and also wants you to know that he's enjoying his summer back on the island. He lives for the lake and only comes out of the water long enough to eat. We spent the morning playing fetch on Juniper Beach. It reminded me of the night you and I looked at the stars on your tenth birthday. I asked you what you were looking at through your new binoculars and you said, "Infinity." I remember that night well, drifting out on the lake in the dark beneath the Milky Way. I remember because I felt God so strongly. You did too, didn't you? How do you say Milky Way in Italian?

My birthday wish for you is that you will always seek Him with all your heart.

Your friend, and your dog,

Danny and Sailor

P.S. Are you still planning to come back to be a veterinarian?

Yep, I am. And Danny still thinks about me. He remembered our night under the *Via Latteo,* the Milky Way. I turn over the photo. There's Sailor sitting in my dinghy with his lifejacket on, like he's waitin' for me to come home and take him driftin'. Tears start down my face until the picture becomes too blurry to see. I fold the letter up, and slip it and the photo back inside the envelope.

Mama and Daddy are dancing by the pool beneath the moonlight, without music. Well, that's probably not entirely true. I think Mama and Daddy hear music of their own.

My eyes shift upward and search the heavens for the brightest star in the Tuscan sky. *I wish … I wish to go back home.*

My weary head drops forward and comes to rest on my desk. A vision from long ago pops into my mind: the television cartoon, *Tooter Turtle*. Whenever Tooter Turtle got himself in trouble, he'd cry out, "Help, Mr. Wizard!" Then Mr. Wizard, a lizard, would say, "Drizzle, drazzle, druzzle, drome, time for zis one to come home!" and Tooter Turtle would be instantly propelled back home. Tonight I wish it were time for this one to go home too.

4

Mamma Mia

Drizzle, drazzle, druzzle, drome, time for zis one to come home....
Dang, I'm still here.

Seeing the photo of Sailor has thrown me into such deep despair,
I may not come out of it until I see him again. Daddy says I can prob-
ably go back to Idaho to attend veterinary school when I'm eighteen.
But that's not for four more years!

Lost in a daze, I'm mechanically shoveling cold cereal into my
mouth when Mama enters the kitchen. "Morning, sunshine. How's
my big fourteen-year-old today?"

I give her the don't-call-me-sunshine look, then report, "Mostly
cloudy with a high chance of thunderstorms."

She has the nerve to tell me I need to snap out of it and go to
Rome with her for Adriana's runway show.

"Snap out of it?" I glare at her. "Snap out of missing my dog?
Snap out of living in a foreign country where I'm considered a freak
of nature? How do you snap out of that? I don't care about Adriana's
fashion show, and it will not help me one bit to go to Rome."

"My, my, who's been rattling your cage, young lady?"

"Nobody's been rattling my cage, but everything here is rattling
my life."

"Oh, A. J., everybody has a bad day now and then …"

"A bad … *day*? I don't just have a day, I have *weeks* … no, I have *months* … make that, I have *years,* Mama. And I have *four years* of *bad days* ahead of me before I have something to look forward to again!"

Pushing my bowl of cereal away, I run out the front door. I keep running, all the way to the convent. With great determination I climb the wall, stone by stone, and sit on the ledge at the top. Hoping Sister Aggie is on laundry duty, I scan the courtyard. No one is out this morning except a few sisters singing as they work in the garden. I'm on my own.

Closing my eyes, I try to picture what I look like before God right now. There He is, sitting on His big throne, and here I am, a teeny-tiny person sitting on this stone wall. My arms and legs hang limp, like a weary rag doll. Any minute now I'm going to topple off this wall like Humpty Dumpty, and all the kings' horses and all the kings' men won't be able to put me back together again. What would God do? What would He say?

… I think He'd bend down from heaven and scoop me up with his big hands. He'd hold me out up in front of Himself, and my weary little head would just flop to one side.

"Hey there, little Raggedy A. J.," He might say. "You're still the apple of my eye."

"That's sure nice to hear," I'd say.

Then He'd set me on His big lap for a while, and I might just curl up and take a nap. When I'd awake, I'd lean on His big shoulder. I'd tell him how lonely I am. How it feels to leave my home and dog, and everything familiar, and how it feels to change schools ... again ... where no one seems to understand me. How I feel so detached, like no one really knows me anymore.

Then God would remind me, "I know you, A. J. I know everything about you. Would I not keep a close eye on the keeper of My critters?"

A gentle breeze rustles through the olive trees. Angelic voices rise up from the convent. The sisters' songs sound like Italian lullabies to my weary ears.

Sister Abigail, from Indian Lake, once said, "Did you know that God sings songs over us?"

"No, I didn't know that," I told her back.

"He surrounds us with songs of deliverance," she assured me.

That's good to know, because right now I need to be delivered from Italy back to Idaho.

⚬⚭⚮⚭⚬

By the time I return home, Mama has already left for Rome. Daddy is standing out on the balcony, looking out over the hills with his giant coffee mug in hand. This is how he drinks his coffee every morning—looking over the hills, enjoying the view.

"Morning, *ficuccia*," he says, without turning around.

I join him, leaning over the rail. "Mornin'."

"How's life, Little Fig?"

"About a two on a one-to-ten."

"That good, huh?" Daddy keeps staring out there, sipping his coffee.

"No. That bad."

Daddy turns and zeros in on me with that father-daughter look.

Here we go.

"You know, A. J., I've seen people who have everything they could possibly want in life. They're some of the most miserable people I know. And some of the happiest people I know have very little, but they're thankful just to be here."

"Why is that?"

"Different perspectives. It's all about how one chooses to look at things. Happiness has very little to do with what one has, but everything to do with how you choose to look at what you have."

"But it's not something I have or don't have that's making me miserable—it's about where I want to live and can't."

Daddy sighs. "So you're going to dismiss all of this beauty and this short time of living with your family—in a castle—in the Tuscan countryside—because you aren't on an island for a few years out of your life? You know how many people would give their right arm to live in a place like this?"

"I'd give both arms to be with Sailor on Indian Island."

"Then how would you pet him?" Daddy smiles. "A. J., it's all summed up in what a good man once said: 'Folks are about as happy as they make up their minds to be.'"

"Who said that—Jesus?"

"Abraham Lincoln."

Hmm. My favorite president. Interesting.

Daddy swigs down the last of his coffee. "Looks like a good day to add another brick to the ol' castle. What do you say we meet back here around dinnertime and try to catch a glimpse of your sister on TV?"

❧❧❧

According to Mama, Adriana's fashion show is the biggest annual fashion event of the year, and Models of Milan is representing the best new lines. Daddy and I have decided to pop up some popcorn and watch the big event as long as we can stand it, hoping Adriana is in the early part of the show. The boys would rather swim, and told us to holler at them when she comes on. They'll try to race to the house in time to catch a glimpse of her. Brotherly devotion at its best.

Neither Daddy nor I are ones for the big city, but Mama thrives on this stuff and is just tickled pink that her daughter could get her free tickets for the show. I, for one, enjoy the opening riffraff more than the actual show itself. I'm catching all the hoopla of the glamour queens arriving on the scene in limos while Daddy's popping up the corn. "Make that with extra butter, please," I yell toward the kitchen.

"Yes, ma'am," Daddy yells back.

There are some really kooky people in this fashion business according to Adriana, especially some of the designers. "They're like this class of people stuck somewhere in between feminine and masculine," she'd told me.

She works with a male designer named Marcello, who wears sequined jackets and has a long ponytail halfway down his back, and is married to Chanay, who wears jean jackets and has a short, chic haircut. Sounds confusing, but I'm beginning to get the picture. There are some real characters strutting in front of the cameras. They are mostly young and very thin, with outlandish getups. The reporter is talking to a gal with a ponytail sticking straight up out of a six-inch tube before it fans out at the top. He's trying to get her name, but there is some big commotion going on off screen that everyone is running off to—including the reporter, who just cut off what the whale-spout lady was saying.

He informs the crowd that there's a celebrity movie star attending the show and they're trying to confirm who it is. The cameras swing to the gathering crowd and zoom in on the unexpected guest …

Oh, no … it can't be … it's … "Daddy! Hurry, come quick!"

Daddy comes hustling into the room. "Is it Adriana? Is she on?"

"No, Daddy, it's not Adriana … it's Mama!"

"*Sophia?*" Daddy swoops in front of the television to get a closer look.

"I can't believe Mama's pulling her Sofia trick on *live TV* … look, she's signing autographs!"

"*Bravissima*, Sofia!" The reporter goes on to confirm that they have Sofia Loren right there in her home town of Rome … and what an honor it is for her to so graciously sign autographs for her fans.

The camera zooms in on my Mama and there she is basking in all her glory, just signing away like this is what she was born to do. "She had better get out of there before this goes too far …"

Daddy sinks onto the couch, shaking his head in amazement. He looks like he's not sure whether to laugh or go haul Mama out of Rome.

Now the paparazzi are storming in for photos. Mama is creating a scene, and the reporters have to yell over the crowd just to get a few questions to her.

Mama turns and blows a kiss to the crowd. Her trademark tactic for avoiding conversations. She's said it before: "It's one thing to pull off looking like Sofia, but they can't expect me to sound like her too."

As the crowd starts to close in, Mama has claustrophobia written all over her face. She loves a crowd, but this is more like a mob. Her eyes dart around nervously. All of a sudden Mama makes a mad dash away from the cameras, trying to shake off the crowd.

"I think your mother bit off more than she can chew this time," Daddy says.

The crowd chases after her until she runs out of view. That's the last we see of Mama. The cameras swing back in on the fashion event, and the reporter tries to resume his former interview, but the little whale-do lady looks totally put out that Sofia stole all the thunder.

The very moment the whale diva regains her composure, here comes Mama back into the camera frame behind her, with police escorts on each arm. She is being personally escorted into the show. Mama carries herself with so much class it's hard for these young waifs to hold a candle to her.

I look over at Daddy, who is just beaming with pride. "A. J., there goes a real lady if I ever saw one."

Once the show is under way, the camera only occasionally flashes to the audience, but when it does, you can bet where it lands. Right on Mama. We don't have to wait long to see Adriana either. Models of Milan is first to present the new fall line, and Adriana is leading the lineup in a dazzling fuchsia pantsuit with big flaring legs. She struts to the end of the runway and takes a turn in front of the crowd with the confidence of a queen, and I know exactly who she gets it from. She and Mama are two peas in a pod. She could even make my jumpsuit look good.

Daddy looks over at me. "Is that something you'd like to do someday?"

I give Daddy a blank stare. "Is that a joke?"

"No, I think you have the cutes for it."

"Daddy," I sigh, "I can appreciate your attempt to try and salvage my fragile ego from the trauma of having a sister who is taller, prettier, skinnier, and richer than I am. But let me assure you that cutes only go so far in life; short is forever, and neither will get me very far in the world of fashion. *However,* do take comfort. As the younger sibling of a fashion model, I have neither envy nor desire for her life. All the glamour getups and sequins would only get in the way when delivering ponies and stitching up bloody canine accident victims." *Dramatic sigh.*

Daddy looks over and smiles at me. "Popcorn?"

"Sure."

Two hours later the phone rings. "Hi, Mama … Yes, Mama, we saw you—the whole world saw you … Yep, saw the police escorts, and the paparazzi, and the reporters—saw it all, Mama … Yes, Daddy saw the whole thing too. Here, I'll let you talk to him."

Around noon the next day, the bread man arrives with our fresh bread delivery—but that's not all he brings us.

"A. J., what's wrong?" Daddy asks.

"I'm not sure you want to know."

Dino snatches the newspaper from my hands. "Oh man—that's our *mom!*"

Daddy grabs the paper from Dino and reads aloud: "Sofia Loren impostor takes Rome for a ride."

The front-page story explains how everyone fell for the grand movie star appearance at the fashion show, until reports verified that the real Loren was nowhere near Rome. By then the impostor was nowhere to be found.

Suddenly the front door flies open. "I'm home," Mama yells.

We all jump up and show her the morning paper.

"I know all about it—saw it over coffee this morning and fled for the hills. Everybody just lay low until they call the dogs off—I don't think anyone followed me here." She pulls off her dark glasses and head scarf. Then she beams and says, "So did you all see me?"

"Soph," Daddy says, "you looked terrific, but don't you think you took it a little too far this time—I mean you created a real mob scene."

"Yeah, Mama, you could go to jail for pretending to be someone famous and disrupting the public like that."

Mama waves us all off with her hand. "Jail, schmail. Nobody seems to understand that I did absolutely nothing illegal at all. There I was, minding my own business, trying to see my own daughter in her big fashion show, and some nut yelled out, 'It's Sofia Loren!' Everybody went crazy."

"Well, you didn't have to play along with it," I tell her.

"Listen up, toots. They would have mobbed me either way—just as they would if the real Sofia tried to deny it—they'd think she was just trying to get the paparazzi off her back. Now, I had the choice of having everyone touch and paw me to death, or sign autographs."

"But you could be arrested for forging her signature."

"A. J., you should know by now that I only sign my first name—which happens to be *Sophia*." She gives me her most innocent smile.

5

Villa Rosa

Mama has been whirling around her guesthouse all week like a spinning top; scrubbing, polishing, decorating. Her first reservation for the *Ritz*, as us kids have dubbed it, is for a family of three from Kansas. Daddy says it's probably Dorothy, Auntie Em, and Toto, too.

"No, this is the Rizzatti family," Mama tells him. "He's a doctor from the States who has relatives here they've come to visit. They're only staying with us for the night to break up their long drive."

"The Rizzattis visit the Ritz." *Hmm. Could be a good name for a novel.*

Mama takes a good glance around. "Well, everything is ready to go—except for that big blue eyesore on the hill, but not much can be done about that."

"Don't worry, Soph, I've got you covered. I planted the dynamite pack—it's ready to blow the minute the Sophronias leave town."

I'm visualizing the big blue palace exploding over the hills of Tuscany.

"Don't bother," Mama says, "they'd just rebuild it and paint it something worse—like lime green."

I take all this to mean that Mama is still not on speaking terms with her sister.

"Mama, what will there be to do for all of the guests that stay here? It's not like there's anything exciting to do out here on this boring hilltop. Wouldn't they rather stay in Florence or Rome, where all the action is?"

Mama is still fluffing and straightening everything for the hundredth time. "Oh, some guests will just want the peace and quiet of the countryside. Others will use our place as base camp to visit Florence and Pisa and all the tourist attractions. We're centrally located to many of the big cathedrals and, of course, the *David*."

Oh, yes, let's not forget the *David*. When we first moved here that's all everyone ever asked me—have you been to see the *David?* The *David*, the *David*, the *David*. Finally, we went to see the *David*—on a rainy afternoon—the same time an Italian cruise line bused their tourists in to see it. So there we stood, in the pouring rain for hours, behind five hundred matching red umbrellas, all sporting the cruise-ship logo. After dripping like drenched rats all afternoon, we finally got to see the *David*. Stomping inside, sopping wet, I found myself staring at a *buck naked* statue of a man, showing *everything*—and I mean *everything*.

I remember thinking, *So this is what everyone stood hours in the rain to see—some naked guy made of stone? Ewww.* Is the world full of nuts or what? I don't know what I expected. Maybe some huge statue made of gold, with velvet robes and the crown jewels. It was, after all, *King* David. For Pete's sake, at least put a fig leaf on the king. Maybe this is where they got the idea for that fairy tale—*The Emperor's New Clothes.*

Mama even bought a two-foot tall marble replica of David and put him in her bathroom beside the bathtub. I guess if you're naked, the bathroom is the right room to be in. Now, why a married woman would want a statue of another man—naked—I just don't get it. Even Nonna, who is obsessed with statues, refused to get one of the *David*. When she saw it in Mama's bathroom, she tied a handkerchief around his waist, and said only a pervert would want a statue of that. The *David* is one thing Nonna and I have always agreed on— maybe the *only* thing we've ever agreed on.

As far as the whole tourist scene goes, I have seen it all: the frescoes, the *duomo* in Florence, the Ponte Vecchio bridge over the River Arno, you name it—I've seen it. We've even been to what Benji calls the Leaning Tower of Pizza, in Pisa. So now that we've seen everything there is to see in Italy, I'd say it's time to go back home. I just can't get anyone else to see it that way.

❧❦❧

Saturday afternoon I'm lounging out on the terrace engrossed in a five-hundred-page Russian saga, when a small black sports car roars up our hill and pulls in front of Mama's pink villa. Now when I say pink, I don't mean bright pink like bubble-gum pink. I mean a soft pink called *rosa*—like rose-petal pink. That's why she's decided to name it *Villa Rosa*, but the rest of us still call it the Ritz. I'm watching a man and woman pile out of the car with suitcases. A small girl climbs out behind them. The mother hands her a little crutch, which she uses to limp toward the guesthouse. The girl's complexion is much darker than her parents'. My guess is she's around nine or ten years old.

Mama greets the new guests with the warm welcome spiel, while

Daddy hauls their luggage into the guest suite. I suddenly realize that this motel business is going to add a whole new dimension to my life. I'll have people to journal about again, just like when the summer people came to Indian Island.

Mama's chatting up a storm under the grape arbor with Mrs. Rizzatti. "You might think about taking a little dip in the pool this evening. Very refreshing on a day like today. My kids just live for the water. I'll bet your daughter likes to swim too …"

Oh, Mama, come on, the poor kid can hardly walk.

"Rosa *loves* to swim."

Figures.

Leaving the family in peace, Mama reappears on the terrace. "The Rizzattis will be joining us for supper tonight. Can I get your head out of that book long enough to help set the table?"

That's part of Mama's welcome package; the first meal is with us. This way the guests can see who they're stuck with for their vacation. Wait 'til they meet Nonna.

"Before you start on the table, could you please hunt up a tray for Nonna? I think we'll serve her supper in her own place tonight."

Wise choice. "So what's the story with that little girl?"

"Isn't she a doll? Apparently they adopted her last year from an orphanage in Guatemala."

"And what about her leg?"

"I'm pretty sure they adopted that, too." Mama snickers.

I give her a straight face. The last thing I want to do is encourage her warped sense of humor.

"According to Mrs. Rizzatti, Dr. Rizzatti performed surgery on little Rosa while he was on a medical mission, and they ended up adopting her. Poor little thing will always walk with a limp. They gave her an Italian middle name, Bella, so she's *Rosa Bella,* meaning beautiful rose."

That much I figured out.

"They brought her to Italy to meet their relatives, and booked Villa Rosa because of the name."

"Rosa Bella Visits Villa Rosa." I like it. I think I'll add that to the new novel lineup—after *Moon over Milan* and *The Secret Lives of Nuns.*

෴

I have been put in charge of arranging the candles and place settings in the formal dining room. The table looks like something the knights of the round table ate at—except it's not round. But it is seriously long, and can hold up to fifty people. These Italians are used to big gatherings. We have some pretty neat old candlesticks, dishes, and fancy silverware that we found in the cupboards when we moved in here. It all goes with the medieval-castle theme going on in this place. I hope these folks are into "old."

Mama's decided on spaghetti for supper, since it's the one traditional Italian dish that everyone, especially Americans, seem to like. True Italian spaghetti is nothing like American spaghetti. Italian spaghetti is mostly pasta with a little sauce. American spaghetti is a little pasta drenched in sauce. Mama likes to hit somewhere between the two, then goes wild with the Parmesan cheese.

The guests arrive at our front door just as Mama's placing steaming bowls on the table. "Go call your brothers to the table, A. J., and I'll get the door."

"Dino, Benji, J. R., come-n-get-it!" I holler from the back door.

Mama yanks me back inside. "Angelina, did I ask you to call Rin Tin Tin to supper, or your brothers?"

Is there a difference?

Benji and Dino tromp through the back door, dripping wet. They know by Mama's glare that they'd better shape up and dry off before they come to the table. We were all given *the talk* at breakfast on how to pretend we're from a dignified family who grew up with manners; the best actor wins a prize when the guests go home.

Once the boys reappear—looking like cherubs from heaven—Daddy asks a blessing over our guests and our food. I can't help staring at little Rosa. She looks across the table at me with those big brown eyes. How anyone could give up a child like that I do not understand.

It's nice to be able to speak English with these folks. The best part is Mrs. Rizzatti is a Southerner and has a full-blown Southern accent, which just soothes me to the core. "So, A. J.," she says, "where do y'all ride horses 'round here?"

Every time she talks I smile over at Mama and beam. I know it reminds her of the summer at Indian Island when I intentionally talked with a Southern accent and drove her nuts. When I answer Mrs. Rizzatti, I glance over at Mama and say, "Just over yonder a piece," and point up the road.

I can read Mama like a book. Right about now she's thinking, *Watch it, you're walking a pretty fine line, toots.*

Halfway through supper Nonna wanders in wearing her bathrobe and slippers, holding her empty tray. "Well, it seems I've missed the party."

"This is my mother, Juliana," Mama interjects.

"Lovely to meet you," Mrs. Rizzatti replies. "Won't you join us?"

Nonna sets her tray on the counter and says, "Oh, no, I'm not allowed at the family table anymore. I've been shunned for some time now." She tosses her silverware in the sink, causing a loud clank when it hits the porcelain. "Well, back to my dungeon." Nonna sighs, and shuffles out. Daddy smiles. Benji giggles. Mama sighs back.

⁂

After supper I'm reading by the pool while the boys dive for rings. Little Rosa comes hobbling down the hill in her bathing suit. "How can she swim with that leg of hers?" Benji whispers.

"We'll find out, I guess." I stick a feather in my book and move over by the shallow end. Rosa may need some help getting into the water. When she reaches the patio, she limps right past me to the deep end, executes a perfect swan dive, and comes up swimming like a fish. I'm standing here gawking like an idiot.

"Want to dive for rings with us?" Benji asks her.

"Sure!" Her face lights right up.

I toss the rings in the deep end for her, thinking she might get one at a time. Kicking her crooked little leg like mad, Rosa comes up holding all four rings. I can't help myself from clapping. Dino and Benji are clapping too. "Rosa, does your leg hurt when you swim?" Benji asks.

"Nope. When I'm swimming, I don't feel like I'm crippled. That's why I love to swim so much."

Now that just makes me want to sit here on the pool steps and bawl my head off for *ever* feeling sorry for myself. Rosa's mama is heading down the hill to watch her swim, so I excuse myself and leave Rosa with my brothers to dive for rings. I'm no longer needed to play lifeguard, and I desperately need to get some work done on *Moon over Milan*. I'm giving myself two weeks to finish it or I'm just going to burn the whole thing and start a new novel. I'm tired of leaving my main character in Italy for so long. It's high time she went home.

❦

At dusk Rosa agrees to a short walk with me to meet Caesar and Napoleon. Traipsing up the hill, it dawns on me that it's taking twice as long to cover half the distance with Rosa's gimpy little gait. It sure makes me appreciate being able to walk normal. It also makes me want to run and jump, just because I can. I only wish she could too.

Rosa's like me when it comes to animals. Animals can sense when someone likes them too. Within minutes of meeting the farm family, she has Caesar eating fresh grapes out of her hand, Napoleon bringing her sticks, and the chickens pecking at her feet. They all know a softie when they meet one.

Angelo comes out to say hello, then motions with his hand for us to follow him. Rosa and I follow him into the barn where he leads us to the horse stall next to Caesar's. A sheep dog and her litter of puppies are lying in the straw. "Oh, babies," Rosa whispers.

Just as I'm wondering whose puppies these are, Angelo points to the mama dog. "*Del cane di Carlotta.*" Carlotta's dog. Carlotta is

Angelo's sister. Then he points to Napoleon and flashes his tooth-less grin. "*Papà* Napoleon." The little farm family is no longer so little.

The puppies are so spankin' new and tiny, it's hard to believe they will ever be as big as Napoleon. A cross between a mastiff and a sheepdog should make for some pretty big shaggy dogs. We give the babies a few gentle pats, but Ci-ci gives us the protective-mama look, so we decide to leave her in peace with her family. People do the same when my Mama looks that way. A few Italian men have nearly had their heads bit off over a lingering glance at Adriana.

On the way home we stumble upon a little hedgehog attempting to cross the road. "*Un riccio,*" I tell Rosa. "We'd better move this little fella. Most drivers won't stop."

"I've never seen a hedgehog before," Rosa says.

As soon as I scoop him up, he rolls into a tight little ball. "They do that when they're scared."

"May I hold him?" she asks.

"Sure—he may stay in a ball though."

She hands me her crutch, so she can use both hands to cradle him. I place him gently in her open palms. She begins to walk—much more crooked without her crutch—but she carries that little fur ball like he's the most fragile thing in the world. When we reach the other side of the road, she kneels down to let him go. He doesn't budge, so Rosa gently sets him down in the grass. He slowly unrolls himself, and scurries away.

"I love animals," she whispers.

"I know; me, too." I know a kindred spirit when I see one.

We sit quietly in the tall grass, enjoying the chirping cricket symphony that surrounds us. They start up every evening and play for hours for anyone appreciative enough to listen. Even if only for an audience of two.

"Are you starting back to school soon?" I ask Rosa.

Her smile quickly fades. "Yeah, September."

"Do you like school?"

She shrugs. "Sometimes. But sometimes not."

"Why not?"

Rosa looks down at her leg. "Kids tease me sometimes. They call me Tiny Tim."

Okay, that does it. I want to slug someone. "You know what?"

"What?"

"Kids make fun of me, too."

"They do?" She looks at me wide-eyed.

"Yeah, they call me Yankee Doodle because I'm from the United States, and Barbie because they say I look like a Barbie doll."

"I wouldn't think anyone would make fun of you. I think you and Barbie are both pretty," she says.

Pretty. Wow. That's the first time someone has said *pretty* instead of *cute.*

"Well, you, Rosa Bella, are very pretty, too, so you remember that next time someone makes fun of you, okay?"

"Okay. You, too," she says, smiling back at me.

"Hey, I have an idea."

"What?"

"How about, every time someone makes fun of you, you

remember me and start to whistle 'I'm a Yankee Doodle Dandy.' It goes like this …" I even sing it for her.

Rosa starts to giggle. "Okay," she says. "And when someone makes fun of you, you have to remember me and say, 'God bless us, every one.'"

We both fall back in the grass laughing.

We lie on our backs and watch the clouds together. That's one thing about Tuscany, it has a big sky. "Do you have any pets?" she asks me.

"I have a dog named Sailor, but I had to leave him behind when we moved. I'm planning to go see him again in four years. I hope he'll remember me."

"I had a kitten at my orphanage. I miss her too, but I really miss my friends there a lot."

It didn't hit me 'til right now how hard that must be for her to move away from everyone she's ever known. They were her only family before. I tell her that she can write me letters anytime and I will write her back.

A butterfly circles overhead then flutters off. "How do you say butterfly in Spanish?" I ask Rosa.

"*Mariposa.*"

"I've always wondered why we call them butterflies instead of flutterbys. I mean, a butterfly has nothing to do with butter, but it does flutter by." *Another word to add to my dictionary.*

The stars are coming out and I realize it's getting late. "What time do you have to leave tomorrow?"

"Really early," Rosa replies. "Mama says we have a long drive ahead."

"We'd probably better start back then."

"Okay, Barbie," she says, and laughs.

"Come on, Tiny Tim, let's get on home."

God bless us, every one.

6

Vascanaza al mare
(Seaside Holiday)

Our taxi pulls up before the Grand Old Sea Palace. Stepping out of the cab, I stretch from a long day of travel, and turn to salute the sea. A gust of salty sea air hits my senses and I know I've arrived. The Sea Palace is right smack in front of the Mediterranean with a swimming bay and nice sandy beach—a rare find along the Riviera. This is our third summer holiday at the seashore—another tradition in our family. It's still not Indian Island, but if I have to settle for anything less, this is my absolute favorite place to go in Italy. It's also my last big hurrah before heading back to school—my absolute least favorite place to go.

Nothing inspires the writer in me more than being around H_2O. I am drawn to water like a duck. Maybe it's because my body is mostly made up of the stuff, and like Indian Lake, the sea has this instinctive pull, luring me to its shores. So, alas, here I stand before the sea, mesmerized by the rhythm of the tide—in and out, in and out …

"A. J., get your fanny in gear and help take the bags up to the room!" Mama has a way of squelching the seaside poet in me.

"I'm coming, I'm coming." Entering the gargantuan lobby, I am quickly reminded of what a *grand* hotel this really is. A *grand* old lobby with a *grand* piano. Even the ornate elevator is grand. There's just no other word to describe it, but grand, grand, grand. Wait, yes there is. *Grandioso!*

On the way up to our room, I'm thinking how nice it is to have our whole family here together again. Even Adriana has joined us for the week. She treats me with more respect now that she's moved away from home. I think she's starting to see me more as her equal, rather than just her dumb little sister.

"Move your bags, A. J. I already called dibs on the bed. You get the roll-away cot this time."

So much for respect. I toss my bags on the little cot in the corner. I could have sworn I had the cot last time we were here. I think Adriana has pulled this every time we've come. I remind myself I'm only in this room to sleep anyway. My agenda is to be out on the beach from sunup to sundown.

After throwing on my swimsuit, cover-up, sunglasses, and baseball cap, I pack up my beach bag for the day: *Doctor Zhivago,* my travel journal and pen, suntan lotion, dive mask, beach towel, money for postcards, and my novel—the one that I'm writing. Grabbing my room key, I fly out the door and head for the stairwell. I have no patience when it comes to waiting for elevators—even if it means taking five flights of stairs. The beach is calling. In case I forget what my game plan is, I made a list on the train of things to be accomplished today:

1. Go swimming in the pool
2. Dive for shells in the ocean
3. Go for a long beach walk

4. Write the last chapter of my book

5. Eat a greasy Vienna sausage from a beach vendor

6. Burn myself to a crisp from too much sun

Reaching the cabana, I see the twins have already beat me to the pool. This is no ordinary pool—it has a pirate ship built right into the middle of it. The *Buccaneer* looks just like a real pirate ship. Not that I've ever seen one, but I'm sure this is what it would look like if I had. Dino and Benji are in pirate's paradise. A climbing ladder leads to a crow's nest, with a slide that lands you back in the pool. Ropes hanging from the mast swing out over the deep end. There's even a plank for a diving board, which Dino is forcing Benji to walk right now. They appear to be in the middle of a modern-day reenactment of *Mutiny on the Bounty*.

"Die, sucker—the sharks await you below!" Dino always finds a way to torment Benji.

Benji makes a quick move to escape, but he trips over his own feet and grabs onto Dino, and they both fall into the pool together. Their two heads bob back up at the same time. "A. J., come dive for treasure with us," Benji yells.

I loved this treasure hunt game the first summer we came, probably because I went undefeated all week. The game is still the same. There are little gold coins all over the bottom of the pool to dive for. At the end of each day, they tally up your loot and the highest score is displayed on the bow of the *Buccaneer*. By the end of the week, everyone redeems their loot for treasure and the winner gets a bag of "real jewels"—or so they say. But I know differently.

Two summers ago we made our maiden voyage, by train, to the Grand Old Sea Palace. There I was, diving my heart out on the grand ol' *Buccaneer*. All week long I kept picturing this big sack of jewels I'd be toting home with me. Then along comes this kid from Ireland who thinks he's going to beat my score. He was on my nerves from the get-go: a hyper red-headed, buck-toothed kid who was a self-proclaimed leprechaun. He added an exaggerated Irish accent that put my fake Southern accent to shame. I named him Lucky, after Lucky Charms cereal.

Every morning at the crack of dawn, Lucky came prancing out on the bow of the *Buccaneer*, saying, "Aye, mate, me's going to beat yer score t'day." And every morning he showed up sporting more diving gear—fins, mask, snorkel, professional dive bag to collect his loot in.

"Well, shiver-me-timbers," I exclaimed, "where's the wet suit and air tanks?"

"Aye, mate, t'day's the day …" he said one time too many.

There was no way I was going to give my championship to an overzealous leprechaun. "Go ahead," I told him, "they filled the pool with piranhas last night to make it more challenging."

"Did not."

"Did so, but they only like the taste of boys—especially Irish boys." Then I dove in.

Lucky stood on the bow of the *Buccaneer* in his entire diving ensemble, still clutching the dive bag in his little freckled hands. He watched me like a shark while I swam around scooping up the gold. In the time it took him to scan the pool for piranhas, my bucket was nearly full of coins. After asking the pool boy about the piranhas, Lucky informed me, "Ye owes me half yer gold fer lying to me."

"Listen up, Lucky," I told him, "I owe you no such thing. It's not my fault you're a gullible little leprechaun. It's part of the game—real pirates say things like that all the time."

"Then pirates have the right to steal gold from other pirates too," he says.

"Yeah, a lot of pirates die that way," I reassured him.

So one afternoon I was up in the crow's nest sunbathing next to my bucket of gold, when a freckled hand reached in and grabbed a fistful of my coins. That's when Lucky's luck ran out. Unfortunately so did mine. Lucky's mom and dad happened to be watching when I grabbed their son by the arm and hurled him from the crow's nest into the pool, still wearing his dive mask. He walked around with a permanent impression of his mask embedded around his eyes for the rest of the week. I was disqualified from the competition, thanks to parental involvement.

At the end of the week, I traded in the gold coins I'd collected. After all I'd gone through to defend my title and bring home the treasure, I was handed a bag of cheap plastic trinkets that supposedly resembled jewels. Lucky walked away with a bigger bag of the same junk. The next year I became a beachcomber instead. My diving days on the *Buccaneer* were done for.

I wouldn't mind rehashing Lucky-the-leprechaun stories with my twin brothers, but I do need to bow out of the game this time. "Sorry, Benji, I'd love to dive for treasure with you, but the beach is calling." Upward and onward.

Time to set up base camp! Lounge chair? Check. Umbrella? Check. Crowd control? I lay my towel out for buffer zone. Check. I'll follow this routine every day. Same time, same station. Parking my stuffed beach bag on my chair, I head for the water. Fortunately everything is within eyeshot from here: the pool, the beach, the bay, the palace, so I don't have to worry about someone stealing my manuscript if I want to take a swim. It's always a concern until it's published and copyrighted.

I am not a dive-in-headfirst kind of gal. I like to test the waters one toe at a time, then work my way in from there. This routine begins by standing at the shoreline, letting the waves greet me. I'm all for the gradual approach. Once my feet are wet, I inch in up to my waist. Oooo-boy! Not exactly bath water—unless you fill the bathtub with cold water. The hardest part is my shoulders, and I still haven't figured out why. I have the same amount of skin on my shoulders as I do anywhere else. I know the best way to go is to just dive in head first and get it over with.

Nope, can't do it. I think I'll just go and lay in the sun until I get hot.

"Bombs away!" Dino comes charging down the beach from the pool and executes a human cannonball, drenching me in ocean spray.

"Thanks a lot, buster." I fling a handful of water back at him, and we're into a full-blown water fight. So much for the gradual approach.

Back at base camp it's time to get down to business. While the sun is busy drying me off, I pull out my spiral notebook titled *Moon over Milan*. I've been working on this novel for three years up in my writing tower and really need to end it. That's my goal for the trip—to finish my novel. I'm planning to send the story synopsis off to a few New York publishers as soon as I can come up with the ending. Grandma Angelina sends me writing magazines from America each month to keep me in the know. According to my latest issue of

Writer's Digest, Moon over Milan is the kind of story editors are dying to get their hands on.

BOOK PROPOSAL: MOON OVER MILAN

Complete Story Synopsis

By Angelina Juliana Degulio

Pen Name: Dorothy Jones

Genre: Literary Romance

Length: However long you want it

Competition: "Romeo and Juliet," "Pride and Prejudice,"

"Wuthering Heights," "Doctor Zhivago"

"Moon over Milan" is a heart-wrenching love saga about a girl named Janeà and her childhood friend, Tanner. Janeà and Tanner grew up together on the tiny seaside island of Boonadogga, meaning "dog bone" in Swanagi (fictional language), because it's shaped like a dog bone. At age ten Janeà is torn away from her beloved little island to move halfway around the world to Milan, Italy, where her father inherited a peanut farm. She has to leave behind her Saint Bernard puppy, Christopher, as well as her soul mate, Tanner. Tanner owns Christopher's sister, Robin, so now he has to raise both Christopher and Robin himself.

As Janeà is being dragged away by her mean peanut-farmer father, she tosses her lucky rabbit's foot to Tanner, making him promise to give it back someday. Tanner promises Janeà he'll come find her when he grows up.

Eight years pass by. One night Janeà is walking through

the streets of Milan feeling alone in the world (her whole family died when the peanut roaster blew up). Suddenly, under the moonlight, she sees someone in the park sitting on a bench. He's playing fetch with two full-grown Saint Bernards. She hears him call the name "Christopher."

That's as far as I've gotten. I'd like to drag it out a little and make it somewhat less predictable. Maybe it will all just turn out to be a coincidence. The guy in the park ends up being someone named Joe, but he's really nice and looks just like Little Joe Cartwright from *Bonanza*. The reader will be torn over what Janeà should do—marry Joe, or hold out for Tanner? I think I'll just go buy a Vienna sausage for now.

Returning to the pool, sausage dog in hand, I find Adriana surrounded by a number of young Italian males. Typical. She's doing her best to ignore them, but they aren't getting the hint.

A small crowd of people have also gathered around the pool cabana, with my Mama in the middle of them handing out little pink cards. They're all smiling and nodding their heads. *What is she up to now?* Looking up, she spies my sausage dog and saunters over for a bite. "I hope you're planning to share some of that with your poor starving mother."

"Mama, what were you handing out there?" I ask, while offering up a bite.

Half a sausage dog later, she says, "Business cards. I am just letting these traveling folks know that if they ever need a place to stay in Tuscany, Sophia's Villa Rosa is up and running."

"Oh, now it's '*Sophia's* Villa Rosa'?"

"Whatever sells soup."

"Okay, well, I'm going for my beach walk now. Where's Daddy?"

"Your father is hiding behind his magazine right over there, hoping I don't start another scene. I let everyone know right off the bat that I am not the real thing. Besides, even if I were, beach people are far too relaxed to work themselves into a frenzy. They are enjoying the resemblance though."

Heading down the beach, I spot J. R. involved in a volleyball game. There seems to be something here for everyone. I'm fascinated by all the different boats out on the water: yachts, sailboats, ski boats ...

"*Buongiorno, signorina.*"

Startled, I turn and find a guy walking behind me. "*Buongiorno*, yourself."

He starts rattling something off in Italian about his uncle's boat, then in English asks, "Want to go up in the air?"

"Um, *non capisco.*" I understand the language, but have no idea what he's talking about.

He takes me by the arm and turns me toward the bay, then points up.

Holy Toledo! There's a man tied behind a boat, flying in the air like a kite!

"My uncle's boat," he says, and asks again if I want to go up in the air.

I'm speechless. I recall hearing about something like this when our cousins got back from Mexico. Cousin Nicky said he did it and had a blast. And now it's made its way to the Riviera.

The guy hands me a flier with the rates on it, and points down the beach. I can see others waiting, so that must be where the boat takes off from.

"Grazie!" I take off running toward our hotel. I figure if Cousin Nicky could do this, there is no reason why I can't. I have always dreamed of flying and this is probably as close as I'll ever get. The more I think about it, the faster I run.

"Hey, Daddy!" I bellow, the minute I'm within yelling distance of the pool. "I want to go up in the air behind a boat!"

Daddy casually lowers his magazine. "Do what?"

"Fly behind a boat like a kite on a string! Remember what Nicky did in Mexico?"

"You mean parasailing?"

"Yeah, that's it—*parasailing*! Can I go?" I hand Daddy the rate sheet.

He does not appear enthused. "It's not cheap, is it?"

"I can pitch in some of my birthday money—I've got a small wad leftover."

"Are you sure you want to do this? You'll be up there pretty high."

"Sure I'm sure. It's only water below, right?"

He sighs. "Well, let's see what Mom has to say about it."

"Are you nuts, A. J.? That's the craziest thing I've ever heard—a human kite?"

"Oh, Mama, if Cousin Nicky did it, anyone can. Daddy says I can if you let me."

"Oh, he did, did he?" Mama glances out from under the rim of her big sun hat, trying to spot Daddy. She's on the sunny side of the pool, Daddy's on the shady side.

"Well, I'll tell you what, if Daddy says he's willing to go with you and watch, then you go right ahead, but don't expect me to watch you dangling from a string in the air. I don't think my nerves could handle it."

"Thank you!"

I run back over to Daddy. "Let's go!"

Ten minutes later I am headed down the beach, followed by Daddy, J. R., Dino, Benji, Adriana, and yes, even Mama. They've all come to watch me fly.

After I've asked the man to repeat the instructions for the fifth time, he signals to his crew to take over. Three big guys strap me into a harness, and get ready to launch me.

"Daddy, are you sure they buckled me in here right?"

"You look good to go, kid."

"Are you sure—" Before I can finish my personal safety check, the boat takes off. The three guys are running down the beach along-side me, holding onto my harness. Then the wind catches my sail, and I am instantly swooshed into the air. My cheering section below is going wild, especially Mama, but I'm not sure if she's cheering or screaming. I continue climbing higher and higher … and higher. I'm presently feeling a little dizzy … and a little queasy … *quizzy*. Come to think of it, I do have a tiny fear of heights. The higher I go, the quizzier I get.

Passing through the ozone layer, I beginning worrying about the tow rope detaching from my harness … and if it does … I'll be carried out to sea by the wind in my sail … and won't come down until I'm way out in the middle of the ocean … sharks … *I can't breathe* …

"*Help!*" I've changed my mind. Screaming at the top of my lungs, I'm kicking my legs and waving my arms like a puppet on a string. A tangled string! Oh, this blasted contraption. "Get me down!" I don't want to fly, I don't want to die … "Mama!"

Can't they hear me down there? Whoa … looking down makes my head spin, so I close my eyes. Oooh, it can get worse. I open my eyes. Whose idiotic idea was this, anyway? People weren't meant to fly. "Mama, help me! Stop the boat! Get me down!"

No one's listening. No one cares. I might be passing out … then I'll drown … surrounded by hungry sharks …

After ten full minutes of mind-blasting torment, the boat slows up along the shoreline. *Finally.* I'm floating down … slowly, slowly, down toward the beach. I look for the big guys whose job it is to catch me, and spot three tiny dots waving their arms. If this were Adriana, there'd be twenty of them fighting to catch her. I picture myself coming in for a landing while they all stick their hands back in their pockets, arguing over who's going to catch me.

"You get her."

"No, you get her."

Then they'll all back away, and watch me splat face first in the sand. The shell seekers along the beach will be shaking their heads: "If only she looked like her sister, this never would have happened."

I'm floating down over the beach trying to convince myself this would probably not *really* happen, when a huge gust of wind sweeps into my sail and jolts me back out over the water. *What the heck?* I'm too paralyzed to even scream. *I'm doomed. I'm going to die. Sharks ...*

The cool water quickens my senses, which is the only reason I've come to. I feel myself being reeled in toward the boat by my harness, then I'm hoisted up and over the side of the boat like a trophy fish on a hook.

Speeding back toward land, I spot my family on shore. Talk about humiliating. I'm so embarrassed I could die. Mama will say, "I told you so." Daddy will say, "What a waste of good money." The boys will say, "What a *girl.*" Adriana will say, "What did we expect from our drama queen anyway?"

Climbing out of the boat, I turn to face my accusers. Instead of sneering ... they're all cheering for me.

"Bravo, kiddo!" Mama lets out one of her big whistles.

"Was it cool up there, or what?" Dino asks.

Or what! Didn't they hear me screaming for my mama like a two-year-old? Didn't they see the flying nutcase? ... Guess not. Maybe they couldn't hear me from way up there . . .

"Uh ... yeah, it was ... unbelievable."

"I even heard you calling my name," Mama says, "so I finally uncovered my eyes and saw you waving at me. You looked like you were having the time of your life up there."

" ... I sure was."

7

Postcards from Paradise

Dear Danny,

    We're on vacation. Here is a picture of our hotel and beach. If you look at the little white cloud in the sky at the top of the postcard, that's where I was yesterday. I went parasailing—as in: a human kite tied behind a boat. Not as fun as it looked. Landed in the bay. Lucky to be alive. If you ever get asked to try it, just say no.

                    Wish I were there,

                    A. J.

Adding a personal touch, I draw a little stick figure of myself up by the cloud, hooked to a sail, with sharks circling in the water below. I add a little word bubble, "Help!"

I've decided to keep my feet on the ground today and come up with an ending for this dang novel. Now I'm torn between two new endings.

Unpredictable Ending: Janeà sees the guy in the park with the dog named Christopher. She runs to him ... but when she reaches him ... it's not Tanner. It's Joe. Even though Joe is really cute, his dogs remind Janeà too much of her past life. "So long, Joe. You really are cute, but ... your dogs bring back too many memories from the corners of my mind."

"B-but, Janeà ... we can make this work ... I'll trade them in for poodles ... "

"Forget about me, Joe ... I hate poodles." Janeà jumps on a ship and sails back home. She shows up back at her island and everything has changed, except the little hut that she grew up in. "Anyone here?" she yells. The two dogs come running out to meet her. But where's Tanner?

She notices a note tied to Christopher's collar. "I've gone to Milan to search for Janeà. Please feed the dogs."

The End

I think I'll go mail my postcard.

On my way through the lobby, I pass the gift shop where I plan to buy all of my souvenirs before returning home. Scanning the items in the window display, my eyes catch on a painting titled *Paradise*, and I put the skids on my sandals. It's the same image I've had in my head ever since I was a kid: a small child wearing a white robe, leading all of the animals through paradise. This is how I picture heaven, and what I hope to be doing once I'm up there.

What I really like about the painting are the bright colors. Crystal prism colors; like the prisms in the movie *Pollyanna*. Red, orange, yellow, green, blue, indigo, and violet, all in a gold frame ... I'm fascinated how the little child is leading the animals toward a bright sunset—so bright, it leaves you feeling like they're being led to Jesus. That's what good art should do … leave one feeling led to Jesus. After all, God created the artist and gave him the gift, and if he uses his gift to inspire, it should reflect his Creator …

"Hey, A. J., I gotta go to the bathroom. I need your room key. The pool bathroom's being cleaned."

Dino is dripping wet in his swimsuit, with a towel draped around his waist. Handing off my key, I focus back on the masterpiece in the window. "Hey, Dino, what do you think of that painting?"

Dino cocks his head to one side. "Pretty dumb." He drips his way down the hall.

Another inspired moment snatched away by a pesky brother. I check the price. Too much. Back to plan A. Cheap trinket souvenirs.

❦

"One postage stamp please."

The man at the concierge desk hands me a stamp.

"Charge it to room 503."

The man frowns at me. "You're from room 503?"

"Yes, sir,"

"I have a phone message for you." He takes a slip of paper from our room box. "Do you know this person?"

I look at the name. Juliana Gulliano. "Yep, that's my Nonna."

He glares at me. "She said her family abandoned her and left the country."

I just smile. "Yep, that's Nonna. I'll give my folks the message.

Thanks." It's really not worth the energy trying to explain Nonna to people.

Returning to the pool, I notice Mama's engaged with more tourists, so I just hand Daddy the message. "She told the desk clerk we abandoned her and left the country."

"Again?"

"Yeah, she talked to a different desk clerk this time. By the time we leave, no one will be smiling at us anymore. Are you planning to call her back this time?"

"No, it didn't help last time. I'm sure she'll be just fine at Aunt Gen's until we get back."

Daddy crumples up the note and goes back to his crossword puzzle. A few minutes later the desk clerk comes out and waves me back into the lobby. He sends me back to the pool with a pool phone on a very long cord. "Daddy, it's Aunt Genevieve this time."

"Oh, great," he mumbles. "Hello, Genevieve, what's going on?"

Leaning closer, all I catch is Aunt Gen's high tones of hysteria.

Daddy calmly replies, "She always does that, Gen, just take the scissors away from her and hide them."

Mama comes over and I tell her it's her sister. She sits next to Daddy and tries to listen in too.

"Well, if you don't want her cutting paper doll chains out of your bed sheets just give her some paper instead."

All I can catch is, "*Something, something … statues.*"

"Don't worry, she won't take your statues with her, she just misses having her own to talk to."

Daddy cups the phone, and whispers, "She rounded up all the

Greek statues in the house, dragged them to her room, and is now cutting the bed sheets into paper doll chains."

"Oh, for crying out loud, give me the phone."

Daddy willingly hands over the phone.

"Genevieve, I have been caring for our mother for over three years now. You've had her for what … *two days*? And you're calling us on our vacation to whine over a few bed sheets? Grow up." Mama hangs up.

Nice to see Mama's talking to her sister again.

Daddy looks over at Mama and says, "Soph, I think there are very few people in this world gifted enough to deal with your mother … and you may be it." Then he stands up and holds out his hand to her. "So what do you say we hit some waves?"

Mama and Daddy are splashing each other in the waves like a couple of kids. It's so weird to see grown-ups not acting their age. At least they have each other to help get their minds off Nonna and the strange relatives we aren't talking to.

Sinking comfortably into my beach chair, I immerse myself in *Doctor Zhivago*. I am really enjoying where Yuri and Lara find each other again after the war ends. He shows up on her doorstep as a human ice cube, then he goes inside to defrost in her cozy little apartment. But pretty soon I'm thinking, wait a minute here, this Yuri guy is married to sweet Tonya now, and here he is back with Nurse Lara. But you almost want him back with Lara because they loved each other before. Then I realize how horrible it is to make your reader like both women and you don't know which one he should pick. But, really, Yuri's a jerk for being with both of them since he's married to Tonya. I'm so disturbed over having my emotions compromised!

I slam the book shut, refusing to finish it. I will not put my readers in a compromising situation like that in *Moon over Milan*.

Adriana comes over and pulls up a chair next to me. "What are you reading?"

"Well, I was reading *Doctor Zhivago*, until Yuri decided to be in love with that Nurse Lara again after he married Tonya. I refuse to spend my summer vacation with a two-timing doctor who can't make up his mind."

"Yeah, well, if that bothered you, it's probably best to quit now then. I saw the movie—it only gets worse."

"Sounds like another love tragedy gone wrong." I'll have to end *Moon over Milan* on a happy note to help balance the scales with these tragic love stories they keep coming out with.

"So, speaking of tragic love stories, how would you like to go dancing at the beach club tonight?"

"How is that related to tragic love stories?"

"Well, when you dance with the Italians, they always convince themselves they're madly in love because foreign girls seem so intriguing to them. They'll tell the story for generations to come about the American girl they once danced with who stole their heart and left them. They love the drama."

"Well ..." Adriana's never invited me along before. "I don't know."

"Come on. It'll be fun."

"But I don't know how to dance anything but the *kalamatianos*."

"Oh, just come anyway—I don't want to look like I've shown up alone."

Okay, I get it. It's not sisterly bonding she's after—she just needs me there as a fixture to keep from looking stupid. Whatever. Back to my novel.

Romantic Ending: Janeà walks by the park and two big Saint Bernards come running over. They jump all over her like they can't get over seeing her again. Then some guy yells, "Christopher, Robin, get down!" He comes over to apologize for his dogs, but suddenly stops. "Janeà?" He whispers. "Can it be?"

"Tanner? Is it really you?"

He reaches in his pocket and pulls out the lucky rabbit's foot. "Here, you made me promise to give this back to you someday. I've been to Kingdom come and back looking for you. It's been gnarly, but here I am."

Like two magnets attracting from opposite ends of the earth, Tanner and Janeà fall headlong into an embrace. Tanner takes Janeà's face in his hands and looks into her sparkling chartreuse eyes. "You could have left a forwarding address, you know?"

She looks back into his hypnotic hazelnut eyes. "But then you would have mailed it back. This way you had to come in person." She looks down at the rabbit's foot that brought them back together, and a tear falls from her eye. "You got it all dirty ..."

"You're such a girl," Tanner replies. He draws her lips to his and gently devours them, while Christopher and Robin bark for joy under the moon over Milan.

The End

I can relate to how Herman Melville must have felt the day he finished writing *Moby Dick*. What a relief!

On the way to dinner we pass by *Paradise* again. I linger a bit as we walk by. *I sure would like to buy that.* Maybe if I bought it, it would help remind me to pray—for my enemies, like Annalisa. Help pray her into heaven. Actually she might already believe, in which case I'd have to pray that she likes me by the time we get to heaven or that we live at opposite ends. Maybe Daddy would loan me some money to buy it—I could tell him I'd pray for him more often if I could borrow the money …

"Get along, little doggie, you're holding up the whole herd."

This probably isn't the time to ask him for the money.

After dinner Adriana tells Mama and Daddy that we're going for a beach walk. We end up at the *Sea Palace Beach Club*, a dance club cabana with a live band. Adriana leads me to an outside table, where people are actually dancing barefoot in the sand. I must be the youngest person here.

After our sodas arrive, two guys come over and sit at our table, uninvited. They start speaking to us in Italian. Adriana responds in pig Latin. The guys look completely baffled. Even I can join in on this one. So I ask her in pig Latin why she doesn't want to talk to them.

"Arried-may," she says.

I look at their hands—ep-yay. Yep, wedding rings. "Uck-yay!"

They finally get the hint and go away.

Moments later a dreamy guy—with no wedding ring—asks Adriana to dance, and she accepts. That leaves me sitting here alone. Before long, the parasailing salesman wanders by. "*Buona sera,*" he says.

"Oh, hi ... er ... *buona sera.*" *And no, I don't want to go parasailing in the dark.*

"*Vuole ballare?*" Would you like to dance? he asks.

"No."

"*Neanch' io,*" me neither. He says his name is Antonio, and that he doesn't like to dance. "May I sit at your table?"

"Go ahead, just don't ask me to go parasailing again."

He points to the guy with Adriana and says that's his uncle.

"*That's* your uncle?" *The guy who drove the boat for the lunatic in the sky?*

He nods.

Great. They probably both had a good laugh over what a screaming ninny I was.

He says his uncle wants him to practice speaking English so he can talk to the American tourists about parasailing. Since parasailing is very new along the Riviera, most tourists have never heard of it before. In perfect English he says, "My uncle said you were very brave—especially when you had to land in the water."

"He ... said that?" *Apparently he didn't realize I had passed out from fear.* "Your English is so good—why have you been speaking Italian to me all this time?"

He shrugs. "Just embarrassed."

"Of what?"

"Of … how I sound."

"Your English sounds better than my Italian, that's for sure." I laugh. "Can I ask you something, Antonio?"

"What?"

"If someone were up in the air, and suddenly started screaming her head off, would anyone in the boat or on land hear her?"

"The people in the boat wouldn't hear much except the motor, and the people on the beach wouldn't hear too well because of the distance and wind. They might know someone is yelling, but not what she's saying."

"So let's say if someone were up there yelling 'Help, get me down, I don't want to die or get eaten by sharks!' you might not be able to tell what she was saying?"

Antonio looks at me and smiles. "No, I didn't know what you were saying …"

"Oh." *I guess I could have handled that inquiry a little better.*

"Don't worry, I won't tell. You were brave enough to go up. I haven't even done that yet."

"*Really?*"

"Really—afraid of heights." Antonio looks up and sees his three brothers and hails them over to the table. "Would you like to meet my family?"

"Uh, sure." I quickly recognize them as the guys who launched me off the beach.

I'm sitting here at the Sea Palace Beach Club, laughing my head off with four *grandioso* Italian guys who all look like they starred in *The Godfather,* when who should walk up to our table but Daddy.

Daddy personally escorts me and Adriana back to our hotel room. He stops by the cabana just long enough to inform Mama that Adriana's beach walk resulted in my entertaining the Italian Mafia at our table—solo. Speaking of solo, not one to miss out on an opportunity, Mama's dancing her way, solo, through the poolside cabana, handing out her business cards to the night crowd.

When we get back to our room, escorted by Daddy, we get the lecture of our lives. There will be no more beach walks after dark on this trip.

I'm trying to think of a creative way to remember this night and it finally comes to me. I've always wanted to know what it feels like to receive a postcard from an exotic destination. And knowing that Daddy picks up the mail makes this idea even more fun. I go to the lobby and pick out a postcard with a scene of the Sea Palace Beach Club on it. Disguising my handwriting, I write:

Dear A. J.,

It was a pleasure to meet with you at the Grand Sea Palace Beach Club. I'm so pleased you've made the decision to join our organization. You seem like such a brave girl, I'm sure you will be an asset in helping to advance our cause. Welcome aboard. We'll be in touch.

Fondly,
Your Godfather,
Joe Spumoni
Italian Mafia

8

A Grand Old Hallelujah

As of this morning I have moved base camp to the to the pool area. Since completing *Moon over Milan*, I no longer need the privacy required by an author when working on a novel. At my new camp I've discovered a small gray mouse staked out in the shrub beside my chair. I've been watching him all morning, skirting back and forth beneath the lounge chairs of a few unsuspecting Frenchwomen. He scurries around gathering their fancy French pastry crumbs, and hustles back under his shrub. I panic every time someone nearly steps on him, which is why I plan to keep my camp right next to his hideaway. I'm playing lifeguard for the little fella. Pretty sure I'm the only one who has noticed him so far.

If he were discovered, most tourists would scream, then insist on having him exterminated. That's what separates the merciful from the morons in this life. "Hey, Dino, save me the crumbs from your box of animal crackers, will ya?"

"What for, so you can feed them to the dumb mouse?"

"What mouse?"

"The one that swiped all of my peanuts yesterday while I was busy diving for gold."

"How do you know it was a mouse?"

"Do you have a better name for that furry little gray thing with two tiny ears and a long tail?"

"Where?"

"Staked out in the bushes right next to your chair."

"Oh, fine. Just save me the cracker crumbs, will you?"

Dino hands me the little box with a few whole crackers still left.

"Thanks." I discreetly toss the crackers into the bushes.

❧

After getting sunburned on both sides of my body, I feel like a well-done rotisserie pig and pack it all up for the day. To avoid going by the gift shop altogether, I take the stairs instead. I'll take my money with me and buy my souvenirs after supper. I won't look at *Paradise*—I'll walk straight in, look only at the souvenirs, and purchase them. Jesus would not want me to go in debt to buy *Paradise*.

An hour later we're on our way to dinner. *Don't look … don't look … it's …* "Oh my gosh—it's on sale!"

"What's on sale?" Mama asks.

"*Paradise*—they're clearing out *Paradise*! I have to buy it …" I pull out my wallet and start through the door.

"A. J., we're going to eat."

"Hold on, Daddy, I need to buy *Paradise*."

"Paradise? I didn't realize it was for sale."

"Well, it is, and now it's half price."

"Really? The Lord must be having a hard time getting occupants up there."

"Oh, Daddy, that's not even funny to make jokes about heaven."

"Can't we deal with heaven later?" Adriana moans. "We're all hungry and want to eat right now."

"Yeah, bag heaven, I'm hungry," Dino adds.

Something inside of me snaps. "How can you all stand here and say that eating is more important than heaven? Don't you care what Jesus went through to be able to get you there? Do you think He was *comfortable* up there on that cross? Does this mean *nothing* to you? Is that all you care about—*food?*" Now I'm crying while I'm at it.

My sister has that look that tells anyone walking by that she is *not even remotely* related to me. The rest of the family looks like they deserve all the pity they can get because they *are* related to me.

"A. J.," Daddy says, quietly, but firmly, "is there a reason why you can't wait until after supper to buy this?"

"Yes, there's a reason. I've had this vision in my head ever since I was three years old. It's been my calling to be a keeper of His critters. That's why I rescued Sailor, that's what my critter cemetery is all about. I want to qualify for the animal-keeper position in heaven. I've walked past this painting all week but couldn't afford to buy it. And here it is on clearance. If I don't buy it, someone else will, and if they do, I will be so upset I'll probably go absolutely insane and out of my mind!"

Daddy looks over at Mama. "I'm fairly sure I would go absolutely insane and out of my mind without heaven too."

Mama cocks her head to one side. "Isn't that an oxymoron? Buying paradise?"

Everyone looks at each other.

"It just strikes me funny—getting material over paradise." Mama shrugs.

I take her shrug as a green light.

All eyes are on me as I slip inside and place my lira on the counter. The shop lady heard it all and has already pulled *Paradise* out of the window display. She wraps it up in butcher paper and tapes it up for me. Then I set off with my family for the Grand Old Sea Palace Restaurant as the proud new owner of *Paradise*.

After stuffing myself silly on *gnocchi* and *polenta*—potato dumplings and cornmeal mush—I set out on a sunset stroll for my last evening at the sea. One of the highlights of my trip has been observing the wildlife around here—the mouse by the pool, sea birds at sea, and dogs playing on the beach, fetching sticks like Sailor always did. There are some gigantic seabirds that look like they could carry a whale in their beaks. They even take their naps perched on the bows of wooden fishing boats anchored in the bay, where they're rocked to sleep by the waves. It's very peaceful to watch. Funny thing, they don't seem afraid of humans at all, and I'm wondering just how tame they are. I've decided to find out.

One of the birds by the rocks doesn't even budge when people walk by, so I'm slowly working my way over there without scaring him away. I start to talk to him in a soft, gentle voice, hoping to gain his trust. A young fisherman is loading up his net near the rocks where the bird is resting. "*Scusate, signori?*" I ask.

He looks up and nods.

I ask him if the birds are friendly.

"*Sì, molto amichevole.*" Yes, very friendly, he tells me.

"Really? They won't bite me?"

"No," he says. He motions for me to pet the bird, and smiles kindly.

As I inch my way closer, the bird eyes me back, cautiously. His head is so cute and fuzzy up close. He really does look friendly. I reach my hand toward him…. Suddenly his huge beak opens, then nearly snaps my hand off. Jerking away, I shoot a glare over at the fisherman. He's laughing his head off, like this is just the funniest joke he's played on anyone in a long time. He walks over to the rocks and holds his hand out to me, still laughing. "*Sei una grande, signorina*," he says, which means that I'm a good sport.

No, just really stupid.

He gives me a hand up the rocks. "*Voi Americani matti volete toccare tutto.*" You crazy Americans want to touch everything.

⌬

I awake to the sound of the wind. My last day at the Grand Old Sea Palace. Looking out at the bay, I realize this is going to be one wild day at sea for those fishing boats. I have been waiting all week for those waves to pick up enough momentum to take me bodysurfing. On an average day this bay is too calm to get a ride back to shore on the crest of a wave. But today is the day.

I gobble up the last bite of my croissant, gulp down my orange juice, wipe my mouth, and announce: "Welcome to the 1972 Grand Old Surfing Championships on the Grand Old Salty Bay—first contestant up, A. J. Degulio. In other words I'm going surfing."

Mama looks up from her morning paper, takes a sip of espresso while peering out at the bay. "A. J., those do not look like friendly waters today, at all. The pool might be a better option until that wind dies down."

"But that's why I'm going in the bay. I've been waiting all week to catch a wave. Don't worry, I'll be careful."

"Yeah, I've heard that before. Remember, this is our last day, so don't do anything idiotic. And remember, we all have to be packed up and ready to check out by noon."

Entering the bay, I notice I'm not the only daredevil out here, which is a good sign. I plunge fearlessly into the icy waters of the Mediterranean and kick my way out to the breakers and catch a wave. The first swell is a snap. You just have to know when to start paddling back toward shore—before that wave crests on top of you. You also need to know when it's time to bail, before it curls on the shoreline, rolling you along with it.

Heading back out, I spot a set of swells mounting in the distance. Must be from some cargo ship or something big. If I can catch one of those waves after they've taken on some wind, I should have a pretty darn good swell to ride.

About halfway out I realize I'm the only surfer still in the bay. *Where'd everybody go?* Maybe they all chickened out. I've been swimming my entire life and have overcome the worst of wind and water tragedies. I can pretty much handle anything the water has to throw at me.

After sizing up the set of swells rolling in, I am ready and waiting. Swimming out to greet the first wave, I vaguely hear someone who sounds like Mama, yelling something that vaguely sounds like my name. Not a good time to get distracted. At this point it's either sink or swim.

But between the time I thought this would be a good idea and now, the wave has somehow doubled in size. Swimming like crazy for shore, I have a sinking feeling: too little too late. I'm riding this wave whether I like it or not.

The monster swell catches up with me. I'm helplessly swept up into the mini-tsunami heading toward shore at a very forceful rate of speed. The picture of *Paradise* flashes through my mind. About the time I decide I'm not quite ready to die, I'm lifted up into the crest of the wave … higher and higher … and higher. Forcing myself to open my eyes, I find myself surprisingly … surprised. I can actually see where I'm going from up here. My fear unexpectedly turns to exhilaration. I'm riding on top of the world … fully free … fully alive … then the wave curls. In an instant I'm slammed to the bottom of the ocean by the sumo-wrestler wave.

Down …

Down …

Down …

Doomed.

Preparing myself with the notion of being buried alive in an underwater grave, I'm suddenly jerked back up … then twisted … turned … and re-slammed. I believe that was the second wave that just broke. Fighting to surface for air, I lose the sense of which way is up. Seconds short of my lungs bursting, I am spit up on shore like Jonah from the belly of the whale. The wave retreats after its merciful delivery, beaching me on the wet sand … I'm alive … I think … *Hallelujah*.

Mama is all over me. "A. J., are you breathing?"

I nod, face down in the sand.

"How could you do something so idiotic? Didn't you hear me yelling to get out of the water?"

While I'm busy coughing and urping up half of the sea, Mama sends Benji to run and get me a towel. She helps drag my battered body back to the pool area. It won't surprise me if a fish flies right out of my mouth. I probably have an entire aquarium swimming around in my stomach. It's always nice to bring back a little memento from the beach. So this is the note I'll be ending my holiday at sea on.

Travel Journal Entry
Train Ride Home, August 1972

Highlights from My Seaside Holiday

The first thirty seconds of parasailing

Riding the crest of the wave

Almost petting a sea bird

My first dance club experience

Purchasing "Paradise"

Lowlights from My Seaside Holiday

The last nine and a half minutes of parasailing

Riding out the curl of the wave (I'm still picking sand out of my teeth)

Almost getting my hand bit off by a sea bird

My last dance club experience (highlight within the lowlight: Adriana took the fall for endangering and corrupting her innocent little sister)

One might read my journal someday, after I am long gone, and wonder:

"How can her highlights also *be* her lowlights?"

"How could all of this happen to the same person on one short holiday?"

"Doesn't this kid ever learn?"

To you I would have to say this:

I am a risk taker. Some people might choose to spend their holiday with their feet on the ground, lying on the beach, and playing it safe. But is that truly living?

The true thrill seeker often appears to be the idiotic one in life, but one must ask, "What is more important in life—feeling safe and bored out of your skull, or being fully and vibrantly alive?"

I say, go big or go home. I can honestly say it was all worth the risk to taste an instant of "Yikes!" I went big. And that, my friend, is one grand old hallelujah.

9
Chutes and Ladders

No matter where you go in life, there is nothing quite as nice as sleeping in your own bed. Especially after a week on a cot. When you check into a place called the Grand Old Sea Palace, you kind of expect to be sleeping in a canopy bed made for a queen. Except when you have a sister like Adriana, who always pulls rank on you. But back at the castle, I am reinstated as Princess Dorothy, where no one can pull my name or rank. Up in my tower with *Paradise* hanging above my bed, no one is even allowed to enter without being summoned by the princess.

"Hey, A. J.!" J. R. bursts into my room. "We need to use your laundry chute." Without waiting for me to extend my scepter, my three brothers tromp into my room, dragging a long knotted rope behind them. In the good old days they could have been beheaded for this.

"What on earth are you up to?"

"C'mere, we'll show you." They head over to my laundry chute. "Okay, Benji, you're our man."

Benji opens the little door, while J. R. and Dino unroll the rope. "Wait," Dino says, "we'd better throw a bunch of clothes down first, in case he falls."

"Good idea. A. J., toss down some of your clothes."

"Wait—you're sending Benji down my laundry chute on a rope?"

"Exactly." J. R. helps load Benji onto the knot. "Just sit on that knot and hang on."

I have only one question. "Why?"

"Because Fabrizia has locked us out of the kitchen again. She does that every time mom and dad leave, and we want to know what she's up to in there." The chute opens into the kitchen on the second floor, then continues on down another floor to the laundry room.

"But it's three stories down to the bottom."

"So?"

"So—what if he falls?"

"That's why you're throwing clothes down there." J. R. and Dino both hold the rope and start to lower Benji down the chute. "Benji, once you get down there just crack the door enough to see what Fabrizia is up to, then jerk on the rope and we'll pull you back up, okay, buddy?"

"Okay."

I quickly toss my pile of dirty clothes from the trip down the chute.

"Hey, that's my head your stinky clothes are landing on!" Benji yells.

"Shhh!" I hiss down the chute. Fortunately Fabrizia has Italian opera music playing and is trying to sing along. "Sorry! Drop them on down below," I whisper back.

Fabrizia is our very heavyset housecleaner who comes once a

week to dust and mop the villa. She's supposed to clean the whole villa, but for some unknown reason, she always gets sidetracked in the kitchen.

The boys are letting out the rope foot by foot. Leave it to Benji to be their man—he has been "their man" for every experiment they've ever done. The little guy has no fear. He's always the one who gets sent up on rooftops, treetops, anything involving heights, and he never complains. He'd be a fearless candidate as a Hollywood stuntman. The only problem is he's kind of a klutz, which worries everyone but his brothers.

I stick my head down the chute to see how he's getting along. It's too dark to see that far down. "Hey, Benji, where are ya?"

"Shhh," he hisses back. He opens the little door and a crack of light shines into the chute from the kitchen.

"He's there," I report.

We get the tug on the rope from Benji, and J. R. and Dino start to hoist him back up. Grabbing on behind Dino, I figure I might as well get in on this too.

"Okay, A. J., back all the way out your door while we drag him back up. We're reeling him in but coming up is a little tougher than going down."

When I back out the doorway, my foot catches on the doorframe and throws me off-balance. "Hold on, I lost my grip!" The rope slides through my hands and we lose a good couple of feet before the boys can get a better grip on it. We all cringe, listening to Benji bang from side to side in the chute.

"Hey, what's going on?" Benji blurts out, in a loud whisper.

J. R. sticks his head down the chute. "Hold on, buddy, we got you."

Inch by inch we pull Benji back up the chute to safety.

"So what's the story?" J. R. asks.

Benji has a big grin on his face. "Mystery solved," he says. "She's got a whole pile of food lined up on the counter and is eating with one hand while she mops with the other. She has all of our pastries and cookies out, and was even gulping our milk from the jug."

"So that's it." J. R. nods. "Fabrizia the food fiend! Well, at least she's not stealing the silverware."

"But no wonder mom's always getting mad at us for eating all the snacks," Dino says.

He's right. It seems like we're always out of snacks—and Mom figures one of us is sneaking them and treats us like we're all guilty. "Now she'll know the truth."

"I don't think so," J. R. says.

"Why not?" Dino asks. "We have evidence."

"That's the problem," J. R. replies. "How are we going to tell Mom that we lowered Benji down a three-story laundry chute on a rope and not get in even more trouble than for eating the food?"

Hmm. Good point. "Maybe we could just tell her our suspicions and she could spy a little herself to find out the truth," I say.

"That might work." J. R. looks at me. "Okay, A. J., it's up to you to plant the idea in Mom's head."

When Mama and Daddy get home, Fabrizia is long gone. And so is most of the food in the house. Daddy unloads the grocery bags on the counter. Mama follows him into the kitchen and starts to put it all away. She opens the cupboard. "Okay, which one of you little oink-faces ate all the pastries this time?"

"Mama," I say, "there's something you need to know."

She looks at me with her *I'm listening* eyebrows.

"Well … when you were gone, we noticed that Fabrizia locked the kitchen door, which she's done before when you've left the house. So after she went home, we looked in here and realized that a whole lot of food was missing."

Mama looks at me and blinks a few times. "Is this some story you and your brothers cooked up, so you could come in here and eat everything in sight, then blame it on the housekeeper?"

"No, Mama, we wouldn't go to all that trouble, and besides, Benji saw her eating all of it." *Whoops.*

Mama's eyebrows are back up. "Benji saw her—when the kitchen door was locked?" Mama looks at Benji. "Well, Benjamin, would you like to explain this to me?"

I quickly butt in to try and save the day. "I can explain it, Mama …"

Mama looks back at me. "I don't recall pulling your string, Chatty Cathy."

That was the name of my doll who had a string you pulled when you wanted her to talk. Mama looks back at Benji.

"Well, it's because … I was … I was spying from the laundry chute."

"The laundry chute? And how did you get into the laundry chute with the kitchen door locked?"

"J. R. and A. J. and Dino lowered me down on a rope."

"You were lowered down the laundry chute on a rope so you could spy on Fabrizia?"

"Well, we didn't know what she was doing in there, which is why we needed to find out."

Mama walks over to the laundry chute and jerks the door open. "So you're saying your brothers and sister lowered you from A. J.'s room down to here ... on a rope?" She swings the laundry chute door all the way open and sticks her head in, first looking up, and then down, to emphasize her point.

Mama pulls her head back out and turns slowly around. Her eyes narrow incredulously. "You lowered your little brother down a laundry chute on a rope?"

I don't like the way she's looking only at me. "Well, it was J. R.'s idea—he just wanted to make sure she wasn't stealing our silverware or something valuable. And besides, we're all tired of being accused of eating all the food, when it's been Fabrizia all along."

Mama looks from me to J. R. "Well, that is certainly worth risking your brother's life for, isn't it?"

"We ... uh, we threw some clothes down there to cushion the fall, just in case." J. R. fumbles the recovery.

"Well, pin a rose on you for being so thoughtful. Excuse me, *son*, but that little pile of clothing on top of a brick floor three stories down wouldn't do diddly-squat if your brother were to fall."

"Oh."

"Oh?" Mama sighs. "I hope you will say more than just 'oh' the day you realize that your brother's life is worth more than a piece of silverware or a French pastry."

"Yes, ma'am, I will."

She looks at me.

"Yes, Mama."

She looks at Dino.

"Yes, Mom."

Mama calls Daddy to the kitchen. "I think I'll let all of you explain this one to your father."

❦

Two days later, when we're no longer grounded, Benji has a visitor. Benji is best buddies with a nine-year-old girl. Christiana lives just down the hill from us. They met when we first moved here, and have spent a lot of time up in trees together. Sometimes when I'm out wandering around the olive grove, I'll suddenly hear giggling up above me. Sure enough, when I look up, there's Benji and Christiana sitting up in an olive tree. It's really pretty cute. They come up with all kinds of games together.

On my way down to the pool, I find Benji and Christiana playing tetherball with an old ball tied to a tree. "Where on earth did you find that old tetherball?"

"Angelo found it out in his shed and gave it to us."

While I'm swimming laps, I hear those two laughing, just having the time of their lives batting that ball back and forth. It makes me think back to running around Indian Island with Danny. There was something so nice about having a boy for a friend—compared to snobby girls. Dorie and Bianca are the only exceptions.

Headed back up the hill, I notice a ladder disappearing into the dense branches of a tall cypress tree and can hear Benji and Christiana howling from up inside the branches. Makes me miss Danny all the more.

I remember the time Danny rescued me when my dinghy drifted down lake in a windstorm. We warmed up by the fire he built, and shared what we wanted to be when we grew up. He's the only one I've ever really talked to about things like that. I'm glad Benji has a friend like Christiana. At least I can still write to Danny.

August 28, 1972

Dear Danny,

How are you and Sailor? I'm fine. Not really. It's the end of summer. That is always my saddest time of year. It was the time we had to leave our cabin on the island and head back to school. You're lucky you get to live on the island all year round now. I sure wish I could. Instead I will be heading back to my new school in a few days where I will be Alien A. J. again. At least I'll have my brother and some of his friends at this school with me. Three years at an all-girl school was long enough to know that boys make better friends. They aren't as tricky as girls.

I was wondering if you could do me a favor? Could you please send me some pictures of the island, and of our cabin, Papoose? And maybe one of Juniper Beach, and one of Sailor playing fetch in the water there? And one of Big Chief, and the Pitchy Pine Trail, and my critter cemetery? If it's not too much trouble, could you just check up on my dead animals now and then and make sure they still have little crosses on their graves and maybe some fresh flowers? And maybe send a picture of you with Sailor so I can remember what everyone looks like? I think I'd just feel a lot better about being here if I had some pictures of y'all back there.

How is your grandpa? Tell him I said, "Hey." And say it
with a Southern accent. I miss him, too. Could you also send me
a picture of him?

                                        Thanks a bunch!

                                        A. J.

10

The Life of a Yankee

Journal of Seasons: September 1972

Fall + Autumn = Fatumn

Fatumn in Tuscany

Why do we need two English names for the same season?
Dunno.

Settembre. September is known for its warm but shorter
days, and slightly cooler, crisp nights. Vineyards are ripe with
fruit, and the air smells like grape juice. Leaves turn to butter
yellow and copper red, splashing color across the golden
hillsides. One is tempted to forsake all other plans and spend
the day wandering through the brilliant, changing countryside
with a good book in hand. What could possibly keep a free
spirit from embracing a day such as this at her own leisure?

"A. J., hustle your buns out the door or you're going to be late!"

Unfortunately today is the first day of school, otherwise known as
Open Season on A. J. Day. I did not end last year on a very good note,
thanks to Annalisa. It's still a mystery what she has against me.

I barely make it to lunch before running into her little swarm of drones buzzing around the beehive, also known as the popular table. I wish I could find Bianca and have someone to sit with. Instead I'm A. J. the sitting duck. Even though we wear uniforms, it is no secret where everyone stands on the social ladder. It all comes out at lunch. The rich kids buy lunch, the middle-class kids bring nice sack lunches, and the poor kids bring the same brown bag over and over. At this coed high school—*scuola media superiore*—the popular people rule one table with Annalisa as the queen bee. The wannabees set up camp one table over and look on longingly, and the social misfits sit together and yet alone, staring at the clock on the back wall.

Mesmerized by the mosaic tile pattern around the wall clock, I hardly notice when Dominic, a very, *very* cute boy I met last spring, wanders over from the popular table—and sits down beside me. This throws the entire caste system in the lunchroom out of whack. While I'm wondering how this unusual event will change the course of history, Dominic starts to tell me how his summer vacation went.

Meanwhile queen bee Annalisa and her little worker bees buzz their way over and decide to ruin my life.

"Buongiorno, Angelina," says the queen, in a voice that lets me know she's about to open fire.

Oh, just get it over with.

She flicks her thick, dark mane behind her shoulders, where it lands in a perfect line against her forest-green sweater. *"Lei è viene dalla famiglia greca con la villa blu?"* … Am I related to the Greek family with the blue villa?

"Più o meno." More or less.

"I hear you're pretty good at Greek dancing. Why don't you show us some of your moves?" Her little drones all laugh.

I'm about to say, *I'd love to, Annalisa, but it's probably too complicated—you have to be able to count to four.* But then I remember Rosa Bella. Instead I just smile and say, "God bless us, every one."

"Huh?" Annalisa scrunches up her face.

"Never mind." I get up and walk out. *Here's to you, Rosa Bella.*

⚓⚓

The day goes downhill from there. Bianca never shows up, no one else talks to me, and by the end of school I'm informed that I have a "Yankee go home!" note stuck on the back of my sweater. Walking out the front door of the school, I feel my head swirling. Someone added an extra shake to the snow globe today.

On my way home I stop by to say hello to Napoleon and Caesar. They're always good company when I need it. Napoleon gets excited anytime he thinks we're heading out on the range. Caesar just looks forward to the carrots I bring him. "I'll be back, buckaroos." I plan to return for an afternoon ride after I change my clothes.

Mama greets me in the kitchen with some homemade *biscotti* and espresso—*biscotti* for me, espresso for Mama—the Italian equivalent of milk and cookies. "How was your first day of school, sunshine?"

"Worst day of life my life, and don't call me sunshine."

"Why? What happened?"

"The entire school knows that I'm related to Uncle Nick, and thinks we're all a bunch of dancing weirdos from the blue villa."

"Oh, A. J., every family has its quirks."

"Yeah, well, there are *quirks,* and then there's just plain *weirdness.* Now I'm just waiting for everyone to find out that my mama is the Sofia Loren impostor from Rome."

"I would think they'd find that somewhat impressive."

"Then you don't know Annalisa. She'll use it to ruin me."

"What does this girl have against you anyway?"

"I have no idea. Just the fact that I'm alive, I guess."

"Why don't you let me have a little chat …"

"No! I can handle Annalisa myself. You would only make things worse—trust me."

"Well, she'd better back off, or I may just show up on her lunch tray at school one of these days."

"Mama, *please.*" I can just see that happening. I'd better plan where I'm going to run away to when it does.

Retreating to my tower, I plop onto my bed and recount the events of the day. My old troll doll on the nightstand reminds me of Annalisa with her scrunched up face. *I wonder if voodoo really works.* I tweak the doll's nose, then toss her across the room and watch her bounce off the windowpane before landing facedown on the floor. Not real mature but it felt kinda good.

Let's see, what to wear … my overalls, or my other overalls? I think I'll wear my … overalls. After changing out of my least favorite outfit into my favorite outfit, I slide down the spiral banister and head for the door. "I'm going riding—be back by suppertime!"

Dino and Benji are sitting at the end of the driveway and turn suspiciously silent when they see me. "Hi, guys. Was your first day as fun as mine?"

"Yeah, fun," Dino says.

"Really fun," Benji adds.

They look guilty as all get out. "Okay, out with it, or I'll tell Mama you're up to something."

They look at each other and smile. "Swear you won't tell?"

"Yeah, yeah, what?"

"Well," Dino begins, "I wanted to be in Benji's class because my best friend, Benito, is in his class, and Benji wanted to be in my class because his girlfriend, Christiana, is in there—"

"She's *not* my girlfriend," Benji butts in.

"Anyway," Dino continues, "at lunch, we agreed to switch classes and see if we could get away with it." They look at each other and grin. "And it worked."

"Really? No one noticed?"

They look so proud of themselves. "Nope, except I told Benito, and Benji told Christiana, but they both promised not to call us by our real names."

These two really did come from the same mold. The only way I can tell them apart is by their cowlicks. Dino's is on the opposite side as Benji's, but no one outside of the family ever guesses them right. Mama's the only one who can tell them apart instantly. But she would know with her eyes closed. Mamas are just like that with their babies. "So are you planning to switch for the whole year?"

"No, just whenever we feel like switching. Benji doesn't like playing *calcio,* soccer, and I do, so we'll probably switch PE on Fridays. And Benji can have my art classes, 'cause he's better at drawing than me. Stuff like that."

"Hmm. Well, hey, I'll see you guys at supper—I'm going

riding." I wish I had a double back in Squawkomish who wouldn't mind living in Italy for the next four years. Maybe I could advertise in the *Squawkomish News Review*. For now, another spying session on the secret lives of nuns sounds like a good distraction.

When Caesar and I arrive at the stone wall, I peer into the courtyard, but Sister Aggie is nowhere in sight. Another sister spots me and comes to greet me. She says the reverend mother would like to have a word with me in her office.

"Oh … okay." *Oh, great, she found out. Sister Aggie probably got fired, thanks to me.* I'm not sure what to do with Caesar, so I loop his reigns around the base of an olive tree and leave him to graze. The sister lets me in the front gate and tells me to follow her. I've always wanted to see the inside of one of these places, but not bad enough to be sent to the reverend mother.

I'm led down a long dark hallway. The place looks empty. No one is just *hanging out* around here. When we finally reach the office, the sister taps lightly on the door.

"*Avanti*," a soprano voice calls back.

"*La donna giovane col cavallo è qui.*" The young lady who rides the horse is here. She opens the door for me to enter.

"*Grazie. Gestiró la questione.*"

She'll deal with what matter? Can I be sent to hell for this?

"*Buongiorno, signorina. Lei è amica di Suore Agastina?*"

"Yes, Mother, I'm Sister Agastina's friend. I'm Angelina."

She motions for me to sit down, then watches for the door to close. "Now then … Angelina, I must make you aware that here at the convent we have certain rules we must abide by."

"Yes, ma'am." *Here it comes … You fired her, didn't you?*

But then she says she doesn't know of any regulations on horse-back riding. "So I'm wondering"—she leans in closer—"if you might take me for a little ride sometime too?"

"… you … ride? I mean, y-yes, Mother, of course, I would be happy to."

The reverend mother claps her hands like a giddy little child. "Oh, *perfetto*!"

We agree to meet on Saturday at dusk. She rubs her hands together like she just sealed the deal of the century. *Funny lady.*

By the time I make it back to Caesar, he's cleared out every blade of grass in range and is about to take the olive tree with him to find some more. I hoist myself back into the saddle, and head off down the hill feeling completely baffled by my visit. What is it with these nuns anyway? There must be something in their pasts … Did they do acrobatics on horseback in the circus, or what? *È assolutamente sconcertante.* It's absolutely baffling.

When I return Caesar to Angelo, I ask him if it's all right if I come back for a sunset ride on Saturday. I figure that way I can just stay out until the sun goes down for the evening rendezvous with the reverend mother. Angelo says he goes to bed with the sun, so he probably won't wait up for me, but I'm welcome to ride. All the better. He won't worry when it gets dark out. He'll be asleep.

Back at the castle I run into J. R. out in the courtyard. He's talking to Nonna, who is talking to both him and Saint Francis—as though she's in a three-way conversation. "So, J. R., tell Saint Francis and me all about your first day back to school."

"Well, school was uneventful," he says looking at Nonna, then turns to Saint Francis, "but walking home was very nice."

"Very *nice?*" I butt in. "Okay, who's the girl?" J. R. doesn't use words like *very nice* when it comes to taking a walk. There's something more to it.

He just smiles. "Someone."

"Is it Celeste—that girl we saw in San Gimignano on my birthday?"

"Maybe." J. R. is impossible to get details out of when it comes to girls.

"Well, *maybe* I'll have lunch with Celeste tomorrow, and *maybe* I'll ask her."

"A. J., if you blow this for me …"

"Don't worry, I just wanted to confirm whom you're all gaga over. And now I know—so I don't have to ask."

"Promise you won't do or say anything to make her think I have a weird family?"

"J. R., trust me, thanks to Annalisa Tartini, Celeste not only knows you have a weird family, she also knows you're related to the people in the blue villa. But if any of that mattered to her, you would have known it by now."

Nonna looks back and forth between J. R. and me. "Listen, J. R.," she says, "you just bring your little friend home with you tomorrow and I'll introduce her to Saint Francis. If anyone can help win her heart for you, it'll be Saint Francis."

"Yep, that would do it, all right," I tell J. R.

"Thanks, Nonna, I'll be sure to keep that in mind." He smiles and gives Nonna a kiss on her cheek.

Mama comes out with a pile of fresh towels for the guesthouse.

"Expecting company, Mama?"

"Late arrival—they're just staying for the night and flying back to the States tomorrow."

Maybe they'll have a girl I can swap lives with so I don't have to face another day at Macchiavelli High.

∽∾∽∾∽

Day two of open season, I intentionally sit at the back table, in the darkest corner of the lunchroom, hoping not to be detected by the beehive in case they decide to swarm again. Somehow Dominic finds me and sits down. Is this some kind of setup? Do they send him over here first to distract me, then come in for the sting?

This time Dominic wants to know if I've been invited to Annalisa's birthday party.

Are you serious? I'm not exactly on her top fifty favorite people list. "Um, not that I know of."

Sure enough, just like clockwork, here comes the swarm, making a beeline right for me. *Bzzzzzzzzzzz.*

Once again the birthday girl is leading the pack. "*Ciao, Dominic. Viene alla mia fest venerdì sera?*" Are you coming to my party Friday night?

Dominic looks at me, then back at Annalisa. "Is Angelina invited?"

Her fake smile begins to quiver. "Um, well, s-sure she is. You are coming, aren't you, Angelina?"

This is where I have the choice to tell Annalisa to buzz off, or go ahead and play this game. *Hmmm.* "Of course I'm coming, Annalisa

I wouldn't miss it for anything." I've been dying to see what goes on at these parties that I'm never invited to.

"Then, yeah, I'll come," Dominic says.

"Great …" Annalisa walks away looking miffed.

Now I'm stuck—but I'm still curious enough to go.

I'm heading down the hall on my way to class when someone runs up behind me and grabs me by the arm, "*Ciao, amica!*" Hey, friend!

"Bianca!" I throw my arms around her. "*Mi sei mancata molto.*" I've missed you so much. *If you only knew.*

"We returned home from holiday late, but here I am. Hey, I just heard Annalisa talking about her party. Are you really going?"

"Amazingly I am. But she didn't want to invite me—she had to, so Dominic would go."

"It doesn't matter." Bianca waves a hand in front of her face. "Let's go together. Annalisa's mom and mine are friends, and every year her mom makes her invite me, and mine makes me go. But no one ever talks to me, so I always feel like an idiot."

"Great, we can be idiots together then."

It's amazing how much difference one good friend can make. I think it's true what they say, that friendship helps the world go 'round. I'm not sure who said it; maybe I just thought it up. But without Bianca, I'd be yelling, "Stop the world, I want to get off right now!"

Friday evening Bianca's car pulls into our driveway to scoop me up for the Sweet Fourteen party at Annalisa Tartini's. After making a mad dash for Mama's vanity, I sneak a dab of her Carnation perfume.

"A. J., Bianca's here!" Mama yells up to me.

Tweaking my crooked French braid one more time, I look in the mirror and flash myself a smile. Yep. The gap is still there. Better, but there. Trying to will my front teeth to move together is like trying to get two continents, oceans apart, to converge. Braces aren't an option because Mama thinks it's cute. Another nonnegotiable. *Oh, well, even if I look like a dork, I'll at least smell good.* I hustle down the stairs and out to the car. Bianca hops out and climbs in the backseat with me. "*Mmm, Carnation?*"

"Yep. My mama's."

"Mine wears that too."

Bianca's mother turns around and smiles at me. She is an absolute French beauty. Graceful and petite, unlike Bianca, who is tall and lanky. They both have cool natural red streaks in their hair. Bianca's is cut really supershort, all spiky, and shows off her big green eyes. Mama says Bianca's the kind of girl who is still growing into her beauty. She has the kind of features that teeter between awkward and gorgeous. But Mama says you can bet your booty that Bianca will probably knock everyone's socks off when she's older. Right now she is on the verge of beautiful, with brains to go with it.

Annalisa is just the opposite. She looks good now, but I think her glory days are numbered. She has a cute baby face, but because of her big teeth, she kind of reminds me of the horse who won the Kentucky Derby. And she is, basically, not a nice person. But Bianca is a true friend. Annalisa started being mean to her when Bianca left the beehive to be my friend. I'm still trying to figure out why Annalisa hates me.

The Tartinis live on one of the nicest estates in Siena. They own Tartini Vineyards. Annalisa's Sweet Fourteen party is sure to be the talk of the town, same as her Sweet Thirteen and Sweet Twelve parties—the ones I was not invited to. The Tartinis are known for throwing *grande feste,* really fancy parties. Pulling up alongside the huge water-spewing lion fountain in the circular drive, I get the feeling this will be no exception.

"*Buona sera, signorinas.*" Some guy who looks like a butler holds the car door open for us while we tumble out. Another house servant directs us to the pool cabana below. The entire pool area is lit up with colored lights that reflect off a twenty-foot rock waterfall that splashes into the pool. A row of torches lights the way to long tables displaying fancy ice sculptures and piled sky high with gourmet snacks—including a cake that looks like something made for a royal wedding. Except—rather than a bride and groom—on the top tier stands a single plastic princess, presumably Annalisa.

I recognize most of the party guests from school, although no one acts as though they recognize Bianca or me. We're not exactly drawn into the center of the action. "Come on," Bianca says, and points me in the direction of the hot tub.

We shed our clothing down to our swimsuits and plunge into the warm bubbles. Bianca tells me all about her "dreadfully boring" summer in the south of France, and I share my harrowing parasailing adventure with her. After a good laugh I volunteer to go on a quick food run, while Bianca grabs us a few sodas. We reunite in the hot tub, happy as two pigs in a poke, left to ourselves.

Our private party lasts only until a few of the guys decide to join us. Why is it every time a guy comes near me, the beehive is right on his tail? Sure enough, as soon as Nicholi and half the soccer team hop in to join us, the little stingers are right behind them. They all pile in as well. I take this as a cue to hop out, before they start making fun of us. "Boy, I'm getting hot," I remark, and make my graceful exit. Bianca follows after me.

We duck into the cabana dressing room, change into dry clothes, then slip back out to look for a new place to stake out. "Angelina!"

Dominic hails us over to a table in the game room where a lively card game of *scopone* is going on. "We need two more players to start a new game."

Bianca nudges me on the way over. "Count me in," she whispers.

Looks like it's me and Bianca against Dominic and Dario. As soon as we're seated, the birthday girl shows up and announces we're all playing Spin the Chianti Bottle instead.

Great. I have never kissed a boy in my life. I glance over at Bianca, who appears as enthused as I am. Annalisa volunteers to go first since it's her birthday. She gives the bottle a spin. If it's possible to rig a Chianti bottle to land on the right guy, she'll be the one to do it. It's no secret to anyone who she'd like to lock lips with. When it slows to a crawl in front of Dominic, he leans to the left, and it lands on Frog Lips Fabio. I smile, while Annalisa has to pretend she's okay kissing a guy with frog lips.

As the bottle works its way around the table, I'm feeling more nauseous by the minute. It's Dominic's turn. The bottle spins wildly out of control, then, as if in slow motion, it inches its way toward me. Before it has a chance to stop, I jump up from my seat like I sat on a thumbtack, and announce, "I have to go to the loo!"

What an idiotic thing to do! I cannot believe I did that. I'm probably the only one here who's never kissed a boy before. I don't care. Annalisa's party is not where I want to lose my virgin lips.

Once in the loo I'm afraid to come out. Everyone knows what a chicken I am. I can just picture Annalisa out there making fun of me … *bock-bock-bock-bock.* Can I help it if I've spent the last three years at a girl's school instead of at coed kissing parties? I start to look for a window to escape through but I'm three stories up. My luck, I'll land on my head, break every bone in my body, and still live to endure the humiliation. *Disfigured Yankee lives after jumping from loo window to avoid being kissed in Spin the Chianti Bottle game.*

After ten minutes of turmoil, someone knocks. "Angelina, it's Bianca. Let me in."

I turn the lock and allow her to slip inside with me. "I feel like such an idiot. What am I going to do?"

"Relax. You're not the biggest idiot here. You should have seen what Annalisa just did. As soon as you left, she barged her way into the spot you gave up, so the bottle would stop on her. Dominic took one look at her puckered-up lips, said he was late getting home, and headed for the door."

"Really?"

"Really. You're off the hook. You were both spin the bottle dropouts, but the game is over, so come on out. Everyone's having cake by the pool."

I crack the door an inch and peer out. Sure enough, the coast is clear. Bianca and I make our way out to the balcony over the pool where we can see but not be seen. It's nice to know I'm not the only one afraid of being kissed. It's not so much I'm afraid as I just want to be in love first, and that hasn't happened—in Italy anyway.

❧❧❧❧❧❧ II ❧❧❧❧❧❧
Gone to the Dogs

The reverend mother hails me over to a stack of wood pallets. In the time it takes me to ride over to her, she's scaled the pallets and is waiting on top to mount Caesar. Where did these nuns learn to climb so well anyway? There are definitely stories to uncover here.

The mother gracefully swings on behind me, habit and all. She's amazingly agile for a sixty-year-old nun. Once she's all straightened around, she gives Caesar a "*Corriamo!*" Off we ride into the night: a Yankee and a Franciscan nun, running through the moonlit hills of Tuscany.

The Secret Lives of Nuns

Entry: September 1972

Something's fishy. Where did these two nuns learn to ride so well? Most people only walk when they first get on a horse. These two nuns love to run like the wind. Besides that, they can scale walls and wood pallets faster than a jackrabbit can jump. Somehow these two nuns are connected—in more ways than meets the eye. Were they, perhaps, former horse jockeys? Are they undercover nuns? spies? KGB? CIA? FBI? the mob? Or, simply two common, everyday nuns who both happen to

be in love with horses and extremely athletic. Doubtful. Very
doubtful. I plan to get to the bottom of this. Nothing a little
detective work can't solve. Agent A. J. is nominated for the job
[I draw a little sketch of me in a trench coat with a curved
pipe like Sherlock Holmes]. I second the motion and accept
the challenge. If nothing else, it will help take my mind off my
otherwise miserable teenage existence.

There is nothing as dreadful as walking into the lunchroom after having chickened out in spin-the-chianti-bottle at Annalisa's birthday party. Passing by the hive, I see the drones are all a buzz. Their beady little eyes dart back and forth from me to their queen; whisper, whisper, giggle, giggle. I may as well just hop up on top of their table and announce, *Here I am, the girl who doesn't smoke, kiss, or cuss!* Let's just get it all out there right now, have a good laugh, and move on.

Instead I make a beeline for Bianca, who is waiting faithfully for me over in the social reject's section. *"Dimmi, amica,"* I say, sliding in next to her. Tell me, girlfriend. "How is it that the birthday girl can throw herself at a boy who runs away from her, and she is hailed the queen, and I'm the one who gets made fun of?"

Bianca ponders the question, and sighs. "The world is full of injustice, dear Angelina. I think it's because she has perfect hair."

"Ah, of course. That would explain it."

We both laugh. "One day, A. J., we, too, shall have perfect hair and the world will be ours. Until then, want to split a Bavarian cream puff with me?"

"Sure."

I'm trying not to drool while Bianca pulls the gorgeous, gooey, fluff-puff apart and slides half of it to me. As I'm about to devour it, Bianca whispers, "Buzz alert."

"*Buongiorno, Angelina.*"

I whip around and find myself graced by the presence of *la primadonna,* the queen bee, herself. She informs me that everyone at her table is having fun coming up with new names for me. I'm touched, of course. I glance over at her drones, who are looking on with smirky little faces. The boys are watching with keen interest as well, minus the smirkiness.

"*Sei un pauroso, Yankee,*" Yankee chicken, she spews, with her scrunched-up, troll-doll sneer.

I think of Rosa Bella, and I try to say, *God bless us, every one*, but instead my arm involuntarily raises and I watch, like a bystander, as my cream puff suddenly leaves my hand, sails through the air, and splatters in Annalisa's shiny locks.

A collective gasp goes up from the drones, along with a burst of laughter from the boys. Part of me is mortified, the other part is gloating, and I'm not sure which side to root for.

"*Peggio per te.*" You'll be sorry, she hisses, just as the bell rings.

I get the feeling she's right.

On my way to the afternoon assembly, I make a pit stop at the girls' loo, only to find half of the bee colony primping in front of the mirror. I dart inside a stall and lock myself in, hoping to wait out their glamour session. No such luck. *Do I skip the hand-washing bit and dash for the exit? No, that's just one more thing they'll announce all over school: The Yankee doesn't wash her hands after using the loo.* Reluctantly I unlock the stall door and head for the sink. And so does the colony.

When I turn to leave, I'm surrounded.

"*Ciao,* Yankee." Annalisa is standing in my way. "Have you ever wondered what you'd look like with short hair, Yankee?"

"No."

I'm waiting for a pair of scissors to appear. Instead Annalisa puts her arm around my shoulder. "You know, I think you'd look really good with short hair, don't you all agree?" She tightens her grip on my shoulder while her three worker bees paw at my hair.

Tia holds my hair up to my ears. "Definitely better short," she remarks.

They finally let go, then file out behind their queen, laughing.

Annalisa turns back and smirks at me. "*Ciao.*"

I'm standing in front of the mirror with four wads of gum stuck in my hair. I get the feeling that by the time I get all of this out, I'm going to know what I look like with short hair.

Thank goodness the only thing I'll be missing for the afternoon is a school assembly, and maybe no one will notice that I'm missing. Looking both ways down the hall, I make a run for the side door, and just keep running. Instead of running home, I end up in Angelo's barn, in front of a dusty, cracked mirror in his washroom. There are some things I cannot tell Mama, knowing that the reaction would be worse than the problem.

After half an hour of tugging, twisting, and snipping away with an old pair of garden shears, I finally give up. Dropping the shears, I pull what's left of my hair, gum still intact, into a ponytail, then take off down Poppy Hill.

I show up on the doorstep of the convent in desperate need of a visit with Sister Aggie. Sister Superior greets me at the door and says she'll ask permission for Sister Aggie to break from her chores. I'm told to wait in the *atrio,* an indoor garden of bright lilies in a sunroom near the entrance. It helps add some life to this cold, drab monastery.

Sister Aggie returns shortly, looks at me oddly, and directs me out to a small table on the patio. "We'll have some privacy here."

I stare across the table, expecting Sister Aggie to comment on my hair, which is obviously sticking out in all directions.

"So, Angelina, what's on your hair … er … heart?"

"Well, it's like this …" What I thought would be just a few words, turns into a blow-by-blow account of my entire mess of a life. I launch out with Annalisa's party, followed by the embarrassing names at school, and work into the cream-puff incident. "I don't know what came over me … it was like part of me wanted to do the right thing … but … there was this other force … and before I even realized what was happening, I threw the cream puff at her instead. It almost felt like … I'm wondering if maybe I'm … *possessed* or something … ?"

Sister Aggie has an expression on her face that is not easy to read. "Angelina," she says, "you love dogs, right?"

I nod.

"There's an old story about a man who said he often felt a tug-of-war going on in his soul. He said it felt like there were two dogs inside of him, a white dog and a black dog, that were always fighting with each other. Does that kind of describe what you were feeling?"

I think about that for a minute. *Good dog—bad dog* ... "Yeah, that's pretty much exactly what I was feeling. Which dog did he say usually wins?"

She looks over at me and smiles. "The one he feeds the most."

Ah.

"You're not possessed, Angelina. You've just described our struggle with human nature. Saint Paul admits to having the same problem."

"What do I do about it?

"Well, you feed the white dog, and you starve the black dog."

"Like how?"

"Have you ever heard, 'As a man thinks, so is he'?"

"I think so."

"There are two ways of looking at everything under the sun. God leaves it up to you to decide how you're going to react to life. Feed the white dog; life is good. Feed the black dog; things won't go so well."

"So, white dog, black dog; good dog, bad dog; good and evil?"

"That's it. Sometimes it's easier said than done, but you should notice a difference in your thinking when you apply it. And the way we think affects our actions."

Anything that can keep cream puffs from flying and hair on my head is worth a try.

Sister Aggie tilts her head to one side. "Angelina, did ... something happen to your ... hair?"

Oh, that. "Revenge, Sister. Revenge of the cream puff happened to my hair."

"Ah." She smiles. "Let's see if we can't fix you up a little before you go."

What took four mean girls two minutes to do takes four kind nuns and a bottle of olive oil an hour to undo. I'm struck by the difference in the feel of hands intending harm versus hands that minister love. Black paws, white paws.

❦

Walking out the front doors of the convent, I linger a minute. Just standing on the front steps of a place like this fills me with something good. It feeds my white dog.

Passing by Angelo's farm on my way home, Angelo comes hobbling out, terribly upset. "*Cucciolo di Ci-ci.*" Ci-ci's puppy, he says.

Something's happened to one of the puppies. I follow Angelo out to the stall, and realize there are only three puppies. The runt is nowhere in sight.

"*È persa?*" Lost? I ask.

Angelo nods.

I take a quick look around the horse stall and corral, then tell Angelo I'll be back with my brothers to help look for him. It's turning dark and cold—too cold for a small puppy to be out on its own.

I run home and round up Dino, Benji, and J. R. to come help in the puppy search. This is one of the few favors I've asked where they've hopped right to it, no questions asked. Babies and puppies are a few of the things considered sacred to our family. Even Mama's concerned. She helps the boys round up their jackets, then whisks us out the door. "What's that in your hair?"

"Olive oil," I tell her as I whip past. "The nuns say it's good for you."

"Maybe on a salad, but in your hair?"

"Makes it soft," I yell back, and keep on running.

When the four of us reach Angelo's place, we spread out to cover everything within a puppy-roaming range. Mama Ci-ci anxiously herds us around the property, nudging us on in the search. I'm wondering why she can't sniff the little guy out.

After nearly an hour of searching, it's too dark to see anymore and the temperature is dropping quickly. I hate to tell Angelo that it's about time for us to go home, and I can't stand leaving, knowing the lost little pup is still out there ... somewhere. It suddenly dawns on me to try praying. After all, God knows exactly where he is. *Lord, It's me again. I know I've been feeding the wrong dog lately—the black dog had a big meal today—and I'm sorry. But there's this lost little runt out there right now, and if you could just help ...*

"A. J., look!" Benji is standing by the water trough holding one sopping wet, shivering puppy.

"You found him!" I grab an old blanket hanging by the horse stall and hustle to the trough. Ci-ci's already there, yipping like a protective mama, scolding her baby.

"He fell in," Benji says. "I heard a whimper when I walked by the trough, and there he was, just standing there, with the water almost up to his neck, shivering himself to death."

I take the blanket and gently scruff him dry. Wrapping the little guy up, I hand him back to Benji. After all, he was the rescuer. "Let's wait in the horse stall with him until he warms up."

The rest of the rescue crew gathers round to give the puppy their regards, then they head on home for supper. Benji and I sit side by side on a hay bale, taking turns warming the puppy up. Ci-ci is nestled at our feet with the rest of her litter, keeping a watchful eye on us.

"Boy, if he'd gone much longer, that water would have started to freeze …" Benji can't even finish the sentence.

"God helped you save him, Benji. I had barely gotten my prayer out when you found him."

Benji says, "Does he have a name yet?"

"I don't think so."

"I think we should call him Luigi. Little Luigi."

"I think that's a good name for him."

Angelo comes over after closing the stall door and thanks Benji for finding Ci-ci's *cucciolo*.

"Luigi," Benji says.

"*Si, Luigi*," Angelo nods.

Once Little Luigi is all warm and dry, we tuck him into the middle of his brothers, all snuggled up to Mama for the night. "*Buona notte e sogni d'oro, Luigi*," Benji whispers. Good night and sweet dreams.

I look over at my little brother. I've never seen Benji take to an animal before like he has with Luigi. He sure seems attached to the little guy…. But it makes sense, after all—Benji's the runt in our family too.

12

La Principessa Dorotea (Princess Dorothy)

Falling into Winter

Fall + Winter = Finter

Finter 1972

Secret Lives of Nuns

October evenings are really too cold for any more secret rendezvous with the nuns. I let Sister Aggie know that our only hope for another ride would have to be on a sunny afternoon, in broad daylight. After discussing the matter with the reverend mother, Sister Aggie hailed me down on my last ride and let me know that she and Reverend Mother are willing to risk an afternoon ride together before giving it all up for the winter. I'm not sure who they are worried about being seen by: the other sisters, the bishop, the public ... or all of the above.

They've decided they would like a picnic in the country, which they have agreed to provide since I'm supplying the horse. We have it all planned out. I'll pick them up Saturday, one at a time, and deliver them to a favorite lookout spot on

Cresta di Papavero, Poppy Ridge. Once we're all together, we'll feast on fresh fruits and the fine fare of finter.

※ ⁂ ※

While I'm saddling up Caesar, Napoleon is no longer the only one pacing back and forth, waiting impatiently for us to head out. Now the four puppies pace back and forth along with him. They're learning the ropes from old dad. Little Luigi has made a full recovery. It takes him twice the effort to keep up with his siblings, but that's only because he's the runt. He's a real trouper.

Once I've explained to Caesar that he's gotta be on his best behavior today for the nuns, we hit the trail with Napoleon and his four boys trotting along behind us. I can only imagine what we must look like passing in front of these villas along the way. *Look, Mama, it's a parade!*

When we reach the convent, the reverend mother is waiting in the olive grove, all packed up, ready to go. Standing on the wood pallets, she loops her knapsack over the saddle horn and hops on board. With her familiar *corriamo* command, we set off. Caesar, Napoleon, the reverend mother, four pups, and me, all take to the hills. The Pied Piper, the nun, and the pony and puppy parade. *Oh, what I would give for a picture of this.*

Cantering up a gentle slope, we crest the ridge top. The view from here is a definite *bella vista*, overlooking gentle slopes and streams that meander all the way down to the valley. Rays of sunlight reflect off fields of gold. Finter at its finest.

We deliver the reverend mother safely to the banks of *Ruscello di Sole,* the Stream of Sunshine. She breathes in the country air, and begins unpacking her knapsack with an expression of sheer joy on her face. I leave her to set up camp, and head off to round up Sister Aggie.

In record time we arrive back on the banks of the *Ruscello di Sole* with our procession of pups and Sister Aggie. Set before us on a starched white tablecloth are plates of salami, cheese, fresh berries, grapes, olives, bread, and a fresh bottle of grape juice. *"Mangiare, mangiare!"* Eat, eat! the mother says, just like an Italian mama. So we bless the food and we eat! It all tastes so good up here in this crisp country air with the sunshine beaming down on us. Thanks to these nuns, I am beginning to experience some of the finer things Italy has to offer. It helps to counteract all of the not-so-fine things.

The sisters are thrilled over Napoleon's new family, who end up with a good deal of the salami. I'm big on salami myself, but the grapes are especially *delizioso*. What a great word, *delizioso*. Grapes are always *delizioso* this time of year. It hasn't been long since the harvest. The air is filled with the lingering fragrance of overripe grapes. My senses are on high alert, but so is my curiosity about these nuns and their riding fetish. *I have to know what the story is, and now is as good a time as any to find out.* "So ... where in the world did you both learn to ride so well?"

The mother and the sister look at each other and smile. "Go ahead, Sister Agastina," the reverend mother says, "you tell her."

Sister Aggie rearranges herself on the blanket, so I do the same. It reminds me of getting ready for story time in kindergarten. *Where's my little green blanket?*

"Do you know much about World War II, Angelina?"

"Some. I know about the Nazi nut, Hitler, and how he hated the Jewish people and tried to kill them all."

"Yes, well, near the end of World War II, in 1943, the reverend mother and I were both young sisters of Cuneo. Our convent was near the base of the mountains. The Nazi forces were moving across Europe and thousands of Jewish refugees were fleeing over the Alps into Italy to escape the death camps. Italy was their only hope for a safe haven. But almost as soon as they arrived, the Germans rolled into Italy and took occupation of our town. They invaded the homes of the Italian people, and took away all the Jewish people they could find.

"Our secret mission was to hide the Jewish children from the Nazi soldiers. Desperate parents gave their children to anyone who would help them escape. Many Italians were trying to hide them. But if they had nowhere to hide them, they brought the children to our convent, where we kept them until nightfall. After dark we rode the children on horseback to farmhouses farther out in the hills and valleys, to places known as safe houses."

So that's why they like the night rides. Well, and probably the embarrassment of being seeing in public riding in a habit. Glad to know it's not because it's a sin to ride horses.

"The Nazis would raid our convent every few nights, trying to find any children that were being hidden, but they never once found them there. The children were always gone by the time the soldiers came."

"*Grazie a Dio.*" Praise God, the reverend mother whispers.

"Weren't you scared?" I ask her.

"*Eravamo spaventati da morire,*" she replies. We were scared out of our wits. "But we didn't want to scare the children, so we made a game of it. We told them we were on an adventure and had to sneak away from the other team. So the children knew they had to be very quiet. They thought it was quite exciting to ride horses in the dark. The other team, of course, was the German soldiers, but the children never realized that."

"Where did you find enough houses to hide all of them in?"

"If there wasn't room in the houses for all of the children," Sister Aggie says, "we'd hide them in barns and lofts and attics, anywhere we could—sometimes we'd have to hike into the hills to get far enough away. We climbed mountains with children on our backs— even scaled a few rocky cliffs."

So that's where they learned to climb.

"Finally, in 1945, the allies liberated our town and all of the children came pouring out of the farmhouses one by one. They say the Italians helped to save forty-five thousand Jewish lives."

Wow. That pretty much answers all of my questions about the secret lives of nuns. *Meraviglioso!* Marvelous.

⚜

When I return home, there's a letter from Indian Island waiting for me. I run up to my tower to read it.

September 20, 1972
Dear A. J.,

How are things at the castle? I need to ask you a favor. Would you pray for a guy named Chuck? He's a kid I met

at school who's kind of a loner. A few days ago some of
the jocks started picking on him, so I stepped in to help
him out. The next thing I knew, half of the football team
showed up, ready to take me out. One of them held my
arms behind my back so the others could take their best
shot at me. Suddenly I heard someone yell, "Let him go." It
was this guy I recognized from my youth group. Turns out
he was the captain of the football team. It was a miracle he
showed up when he did. Anyway, Chuck agreed to come to
youth group with us. Please pray for him, that he'll be open
to knowing God.

I hope things are going okay for you at your new
school. It's never easy being the new kid. Sailor is great and
says hi. I shot the pictures you'd asked for and will be sending them as soon as I get them developed.

Give my best to J. R. and your family,

Danny

Well, that is interesting. Seems Chuck and I have a lot in common. I wish Danny were here to step in for me. Maybe there is a way
to ask for help without having to reveal the whole sad scenario that
defines my social life right now. I hope one day I'll have a heroic story
of my own to tell, but for now, we just have to face the facts …

October 15, 1972

Dear Danny,

Thanks for the letter about Chuck. I will be happy to pray
for him. I know someone who needs some prayers too, and was

wondering if you could pray for her? Maybe you could ask your youth group to pray for her too. She might not want her name mentioned, so I'll just call her Dorothy. She's this really nice girl who is kind of new around school. There's this group of girls she calls "the beehive" who don't like her. They have a queen bee named Annalisa, who they will do anything for—they're her little worker bees. Annalisa has talked them all into hating Dorothy. They torment her daily—especially in front of boys. They call her a Yankee and a Barbie doll—among other names that I won't mention. Their latest prank left her looking like she got her hair caught in a ceiling fan.

Anyway, Dorothy has just had it up the kazoo with these buzzing idiots and could really use some prayer. Please pray that God will rescue her—while she still has some hair left—maybe even send her to America before she gets stung to death over here by the mean bees.

That is really neat that God stopped those guys from hitting you. I hope He'll help Dorothy too. Give Sailor a hug for me.

Your friend,

A. J.

At dinner Mama announces that Cousin Stacy called to tell us she got invited to Rome to attend *Il Premio di Dante*, the Dante Awards, in November for her award-winning poem, "Once upon a Tuscan Hill." Mama says she should have entered her own poem:

Once upon a Tuscan hilla
Sat an ugly big blue villa
It sent the tourists into fits
And ruined business for the Ritz.

Mama is having a hard time letting go of this. She's already been to confession twice over the whole thing and will now have to confess that poem as well. I wonder if she'll actually recite it to the priest.

So far none of Mama's guests have canceled their reservations over seeing the blue villa. They usually just laugh and say, "What a crazy thing to do."

Mama has had a steady flow of bookings ever since she schmoozed with all of the tourists along the Riviera in August, but most of them have booked for the spring and summer months ahead. Mama decided to block November and December from booking guests, so we can relax and enjoy the holidays. Those are usually pretty cold months here, and Mama says she doesn't want to get called at six a.m. to bring someone a cup of coffee in the freezing cold just because they're too lazy to make their own.

Daddy loves to tease Mama about what a gracious hostess she is. "But it's so charming to have you take it to them in your bathrobe and curlers, darlin'."

We've found there are two kinds of guests. The kind you only see when they check in and check out. And the kind who think we're here to entertain them around the clock. We kids don't get a dime out of this deal, so when the guests expect us to babysit, or give swimming lessons to their kids for five hours a day, like some of them did this past summer, we feel like saying, *Excuse me, we are running a motel here, people, not Club Med.* Mama says it more eloquently but gets the point across.

Most of the people are really nice and don't bring a bunch of kids with them anyway. But our last guests thought they could leave their whiny children with us while they went tootling off to Florence for the day. Mama set them straight real fast.

✺✺✺

Saturday morning Daddy pops into my room just as I'm waking up. "Hey, check out the picture in today's paper," he says.

"Mama, *again?*"

"Not this time. Someone took a photo of what he thought was an angel riding horseback through his field, but it turns out to be a nun wearing a habit."

I grab the paper from his hands. "Let me see that." There we are, big as day: me and the reverend mother, galloping across the hillside on Caesar, with Napoleon and his boys trailing behind. At least it's from a distance and no one can see our faces. The caption reads: *Mystery Riders Take to the Hills,* then goes on to say, "A cloaked figure is captured on camera, galloping past Caprinito Brothers' vineyards for an afternoon ride. 'At first glance I thought it was an angel on horseback,' Caprinito said, 'but when the picture came out, it looked more like a nun in a habit riding behind a little blonde girl. I've seen the little blonde gal riding these hills before, but never with a nun along. It's just not something you expect to see every day.'"

I hand the paper back to Daddy.

"Who's your friend, A. J.?"

"What?"

"Come on, I know that horse, and I'm pretty sure I know the kid riding it. So who's the nun?"

I fall back into bed and pull the covers over my head. *Oh, what I would give for a picture of this …* Yeah, I said it … but I didn't mean like this! I can't take any more public humiliation. *Basta, basta!* Stop it, enough!

◦◦◦◦◦◦◦◦◦

A half hour later Mama knocks on my door. "Is the princess in?"

"The princess is sleeping." I just don't feel like talking to anybody right now, unless it's about a one-way ticket home.

"The princess can't be sleeping if the princess is talking."

"The princess is talking in her sleep."

Mama barges in anyway. I'm still lying here with the covers over my head.

She sits on the end of my bed and yanks my covers down. "What are you so mopey about?" she asks.

"Life."

"You haven't lived long enough to mope about life yet."

Staring up at the knotholes in my ceiling beams, I reply, "If you're trying to tell me that life gets worse than this, I'm too depressed to hear it."

"Why are you so depressed?"

"Because I'm not happy."

"… Okay. I'm so glad we've had this little talk, and now that we've cleared everything up, I think it's time to go shopping. Come on, I'm taking you to Poggibonsi."

I remain catatonic but my eyes shift toward Mama. "Poggi-what?"

"Poggibonsi. It's a fun little place to go when you're not happy."

"Oh. Okay." I guess I have nothing to lose.

Mama and I hop in the Fiat, drive down the winding dirt road, out to the *autostrada,* and head north. Twenty-three kilometers later, we exit. *Benvenuto a Poggibonsi,* Welcome to Poggibonsi, the sign says. I step out of the car and take a good look around. It's not a bad little town to be depressed in.

"Come on, I'll show you my favorite shop." Mama leads the way to a little hole-in-the-wall shop and holds the door open for me. I walk into a small, dark, brick room filled with books—shelves and shelves of books, cushy chairs with side tables, and cute little lamps. There's also a coffee bar, with small wooden tables and chairs.

"Wow. This looks like the Seven Dwarves' house, huh?"

"Well, you said you're not *Happy,* so maybe we can figure out which one you are."

"Which what?"

"Dwarf."

It takes me a minute. "Oh, Mama … that was so dumb it's not even funny."

"Okay, *Grumpy,* whatever you say."

"Stop it. I'm not Happy or Grumpy."

"Well, I'm *Sleepy,* so while you pick out a book, I'm going to hop on up to the coffee bar and order myself a shot of espresso." Mama is snickering to herself for being so clever.

I'm just trying not to laugh. I hate it when I don't want to laugh and end up around someone like Mama. She'll make it her quest in life to sabotage my bad mood. "I hope you're big enough to see over the counter," I manage to say, with a straight face.

My biggest weakness—next to rescuing animals—is, of course, books. I love books. I love to read them, I love to write them, I love the way they smell when they're new, or from a library, and I love them even in Italian when I want a new perspective on an old favorite. I'm also very jealous that my cousin is a finalist in the Dante Awards. I'd like to find a book on Dante and find out why there is an award named after him. While a little white-haired lady is looking up my book, I decide to go over and join Mama at the coffee bar.

"Where's your book?" she asks, sipping her espresso.

"Oh, Snow White is over there trying to hunt one up for me."

Mama suddenly spews her espresso all over, alternately choking and laughing herself silly. That gets the attention of the entire shop, which makes it unbearably funnier to her. I'm trying to help Mama to stop laughing so she doesn't choke herself to death, but I'm not having much luck. "It wasn't that funny, Mama, really."

When I finally get her to settle back down, someone who's been watching all this says, "*Lei è Sofia Loren?*"

"Oh, no, not now," I mutter.

Mama takes a few deep breaths and says, "Don't worry, kiddo, I've got it under control." She starts to dig around in her purse. Everyone in the shop is moving in for a better look. Suddenly Mama turns around and flashes them all a huge grin with a set of fake buck-teeth in her mouth. That puts the skids on everyone. The looks on their faces nearly send me through the roof. I grab Mama and drag her out by the arm. We double over with laughter, and stumble out the door—without my new book. Once we make it to the curb, we lean against the car with tears rolling down our faces.

"Mama," I squeal, "I guess I really am *Happy* after all."

Those teeth get me every time. Mama and Daddy have an amazing collection of teeth for special occasions. They especially like to use them to embarrass us in front of our friends when we're late coming home. Adriana saw more than her share of the collection back in Squawkomish. It always made my day when it happened to her.

Pulling ourselves together, we climb back into the Fiat and try to head home. I say *try* because the street only goes one way and it's in the opposite direction from where we want to go. We keep turning to get headed the other way, but all of the streets just lead us in circles. We cannot, for the life of us, get ourselves out of this one-way town.

"A. J.," Mama says, "if we can't figure this out, we're going to have to call your dad and tell him to come get us out of here."

I can just picture our family stuck in this town forever. "Mama, just go ask someone."

"No, they'll think I'm *Dopey*. Let's just follow the car in front of us."

Before long the car in front of us is going in circles too. This is the craziest town I have ever been in. I'm beginning to wonder if this isn't one of those weird nightmares where the same thing happens over and over, but you can't wake yourself up. After driving in circles for a half hour, Mama finally gives in and pulls over behind a police officer.

"*Scusami, il signore*," she begins. "Excuse me, sir, we're having a little trouble with these one-way streets; could you be so good as to escort us out of town?"

"*Non è un problema, Signorina Loren.*" No problem, Miss Loren. He motions for us to follow him.

Mama looks over at me and smiles. "Stick with me kid, everything's going to be all right."

There may be hope for Dorothy yet.

13

An Early Frost

We had a severe temperature dip overnight and awoke to a frosty-freeze world outside. Luckily for the vineyard owners, the harvest is behind them. September was the month of the *Vendemmia* in Tuscany. The big grape harvest. All over Tuscany the grapes have been crushed and barreled, soon to become some of the world's finest wines. The closest I have gotten to tasting wine has been in the communion chalice at mass. I honestly don't see what all the hype is about. It tastes like sour grapes to me—a bitter batch of grape juice. But I don't know what they expect after letting it sit around in those old barrels year after year. Logic should tell you to drink it when it's fresh off the vine. It's just a wonder to me how so many people fall for this stuff.

The one highlight of the early frost is that our little lake—or big pond—is frozen solid. Solid enough to enjoy a good skate after school. I'm digging my ice skates out of the closet so I can set them out to warm up by the fire while I'm at school.

"You're late, A. J.!" Mama yells. She's stationed at her morning lookout spot by the kitchen window, where she sips her coffee and watches the kids walk to school. She always shouts a heads-up when the last of the kids go by.

I go ripping out the door, slip down the front steps on my backside, and slide all the way to the curb. J. R. is up ahead, walking with Celeste. He's made it clear he prefers to walk alone with her. I think he's afraid I might say something embarrassing.

When I reach the top of our hill, I look around for Bianca. She is nowhere in sight, so I end up walking the rest of the way alone. *Does this mean I have to face school entirely on my own today?* It's beginning to look that way.

⚜

The loner lunch tables along the back are covered with posters for some art project, so I have to settle for a table in middle of the cafeteria. I save a seat for Bianca just in case she shows up late. Maybe the frost threw her off course. I look around the cafeteria, but I only see Dominic walking toward the bee colony.

"*Di qua,* Dominic," over here, Annalisa calls from the table behind me.

He makes his way down the aisle, and sees the empty seat next to me. "*Posso sedere qui?*" he asks. Mind if I sit here?

"Nope." I scoot over a little. I can feel Annalisa's eyes burning a hole through the back of my head.

"Cold out, huh?" He sets his lunch tray down and takes off his big parka.

"Yeah, our lake even froze. I'm going ice-skating after school."

He slides in next to me. "Really? You have your own skates?"

"Yep. They're sitting by the fire right now getting warm." *Okay, that's something a five-year-old would say.*

"I wish I had some skates. I'd love to try ice-skating."

"You could borrow my brother's skates." As if he'd even want to …

"No kidding? That would be cool. Can I come over after school and go skating with you?"

"Um … sure. *What?*" I'm suddenly not sure I heard him right.

"Can I go skating with you after school?"

"Yeah, anyone can skate there." *That was personal.*

"Great, I've always wanted to learn to ice-skate. How about if I just walk home with you?"

"Um, okay."

I sit back, remind myself to breathe, then turn to make sure it's really me he's been talking to. Annalisa's staring at me out of the corner of her eye. She's not smiling.

Dominic's friend, Dario, comes by and sits down across from him. That helps take the pressure off me. Now everyone can stop looking at me and Dominic like we're a couple. Bianca will never believe me when I tell her. She thinks Dario is the biggest hunk-a-hunk on the planet. I still can't believe they chose sitting next to me over a personal invite to the bee colony. Sure beats eating alone.

When I'm finished with my salami-and-cheese sandwich, I get up to leave.

"See you after school," Dominic says.

"Yeah, see you." I step out in the aisle in front of Annalisa.

"*Ciao*, Angelina."

I turn around.

"Did you say you're going ice-skating today?"

"… Yeah."

"I was wondering if I could walk home with you after school

and go skating too. I've had private lessons and could teach you how to spin."

I'll bet you could. You'll probably spin me into kingdom come. I don't think I want to skate with someone who'd rather see me dead than alive. "Uh … you might need some ice skates if you're planning to go ice-skating."

"Maybe I'll just slide around the ice in my shoes, and give you some pointers."

Like point me into the thin ice area of the pond? Maybe I'm not ready to die yet. "Um, isn't it a little cold out for skirts?"

"Oh … right. Okay, I'll have my driver bring me over after I change my clothes and grab my skates."

Great. I'm toast. "Uh, well … if I'm already at the pond, just ask my mom for directions."

"Great. Can't wait."

I can, dang it.

☙❧

After school Dominic walks home with me, J. R., and Celeste. We all show up together at the castle.

Mama is in seventh heaven, fussing over us, fixing up little plates of cookies and cups of hot chocolate, like we just got home from kindergarten. She keeps wiggling her eyebrows at me. "Just friends, Mama," I whisper, hoping she will stop before Dominic notices.

I grab the ice skates and tell Mama we'll be at the pond in case Annalisa comes by. "Just point her down the hill."

"Annalisa? Isn't she the one …"

"Mama …" I give her *the look*. I really don't need her announcing everything in front of Dominic.

"All right, go have fun skating. Don't worry about Annalisa, I'll take good care of her."

I don't trust that look in Mama's eyes one bit. She can be a real mama bear when it comes to people messin' with her cubs. Good thing she doesn't know about the chewing-gum hairdo, or Annalisa probably wouldn't live to see tomorrow.

The four of us head down the hill to the pond. J. R. is bringing some wood to start a fire in the burn barrel. It's our skating tradition. Dominic puts J. R.'s skates on and wobbles out on the ice like a newborn calf trying to walk for the first time. I can't help but laugh. "Watch out for that … kid!"

After helping him back up, I give him a few pointers on keeping his skates headed in the right direction. Before long he starts to get the hang of it. Some of the other families on our hill make their way to the pond and join us. By the time the sun starts to set, there are a dozen kids skating, and more warming their hands by the fire.

I try to pull off an impressive Olympic spin in the middle of the pond, and end up spinning across the ice on my tail instead. Dominic comes to offer me a hand up. I grab hold of his gloved hand with my mitten and he pulls me to my feet. Once I'm up, he starts to skate beside me but doesn't let go of my hand. It's a little strange holding hands with a boy for the first time, but we're not, really, since I can't feel his hand. It's kind of nice just skating along talking, holding gloves, just being friends. I'm not afraid of Dominic because

I know he was just as chicken at sin-the-chianti-bottle as I was. We at least have that in common.

When it's time to swap skates with J. R. and Celeste, Dominic and I head to the burn barrel to get warm. I look up the hill at the lights shining from our kitchen window and wonder why Annalisa never showed up. Dominic says he'll walk me back home, then he needs to get home for his supper.

"Thanks for taking me skating, Angelina," he says. "I have a feeling I'm going to be a little sore tomorrow, but I had fun."

I'm feeling a little sore myself.

When we reach the top of our hill, we part ways. "See you tomorrow, Dominic."

"*Ciao*." He turns and walks the other way home.

❧

"Mama, I'm home!"

"Oh, so you are. Did you have a nice skate with your very nice, very handsome friend?"

"Yes, I did, thank you. I'm surprised Annalisa never showed up to try to ruin the day."

"Oh, she showed up," Mama says, casually.

"What? She did … ? What did you do to her?"

"You make it sound like I've got her tied up in the closet or something."

"Mama, I know you—tell me."

Mama gets that little smirk on her face as though she is up to something. "Well, first of all, I did not like the way she came strutting in here sounding like Eddie Haskell from *Leave It to Beaver* … 'Oh, hello, Mrs. Degulio, it's so nice to meet you—I can certainly see where Angelina gets her looks.'"

"And you said … ?"

"I said, 'Angelina looks nothing like me.'"

"That's it?"

"*Mmm* … not quite."

"*What else?*"

"I said, 'Angelina looks like no one in our entire family. We look Italian. Angelina looks like the All-American golden girl, and from what I hear, you have a problem with that.'"

I should have known something like this would happen if I left Mama alone with her. "What did she say?"

"She looked all surprised and said, 'But Mrs. Degulio, Angelina and I are good friends. I even invited her to my party.'"

"And you said … ?"

"Good friends, *my foot.*"

"You didn't."

"I did. Then I suggested it would be in her best interest if she took that little-goody-two-shoes act of hers out the door and trotted along home."

"That's it?"

"*Mmm* … almost."

"Mama, what *else?*"

"Well … just something like, 'If you ever mess with my kid again, you will be sorry you ever laid eyes on my Yankee face.'"

"Oh my gosh—you said *that?*"

"I most certainly did. Someone needs to get that girl under control.

She finally stopped trying to snow me and just asked where the pond was. So I told her."

"But she never showed up at the pond."

"I didn't say which pond I sent her to, did I?"

"Mama!"

"She should be showing up at Pietro's pond any time now."

"You sent her to *Pietro's* pond? That's two kilometers up the road!"

"Exactly. There are just as many kids skating over at that pond. I figured she could use the walk to cool off, and I didn't think you'd miss her company."

Sometimes I just don't know what to think about Mama. She may have just saved my life, but I wonder if she made things better or worse for me by saying all that. I wonder what Annalisa will do when she realizes she's at the wrong pond. Ah, well, I'm not going to lose a lot of sleep worrying about it.

❧⸎❦

The answer to my question comes bright and early at school. Annalisa has suddenly morphed from the queen bee to the ice queen. Mama must have scared the royal jelly right out of her. Now she avoids eye contact with me at all costs. When she passes me in the hallway, she looks the other way. And at lunch she just whispers to her little *icicles* about me. Rather than aggressive rejection, it's now passive avoidance—basically just another form of rejection.

On a positive note Bianca's back at school today, and I have someone to sit with at lunch. Just when I start to tell her about yesterday, someone bonks me lightly on the head with a lunch tray.

"Ehi lí, Angelina." Dominic sits down right across from me.

"Hey there, yourself," is all I get out before Bianca pinches my leg—hard. As Dario slides in across from her, I pinch her back, equally as hard. This just does not happen to people like us—especially in our school cafeteria. I can pretty much say without looking that the ice queen and the entire student body are gawking at the miracle taking place.

"Dario and I were wondering if you and Bianca want to come slide down the ice ditch with us after school? There's a solid patch of ice that runs from the top of the drain ditch to the bottom of the hill."

Bianca and I look at each other, trying to keep our jaws from hitting the floor. She nods casually. "Uh, sure," I reply for both of us.

Dominic and Dario stay and eat their lunches at our table, unaware of the polar freeze that is radiating from the ice queen over at the popular table. I am definitely going down in Macchiavelli history. *Go Yank!*

꧁꧂

In social studies Signorina Rossa gives us an assignment to compare our social system here in Italy with the social systems of other countries. We can use textbook examples as well as personal experience. "What's different? What works well? What doesn't? And what could you do, personally, to help bring change?"

This should be a whiz. I can just draw from experience. I open my textbook, and slip in a piece of sketch paper. Instead of making a list of social differences, I begin drawing our skating pond with two little ice-skaters holding hands.

Signorina Rossa asks for volunteers to share their findings. Since no one volunteers, she picks me.

I take my little skating pond picture and pretend to read from it. "Well, for one …"

"Excuse me, Angelina, could you come up front where we can hear you better?"

Uuugghh. I curl the sides of my paper up so no one can see what I really have for notes. "For one," I repeat, "family structures are different. In Italy most grandparents live with the family until they die, and in America they live in nursing homes. So you're better off being young in America because there's more to do, but you're better off being old in Italy."

"Why is that?"

"Well … nursing homes smell really bad, and there are no kids or dogs around."

"Interesting. Angelina, could you give us an example of how America cares for its needy and unemployed?"

"Uh, s-sure." I stare at my drawing. *No clues here.* I try and recall some of those boring dinner conversations between Mama and Daddy. *Ah-ha, Daddy always talked about the stupid welfare system.* "It's called welfare."

"And what can you tell us about it?"

"Well …" Looking down at my skating pond, I just wing it. "Everyone who works has to pay a bunch of taxes to the government. And they set some of it aside for the folks who don't have jobs and call it welfare. "

"Do you feel it's a good system?"

"Welfare is a good thing for children, and for grown-ups who really can't work, but the whole system backfires for people who can work but won't."

"Can you give us an example?"

Example, example … "It's like this … I once had a hamster named Ruby. She had a cage that came with a food dish, so I always put her food right in the food dish. Whenever she woke up, she went straight to the food dish, stuffed her cheeks, then went back to bed and slept all day. She just got lazier and lazier. I started thinking about how hamsters in the wild have to forage for their food, and how much more productive their lives must be. If they want to eat, they have to work for it.

"I began to see that the food dish was causing a hamster welfare mentality. From then on I made it harder for Ruby to find her food. I scattered her nuts and seeds all over the cage, so she had to hunt for them. And I bought her an exercise wheel to give her something to do besides eat. She seemed much happier after that—like her life had *purpose* to it … If you make something too easy for people, they lose their sense of purpose, feel useless, and become lazy. Everybody feels better when they have to work to achieve something, but welfare gives too many people an easy way out and turns productive people unproductive."

"So, Angelina, is there something you might be able to propose to help change the current system?"

"Actually I'm thinking about sending a letter to the U.S. government with a reform proposal based on my Hamster Welfare Reform Experiment."

"Interesting idea," Signorina Rossa says. "Thank you, Angelina. Anyone else?"

Whew!

"*Il bel disegno,*" nice drawing, someone whispers, as I walk back to my desk.

⁕⁕⁕

Bianca shows up at my locker after school. We're soon joined by Dominic and Dario. As we leave the building, I notice Annalisa and Tia tagging along behind us, hoping, I'm sure, to turn the guys' attention their direction. Annalisa even goes so far as to hint, *loudly,* that they have nothing to do after school, then comes up alongside of us and asks Dominic if he knows of anything going on.

Dominic shrugs his shoulders. "I hear a lot of people are heading over to Pietro's pond."

Annalisa whips her head back around, looking insulted, then rearranges her hair.

Dominic looks at us and shrugs again. He has no idea that Mama already sent Annalisa on a wild-goose chase over to Pietro's pond yesterday.

When we come upon Annalisa's private road, the two of them cross the street, and the rest of us tromp on together. Bianca and I get to endure Annalisa's silent-but-deadly glare as we pass by her gated driveway. If it weren't for the fear of my mama in her right now, I'm sure she'd come up with something to thwart our Dominic-and-Dario ice-ditch date.

As we pass by the *scuola elementare,* Benji and Dino run out to join us.

Dino sneaks up behind me and shoves an icicle down my back,

then darts off. "Oh … brrrr! You rat!" I shake the ice out of my shirt with one hand, and shake my fist with the other. "Tell Mama I'm going to the ice ditch with Bianca, and I'll be home by dark."

"Yes, ma'am," he says, then he turns and gives me the raised eyebrow.

This family and their eyebrows …

Dominic leads us to the top of *La Collina di Papaveri*—Hill of Poppies or, as I call it, Poppy Hill—where the big ice ditch begins. The drainage ditch is about three feet wide and a hundred feet long, with a solid sheet of ice lining the bottom of it.

"*Attenzione.*" Dominic stands at the top of the ditch, rambling off his opening speech. "Welcome to the preliminary time trials for the 1972 Winter Ice Ditch Olympics. Our first Olympic hopeful, Dominic Delossantos, will now attempt his first run for the one-man tobogganless toboggan race."

He gives us a quick good-bye—just in case—while he slides into position. Then he shoves off, hits the first steep incline, and quickly picks up speed. By the time he's halfway down the hill, he looks like a true toboggan racer. Coming into a steeper incline, he becomes just a blur, whizzing through the icy ditch. Near the bottom of the hill, the drainage ditch fans out and runs off into the field—a solid sheet of ice mingling with grass. Dominic hits the field and smashes into a loose hay bale, which explodes into the air and leaves him covered in straw. He stands up with straw sticking out of his clothes every which way.

We are all cheering and howling our heads off at the top of the hill.

"*Lo spaventapasseri carino,*" Bianca whispers. Cute scarecrow.

"Angelina, vai!" Go for it! Dominic yells from the bottom.

I quickly stop laughing. *"Chi, io?"* Who, me?

"Ma perché no?" Why not, Dario asks. "What's the worst that could happen?"

"I could die."

"True." He laughs.

Dominic is waiting with his hands on his hips. "Are you going for the gold or not?" he yells.

I wave back and slide into position on the ice patch. "It's been nice knowing you," I say to Dario, and push off.

Slipping away at a gradual pace, I decide this isn't as scary as it looked. Ten seconds later I am a human rocket. Reaching unearthly speeds, the infamous words of *Wide World of Sports* ring through my ears. *The thrill of victory*—a thick mound of earth and ice rise out of nowhere like nature's idea of a bad joke. I hit the jump like a flying torpedo and take to the air, up and over the hay bale, splatting a good ten feet past Dominic in the grass—*and the agony of defeat …*

Coming to a halt flat on my back, I decide it's a good time to fake dead. I hear footsteps running down the hill. The closer they come, the laughter slowly dies away. "Angelina?"

No response.

"Angelina, are you okay?" Dominic is kneeling over me. Then I hear Bianca and Dario hovering over me. "Angelina? Angelina!"

I can't contain myself any longer. *"Chi sono io?"* Who am I? I whisper, and start to laugh.

I open my eyes and watch their concern turn back to smiles. Except for Dario. It takes him a little longer.

Walking past him, I quietly comment, "You thought I was dead."

"No, I didn't."

"I think you did."

"I think you took the gold." He smiles. That's all I get out of him.

"You still have a chance, you're up next."

He sighs. "After watching you, I think I'd rather try out for the skating event."

14
Nascondino
(Hide and Seek)

October 20, 1972

Dear Danny,

How are you and Sailor? And how is Chuck? I asked the
nuns to pray for Chuck, so good things should start happening
for him any day now. As far as a Dorothy update, keep
praying. No miracles yet. She's not being traumatized in public
so much, but the cold war is definitely on. Dorothy has to live
with a lurking fear that anything could happen at any moment.
The grand total of people who talk to her at school is now up
to three. Pretty sad.

The weather has been icy cold here. Our pond froze
and I went ice-skating with Dominic. The next day, I went ice
sledding with Dominic, Dario, and Bianca. With the exception
of my one girlfriend, Bianca, boys sure are easier to get along
with than girls. And they don't worry about stupid things like
hair.

What are you doing for Thanksgiving? Will you go
home to Oklahoma or will your family come to see you on
the island? I wish I could spend my Thanksgiving there. I

don't know what we'll be doing—no one here celebrates Thanksgiving, except for us. As far as the relatives go, we are going on four months of not talking to each other. I'm kind of wondering how long this can go on. You have no idea how strange it is for people like Mama and her sister to not talk to each other. They used to call all the time just to say things like, "Did you see that ridiculous outfit Carrillo wore today on 'La Dolce Vita' (their favorite Italian soap opera, 'The Sweet Life')?" or, "How many garlic cloves do you put in your Forty-Clove Garlic Chicken recipe?" It's unnatural for them to go without speaking.

Adriana and I are getting along a lot better than we used to. She lives in Milan. She's planning to come home for a few weeks over Thanksgiving and Christmas. The only guy in her life is Pip the Mighty Mutt. I now understand why they call them toy poodles. He's the size of a small windup toy and sounds like one too—the kind you wish the batteries would die on so they'd stop making that yip-yip-yippy noise. Does your brother, Jason, have a girlfriend? Do you?

Well, I guess I'd better go. Mama is yelling downstairs about Grandma Juliana. I'd better go find out what she's done this time. The last time Mama yelled like this, my grandma had painted a pair of pants on Mama's marble statue of David to hide his "indecency."

Write soon,

A. J.

P.S. Could you maybe beef up the prayers for Dorothy? She can use all the help she can get. Thanks.

"Mama, what's all the yelling down there about?"

"Nonna is missing—is she up there with you?"

"No," I yell back, as I'm flying down the spiral staircase. *Missing?* Where would she possibly go?

Sure enough, Nonna is nowhere to be found. The sunshine came out today for the first time in a while, so it's warmer than it's been lately. Mama thinks she may have decided to get outside for some fresh air. Nonna never goes much farther than the courtyard with her statues. Occasionally she'll go out to the grape arbor or the garden, but she's in neither of those places now.

Daddy heads down the hill toward the pond in the Fiat. Mama's going down by the pool—which has been covered up since September. The boys and I start out on foot to look along the road in the direction of the stables. I don't like this feeling. We've never lost Nonna before.

When we make it as far as the stable, J. R. says, "There's no way she could have gone any farther than this."

"Let's just check around here." I start toward the barn. Walking past Caesar's stall, I hear singing. Signaling to the boys to follow me, we peek into the horse stall, and find Nonna sitting on a hay bale in her bathrobe and slippers. She's feeding hay to Caesar, one strand at a time. Napoleon is sitting at her side with his head on her lap. The four puppies are asleep at her feet. And Nonna is singing "Ave Maria."

There are some things in life that are too *preziosi* to interrupt. My brothers and I quietly turn around, and slide our backs down the outside of the stall. Closing my eyes, I picture Nonna singing to the animals. Comforting little grunts and sighs come from the puppies.

"*I miei bambini preziosi*," Nonna whispers to Ci-ci's young family. My precious babies.

My brothers and I exchange glances with one another and add a few sighs of our own.

After Nonna's rendition of "*Arrivederci Roma*," J. R. whispers, "I'd better let Mom and Dad know we found her. Wait here—I'll have Dad bring the car for her."

The twins and I smile at each other as Nonna belts out "*O sole mio*." I can't think of a better way to spend a Saturday morning. I hope I remember this when I'm old. If I'm going to lose my marbles, this is the way I'd like to do it: spending my days sitting on a bale of hay in a horse stall, singing to the animals. Can't get much better than that.

When Daddy pulls up outside, my brothers and I look at each other and sigh again. Taking Nonna by the arm, Daddy gently leads her out to the car; all the while she's accusing him of ruining her perfect day. For once I'd have to agree.

J. R. and Dino ride home with Daddy and Nonna. I walk back with Benji. Halfway home we hear a little whimper behind us and turn around. "A. J., look, it's Luigi." Benji bends down and scoops him up. "Do you think Mom and Dad will let us keep him?"

"I already asked. The answer is *no*. Mama says I'd give her grief on both ends if I got attached to a dog in Italy. She says I'm already torn up over leaving Sailor behind, and I'd be torn up all over again trying to leave another dog. 'You must be out of your mind to even ask,' is how she put it."

"But I really want him." Benji keeps walking toward home, with Luigi in his arms.

Before long Ci-ci shows up, making a big fuss over her baby.

"How did she find him?" Benji asks.

"Mamas know the scent of their own babies," I tell him, "—except when they're up to their necks in a water trough."

"Do you think our mom knows my scent?" Benji asks.

"Sure she does. How do think you she tells you and Dino apart?" I laugh.

"Yeah, well, that's because Dino stinks and I don't."

Come to think of it, mamas have their own scent too. I know mine does. Mama is a cross between Jergens hand lotion, Carnation perfume, and Ivory soap. Mixed all together, that's Mama.

Ci-ci reminds us that we still have her baby and she is not happy about it. "I think you'd better give Ci-ci's puppy back before she goes crazy and shreds you to pieces."

"Yeah, our mom would do the same thing if something happened to one of us, wouldn't she?"

"I'll bet you're right." I think of what Mama just did to Annalisa. "Mamas don't like anyone messin' with their babies."

"I don't want to find out what Ci-ci will do." Benji quickly sets Luigi down beside his mama.

We decide to walk Luigi and Ci-ci back to make sure they get home okay. I think Benji's right. There's nothing in life that can keep a mama from worrying over her kids, and woe to the one who tries to come between the two.

Today is the best mail day of my life since I moved here. Danny's pictures finally arrived. I knew what they were the minute Daddy handed me the envelope. I ran upstairs to savor my former life in privacy.

Laying the pictures out on my bed, I recapture my life one photograph at a time:

1. Little Papoose. My log cabin in the woods. It looks so lonely with no one out on the porch swing.

2. Juniper Beach. The sandy beach I named myself. All of my memories of diving for bottles and star-gazing come from that beach.

3. The Pitchy Pine Trail. The trail lined with pines trees that lead to Juniper beach. I can almost smell that sweet pitchy pine air just by looking at it.

4. My critter cemetery. Where all my dead animals and bugs are buried, including a memorial headstone for my hamster, which reads:

    My Beloved Ruby Jean
    June 1968—August 1968
    Lost at Sea
    RIP

    There are even fresh-cut flowers on each grave. Danny must have taken the time to do that for me.

5. Danny's grandpa, standing on the bow of his tugboat.

And then, there's my favorite, the sixth: Danny and Sailor sitting together down on my old dock. They both look … great. Danny still looks like a blond Little Joe Cartwright. He looks older than I remember him, because he is. He's almost seventeen now—in December. Wow. And I mean *wow*.

I think I'd like to share my photos with Sister Aggie. Maybe she will understand the agony I have to endure living here.

⁐⁐⁂⁑⁑

Saturday afternoons are Sister Aggie's time off, so I show up at the convent, hoping she'll be free to see me. I'm asked to wait in the *atrio* while one of the nuns goes to hunt her up for me. While I'm waiting, I wander over to look at some of the paintings that are hanging in the reception area. I'm fascinated by the paintings of the holy family. One painting of Mother Mary holding Baby Jesus captivates me. Mary's face is expressing both joy and sorrow at the same time. It's a miracle to me that someone can express two emotions at the same time—in a painting, no less.

"Angelina, how wonderful you've come." Sister Aggie greets me warmly, and leads me to a cozy visitor's room. She gestures for me to have a seat on the soft white sofa, and sits beside me. "What have you come to share with me today?" she asks.

I pull out my envelope of pictures and hand it to her. She takes them out one by one, looking intently at each photo while I explain them to her. When she gets to the last photo, the one of Danny and Sailor, she sighs. "Ah, now I see why you are so homesick."

I'm not sure if she's referring to Papoose, the island, Sailor, or Danny. "Why?"

"You had a loyal pet, a true friend, and a beautiful setting all in one place. This island was your paradise."

She gets it. I knew she would. That's why I came.

"Tell me about your island," she says.

"Well …" I tell her everything. I mean *everything*. I tell her about saving Sailor, and about Sailor saving me, and losing Ruby Jean, and about my critter cemetery, and finding my sister and her two-timing island boy, Jason, kissing on my sacred burial grounds. I tell her about Mama's Big Island Bash, and about Sister Abigail, and how I got stuck in the confessional—twice. I tell her about Buzz from the gas dock, about icky little Rodney Gizmode, and the ice bath we set up for him and his hotshot brothers. And then I tell her about Danny, and star-gazing, and how he rescued me and Sailor the day we blew downwind, and how much I wish I was on the island instead of here. I start to cry.

Sister Aggie places her hands on each side of my face, gently, and looks into my eyes. "Angelina," she whispers, "God has something special for you here, too."

"Really?"

"Really. Sometimes all we need is a new light to see our situation differently. God doesn't always change our situation, but He can help change our perspective about it, and that can make all the difference. Follow me. I have something that might help."

Sister Aggie leads me down a long, dark hallway to another room with a desk and a few chairs. The walls are lined with books, shelves and shelves of books.

A library. I'm in heaven.

Sister Aggie pulls out a book and holds it out to me *Il Diario di*

Anne Frank. "This girl was just about your age, Angelina, during the time the sisters and I were hiding children in the hills near Cuneo. Anne Frank lived in Amsterdam at the time, where she was hidden in a home for over two years."

I remember trying to read this book in fifth grade. I could not believe that people could be so cruel to other people—especially to kids who didn't understand why they were hated just for being Jewish. After sobbing myself to sleep reading it each night, Mama took it away from me and told my teacher to give me an alternative reading assignment.

"I believe this was the first book published about the Holocaust, printed two years after the war ended. It was Anne's dream to publish a book, so her father made sure he fulfilled that dream for her. I think this may help you to see your life here in a little different light."

I'm sure it will. I hope I can handle it a little better at age fourteen than I did at age ten. Maybe I'll have better luck with the Italian version.

The minute I get home, I run up to my tower, hang out my handmade *Do Not Disturb the Princess* sign, climb under my covers, and flip on my reading lamp. Nothing beats a good book in bed.

15

Punto di Prospettiva
(A Bit of Perspective)

"What on earth is that kid reading?" Mama asks Daddy. *As if I can't hear her just because I have my head stuck in a book.* Lying across the room by the fire, I'm completely immersed in the tail end of *Anne Frank.*

"Why do you ask?" Daddy replies.

"I just asked her if she wanted some warm *biscotti*, and she looked at me with hollow eyes, and asked, 'How can you be so insensitive?'"

I admit I'm kind of strange that way. When I read a book, I become the main character. After spending three days straight as Anne Frank, I feel like I have spent the past two years in the secret annex and was just betrayed and sent off to die in a Nazi concentration camp. Anne and her sister, Margo, were sent to Bergen-Belsen, where they both died from typhus two weeks before the camp was liberated. She was only a year older than me when she died.

How on God's green earth could this have happened—especially to children? "How could so many people be so evil and stupid all at the same time?"

I didn't realize I'd said it out loud until Daddy says, "A. J., what *are* you reading?"

"*The Diary of Anne Frank.*"

Mama and Daddy exchange glances. "That explains it," Mama says.

"Didn't we deal with this book once before, honey?" Daddy says. "You sure you can handle it?"

"The Franks are the ones who had to *handle* it. At this point I should at least be able to handle reading about it."

Mama has the furrowed-brow feature on her forehead turned on high. They know how anything involving suffering affects me. I'm bad enough with animals, let alone people. Not only did Mama take away books like *Anne Frank*, she also canceled my subscription to *Born Free* magazine because I couldn't stop crying over photos of endangered animals—especially the white tiger cubs. As soon as I'd get over one issue, the next one would arrive in the mail.

By the time Mama canceled, I had already signed up to go to Antarctica to help save baby seals. I figured it was a creative way to get out of Italy. Save the seals and save A. J.—a dual cause. They called Daddy for his charge-card number to help fund the trip. He didn't quite catch their vision. But I sure caught his.

"A. J., didn't you say you had some arithmetic homework to finish tonight?"

"Oh, Mama, how can you expect me to even think about arithmetic problems when Anne Frank just died? Is it really important that I know what time the train will arrive in Florence if it leaves Rome at five in the morning traveling at sixty kilometers per hour?"

"It matters if you're the one on the train, or the one picking up the passenger. It will also matter when your report card comes out. So hop to it, kiddo."

Somehow my mother's concern for me is not working in my favor this time.

One hour of grueling arithmetic problems later, Mama calls me to dinner. After finishing *Anne Frank*, I'm wondering why Sister Aggie had me read this. She tells me to think only on good things, then hands me a book about an evil madman who put innocent people through hell on earth. What was she thinking?

On my way down to dinner, it strikes me that this old castle feels unusually grand and spacious. Aromas of onions and garlic lure me to the table, where I take my seat, and am surrounded by food, *glorious* food. All prepared by loving hands. "Greetings, family. Please pass the eggplant."

Mama looks over, surprised. She knows I never eat eggplant.

I shovel in a big mouthful. "*Mmm-mm-mm.*"

Everyone's looking at me. "What's with her?" J. R. asks.

"She's been reading *The Diary of Anne Frank*," Mama says.

"Oh. That explains it."

⚘⚘⚘

After supper. Wide awake under my soft, warm blankets. Just lying here, philosopholizing. I have a bed. I have a soft, warm, cushy bed—with blankets. I have my own room—in a castle, for Pete's sake. And I am with my family … all safe and warm in our big fat castle. Even my stomach is full and happy … *hold on. I get it.* I finally get what Sister Aggie is up to. Reverse psychology. How brilliant. I need to write about this. I flip on my table lamp and grab my journal.

Journal Entry: Revelations

I feel exactly like George Bailey at the end of "It's a Wonderful Life." Everything I've been whining about, I bet Anne Frank would be grateful for. Compared to Anne, I have no problems. I have everything. And I'm still here.

I'm suddenly thankful to just be alive. Is not life itself enough? Oh, to be truly free from want and greed. In one spine-tingling instant—I am changed. Sister Aggie is a genius. Death to the black dog. The white dog lives!

My door suddenly flies open. A half-eaten bag of M&M's come sailing through my room and hits the floor. "Here's what's left of that care package you got from Rosa," Dino yells from the hallway. I hear Benji giggling beside him.

"You little creeps—those are *mine*—you had *no right* coming into my room and taking my candy! This is *my* tower—*keep out!*"

I run out into the hall as Dino and Benji slide down the spiral banister, laughing their heads off. "Tell Rosa thanks!" Dino yells.

"You spaz—you owe me for this! You can't even get M&M's in Italy! You're probably the one who kiped my Bee Gees tape that I can't find either … stay out of my stuff!"

I storm back in my room, slam my door, and step on the Bee Gees tape lying on my floor. "Great, now it's cracked." It's all their fault.

Oops. Black dog is on the loose …

After school I stop by the convent to return *Anne Frank* to Sister Aggie. She comes out to greet me in the *atrio*. "*Benvenuto,* Angelina." Welcome.

I hand her the book and thank her for loaning it to me.

"Finished already?" She looks surprised.

"I read it fast, so I could figure out what was in there that you thought might help me."

"And what did you find?"

"Perspective."

We awoke this morning to snow. I can't believe it. So much snow dumped on us overnight that school is canceled—*Urrà*! Hooray! The boys and I are running all over the castle gathering up snow saucers, sleds, hats, and gloves. We're going to get out there and make the most of this while it lasts. I told my brothers, "If you help me find the sleds, I'll take you guys to a really steep hill with a drain ditch full of ice beneath the snow." That's all it took to get them into gear.

Gathering up the goods, the four of us head out, caravan style, dragging our saucers and sleds behind us. We've piled extra gloves, scarves, sandwiches, and a thermos of hot chocolate on top—enough food and equipment to last us until noon anyway. The snow is coming down in fine form as we trudge along the country road, and it does not look like it will let up anytime soon—*hallelujah!*

As we crest the hill, it becomes clear we are not the only ones with this brilliant idea. Everyone who lives on our hill has shown up, including J. R.'s sweetheart, Celeste; Benji's buddy Christiana; and my friends, Dominic, Dario, and Bianca. And then … there's Annalisa, in all her pink glory, matching head to toe. She must have run out and bought herself a new snowsuit the minute the weather report hit yesterday. It's the white fur boots that kill me—I think they're real bunny boots, or some animal that could have used its fur more than Annalisa. To think it had to give its life just to keep her royal toes warm … I don't even want to think about it. On the other hand, I'm standing here in my fake raccoon hat with a tail, looking like Davy Crockett. Like Mama says, "It takes all kinds to make the world go round."

"Angelina!" Bianca welcomes me with a cheerful shout, Dominic welcomes me with a snowball, and Annalisa doesn't welcome me at all.

"Bianca!" We twirl in circles, rejoicing in the snow together. Once my head stops spinning, I return the snowball greeting to Dominic, and whomp him on the back—with a lightly packed snowball.

The boys are already busy building a snow jump. Leave it to the male gender to turn everything into a sporting competition. As they're piling snow on the jump, they're rattling off the rules and deciding on the prize for the longest sled jumper. This could get pretty serious by day's end.

The snow jump comes right at the bottom of the steep ice slide. J. R. talks Benji into testing the run for us, which he feels honored to do, of course. J. R. gives him a good, hard shove-off and sends him sailing. Benji is so light he flies down the hill like a blur. Hitting the jump, he shoots into the air and comes to a hard splat a good distance away in the field. It takes him a minute to breathe again, and it's a relief to see that he is, in fact, still breathing.

When it comes to my turn, Dominic says he'll be waiting at the bottom in case I need rescuing, and he heads down the slide before me. As soon as Annalisa catches this, she struts over and looks at me with that sappy sweet smile of hers. "Hey, Angelina, let's go double."

Double ... double ...? Oh, yes, the last time I went double was on an inner tube at the Potholes with Cousin Stacy ... in her heavier days ... and had the wind knocked out of me ... nearly drowned ...

"I'm scared to go alone, Angelina."

Yeah. I trust you about as far as I can throw you. "Um, s-sure, okay." I momentarily hear the scarecrow's song from *Wizard of Oz* playing in my head: "If I Only Had a Brain."

"I'll go in front," she says, and plops herself down on my sled.

Because you're so scared, right? That makes sense.

Dominic signals from below that he's ready for us. I hope he's ready to catch the pink snow queen, 'cause that seems to be her aim here.

"Here we come!" Annalisa yells.

J. R. gives us a shove-off and whispers, "Have fun" to me.

I can't see a thing, thanks to Annalisa's pink fur hat, but I do know that we are ripping down the hill so fast there are probably sparks shooting out from under us. Before I know what's happening we hit a bump and Annalisa goes flying off. I hit the jump alone and sail right past Dominic—the sled goes to the right, and I fly to the left—landing in the field ... on my arm ... and hear a crunch ... I feel nauseous and dizzy ...

Dominic starts over to me. I'm trying not to cry, but it really hurts. Fighting back tears and forcing a smile, I hear a horrendous howl from up on the slope …

"Ouwww—my ankle, my ankle—help, Dominic—*help!*"

Instantly all eyes shift to the screaming pink blob on the hill. Dominic quickly looks back at me, "You okay, Angelina?"

"Y-yeah …" *Hardly. But who wants to compete with that?*

I watch Dominic charge up the hill to the rescue. Annalisa is holding up one leg and balances herself against Dominic, while he wraps his arm around her. Bianca is running down the hill toward me. I slowly climb to my feet, wincing from shooting sensations in my arm.

"What happened?" Bianca asks, when she reaches the bottom of the hill.

"Bad landing. I hurt my arm."

J. R., Dino, and Benji pack up all of our stuff and take turns pulling me home on the sled. Meanwhile Dominic and Annalisa hobble off toward Annalisa's house. I could have sworn she was limping on the other leg at first.

By the next morning the snow is nearly all melted. I show up late to school with a cast on my arm. "A smooth break," the doctor told Mama. "Should be better in about six to eight weeks."

I pass Annalisa in the hall. From her "call of the wild" that echoed down Poppy Hill yesterday, one would expect to find Annalisa in the hospital today. Oddly she seems to have made a miraculous recovery. The second she sees me, a quick limp starts up. "*Lei è stata ferita?*" she asks. You got hurt too?

"Yep."

"I was going to go to the doctor, too, but my leg felt a little better after I got home, so I decided just to brave it out."

"Uhh-huh." Whatever. Spotting Bianca, I make my way toward her.

Before I reach her, a voice in the crowd yells out, "Angelina, *ma che è successo?*" What happened? I'm quickly engulfed by a circle of people. Annalisa looks on longingly, probably wondering where she can get a wheelchair.

At lunch Dominic comes over to my table looking sheepish. "*Buongiorno*, Angelina." Before I have a chance to answer, he says, "*Scusami.*" I'm sorry.

I just nod. I think we both understand what happened here. The funny thing is, I feel more sorry for Annalisa than for myself.

16

Fun on the French Express

"I'm not sure how comfortable I am sending A. J. off alone on a train with her ..."

"Sending me *where* with *who?*" I ask, entering the kitchen, unexpected. I love the way my family makes plans for me without asking me first.

Mama turns around, alarmed to see me. "Nothing."

"Oh, Mama, come on, it's *my* life—what are you doing with it this time?"

Nonna walks into the room carrying her giant coffee mug. "Well, there you are, Angelina Juliana. Are you ready to go visit Sainte Foy with me?"

"Huh?" I quickly look at Mama. "Where am I going?"

"Okay, everyone, just hold on and sit down." Mama pours coffee into Nonna's mug, then gives Daddy a warm-up splash while passing him the baton with her eyes.

On cue Daddy says, "I think it's a great opportunity for Nonna and A. J. to spend some time together with Nonna's relatives. A. J.'s never met her Great Aunt Ada or the Renzos before."

"*More* relatives?" I sigh.

Mama finally forks over the information. "Nonna has been invited to spend a few days visiting her sister in France."

"France? I get to go to France? Wait a minute ... who's Sainte Foy?"

"Sainte Foy is the little twelve-year-old martyr who was beheaded," Nonna chimes in.

"Delicately put," Daddy comments.

"*What?* I don't want to see a twelve-year-old with no head!"

"A. J.," Daddy says calmly, "Nonna's sister lives near the village of Conques. The abbey there houses the statue of Sainte Foy. Nonna wants to go on a pilgrimage with her sister to see the shrine of the little saint."

I'm intrigued. "The statue has a head, right?"

"Yes, the statue has a head. Nonna thought since both of you have such a passion for the saints ..."

"I do?"

"Sure you do," Mama says. "Remember your statue of Saint Francis?"

Um, okay ... I have one statue of Saint Francis back in my critter cemetery ... not sure if that qualifies as a passion, but if it will get me a trip to France ... "Right. So when is this pilgrimage supposed to happen, anyway?"

"That's what we're trying to decide," Mama says. "First we need to feel comfortable about you and Nonna traveling alone on the train for the better part of a day."

"It's not *you* we're worried about," Daddy mutters to me.

Mama continues, "You'd be staying with the Renzo family in Nîmes, then drive on up to Conques and spend a few days together there. It would only be for a weekend, and with the snow starting to fly, the sooner you go, the better—probably this weekend."

"*This weekend?* Will I miss any school?"

"You'd miss Friday and the following Monday, for travel days."

That's two days less torture for me. "I'll go." A train ride with Nonna will be a cakewalk compared to going to school. I mean, how tough could it be?

❧

First thing Thursday morning, I let my teachers know I'll be missing two days of school, in case they insist I do some homework to keep up. My language teacher says we will be analyzing classic works of poetry and has a small collection to choose from. As I ramble through the stack of books piled on her desk, one of them catches my attention, mainly because it's in English. The title piques my curiosity as well. *The Hound of Heaven* by Francis Thompson. Picking it up, I begin to read.

> *I fled Him, down the nights and*
> *down the days;*
> *I fled Him, down the arches of the*
> *years;*
> *I fled Him, down the labyrinthine ways*
> *Of my own mind; and in the midst of tears*
> *I hid from Him, and under running laughter.*
> *Up vistaed hopes, I sped;*

And shot, precipitated,

Adown Titanic glooms of chasméd fears,

From those strong Feet that followed, followed after....

It may be in English, but I can't make any sense of it.

"That is an exceptional poem, Angelina, one of the best, but also one of the most difficult to understand. Here ..." Signorina Luzi hands me a book that explains the poem, which is much longer than the poem itself. "*Hound of Heaven* is a poem written by a young man from London in the late 1800s. He lived a tragic life but envisioned God as the Hound of Heaven, who pursued him with unrelenting love. I wouldn't recommend this to many students, but with your ability, I think you might be able to grasp it with the commentary. Try to read the poem while you're away. We'll have a writing assignment when you return. You'll each be writing a poem, similar in style to the poem you choose but will be relating it to your own life."

That will be interesting.

Friday morning Mama and Daddy wave good-bye as our train pulls away. They have misgivings written all over their faces. Daddy mouths the words *good luck*. I have no idea what they are so worried about. We are on our way to France. I am sitting on a train instead of being harassed at school. As far as I can tell, this is a good trade-off.

"Nonna ... *what* are you doing?"

"I'm changing my stockings." Nonna is rolling her tights down around her ankles, but still has her boots on.

"Nonna, you can't do that on the train, pull them back up."

"Why? I want to wear my red ones instead."

"You can change into the red ones when we get to France—you have to wear black tights in Italy." When dealing with Nonna you have to use her kind of logic if you want to get anywhere.

"Oh." She looks at the legs of a woman across the aisle. Her stockings are black, thank goodness. "Okay." She pulls them back up to her waist. I try to shield the other passengers from having to see her bloomers, which would not be a good way to start anyone's morning.

Pulling out my travel journal, I begin documenting my trip. Nonna pulls a breadstick out of her purse. Everything takes me twice as long with this big cast in the way—at least it was my left arm I broke instead of my right. I'm holding my page flat with the weight of my cast while composing.

Travel Journal Entry: November 3, 1972

A Train to Sainte Foy

I stare out my train window as the November snow begins to fly. I, too, am flying in my soul. I am on my first pilgrimage to France to visit the resting place of the brave little martyr Sainte Foy. I don't know what to think, as I have never been to visit a saint before, or heard of one so young as the little Foy.

As I'm watching the silent snowfall, a quiet hush falls over me, a hush of wonder and stillness ... peace ...

Crunch … crunch … crunch …

Nonna is gnawing away on her rock-hard breadstick.

Crunch … crunch … crunch …

"We can go to the dining car if you're hungry, Nonna."

"Let's do that. I love dining cars."

I pack up my travel journal and help Nonna out of her seat. Navigating the narrow aisles is no easy task, trying to keep Nonna upright and not bonk anyone in the head with my cast. The dining car is at the far end of the train. I'm feeling kind of seasick already.

By the time we arrive, Nonna is still standing and I've only bonked three heads. There are no empty tables, so we ask to join another family. They seem friendly—until Nonna reaches in her mouth, pulls out her dentures, and sets them on the tea saucer in front of her.

The kids' eyes bug out of their heads.

"Nonna," I whisper, "you're not supposed to do that in public. You need to keep those in your mouth."

"Oh." She grabs them off her plate and sticks them back in her mouth.

I'm thinking we'd better leave before Nonna pulls any more surprises. "Nonna, let's go buy some sandwiches and take them back to our seats."

"Why can't I stay right here?"

"Because we have a better view from our window."

She looks out the train window. "You're right." She stands up. "If any of you would like a better view," she says to the family, "you can all come back and look out our window."

They nod politely.

The highlight of the train ride was Nonna's two-hour nap. Running a close second is my sticker-book collection, which has kept her obsessively busy for the past three hours. She has taken every sticker on and off the pages at least fifty times each. I'm just praying the stickum will hold up for the trip home, or we're all in trouble.

The announcement finally comes that we're arriving in Nîmes. I start to gather up our things and put them into our bags. "Okay, Nonna, I need to pack up the sticker book, we're almost there."

"Almost where?"

"Nîmes."

"I don't want to get off. I'm staying here with my stickers; I'm not done yet."

"Nonna, those are my stickers, and you are done for now. You have to save some for the trip home."

"Oh, that's right." She hands it over to me.

There's really nothing to finish—it's just a book full of stickers that you can arrange any way you want. I'm just grateful she seems to think it's an ongoing project. These stickers are worth their weight in gold.

The conductor reaches out to help Nonna off the train. She swats his hand away. "Get your hands off of me, buster."

I apologize for her and thank the man. As soon as we step onto the platform, I start looking for someone who looks like Nonna. Mama says Nonna and her sister could almost pass for twins, but the main difference is their sharpness of mind. According to Mama,

Ada's ducks are still all in a row. I guess it goes without saying that Nonna's ducks have all flown south.

Escorted by a short little couple, I spot a tall woman who is the spittin' image of Nonna heading directly toward us. This must be Ada. "*Bonjour,* Juliana," the short lady calls out to Nonna.

Ada's son and daughter-in-law, Rudi and Gina Renzo, look quite short and stout next to Ada, who stands slim and statuesque between the two. Nonna stops dead in her tracks. She stares at her sister and tears fall from her eyes. "Ada, Ada," she cries, and falls into her arms.

I introduce myself to my great-aunt Ada and my ... *I don't know* ... twice-removed great cousins? Rudi and Gina are ecstatic over having a blonde relative in the family. I'm glad someone can appreciate it. On another very fortunate note, they all know English. "We are so pleased you could come," they tell me. "Come, we will feed you."

And feed us they do. When we arrive at their quaint French cottage, a big feast awaits us. Normandy pork with apples ... peaches in crème brûlée ... yummo! I've decided I like French food. Over chocolate mousse I learn that Gina is my first cousin, once removed. She tells me to just call her Gina. That's a relief.

After dessert, the five of us cozy up in the front room by the fire. This little cottage is full of neat old things from way back. The tables and shelves are covered with knickknacks and dolls and old wooden toys. While I'm busy looking at everything, Gina pulls out the photo albums. "Come see the family."

More relatives? I'm almost afraid to look after meeting everyone on Uncle Nick's side of the family.

"There's something I think you'll be excited to see," Gina says, flipping the album open.

As long as they aren't dancing and roasting animals over fire pits. I sit down beside Gina and try to show some enthusiasm over seeing yet another branch of this ever-growing family tree of ours.

"This is your great-great-Nonna and Nonno Renzo."

I'm completely taken back by the photo. "Are you sure they're *Italian?*"

"Yes, I'm sure," Gina chuckles.

"But they have … they look … they have blue eyes and blonde hair and look like me!"

"I thought that might surprise you. That's why I was so excited when I met you—you are one of the true northern Italians." Gina flips through page after page filled with more of these blue-eyed, blonde Italians who have obviously passed along a recessive gene. I am *floored.* I'm not the only light Italian in the world—there's an entire colony just like me!

Gina has moved on to the plans for the weekend, but I'm still stuck in my new identity. I am a *true* Italian, a northern Italian, with blue eyes and blonde hair and I belong here as much as the rest of 'em! While I'm letting this revelation sink in, I can't keep from staring at these people in the photographs—these beautiful, wonderful relatives of mine. *Hey, people, I'm one of you!*

Meanwhile I haven't heard a word of what Gina is saying, and try to tune back in …

"… So we'll drive up to Conques in the morning and spend tomorrow night at the Château Sainte Foy. It's right across the street from the Abbey Sainte Foy, home of the statue Sainte Foy. The restaurant in the Château Sainte Foy has wonderful food."

Don't tell me … they have Sainte Foy burgers at the Sainte Foy Bistro.

Since we'll be getting up early for the trip to Conques, Gina suggests that we all turn in for the night. It sounds like a good idea to everyone but me and Ada, because we are both still wide awake. We stay and chat in front of the fire while everyone else heads off to bed. There's so much I want to know before I go to sleep tonight.

"Ada, what was it like for you and Nonna growing up in Italy? I've asked Nonna before, but I'm not sure her memory is all that clear." *Understatement.* I can tell right off that Ada is still sharp as a tack, and this may be my only chance to hear the real story. Nonna has her own version, but I have my doubts—unless her father was really the prince of Cimano and raised kangaroos.

"Oh, well, my goodness, let's see … Juliana and I were in a family of six girls, living in the town of Cimano, in northeastern Italy. I was named Immacolata, after my grandmother, which was the traditional way of naming one's children."

Oh, don't I know it.

"In English, Immacolata means *immaculate,* as in the Immaculate Conception."

Okay, that right there is a good reason to be grateful my grandma's name was Juliana.

"Your Grandmother Juliana was the youngest daughter and barely remembers our mother. She died when Juliana was only eight years old. Juliana looked so much like our mother it was remarkable. Mother was very dark and beautiful—and probably responsible for changing the family genes from blonde and blue-eyed to brunette and brown-eyed Italians. Our father loved her very deeply, but his family was against the marriage, so he ran off to marry her and lost his family inheritance. They were poor but happy. They owned a corn mill, and ground flour for the people of the town. When our mother died, it broke our father's heart. He was never quite the same." Ada's eyes tear up.

"By the time Juliana was twelve, I had married, and all the other sisters found work in a brick factory in Austria. Juliana was Father's only consolation, and he loved her very much so she stayed home with him. But Father got very ill and could hardly care for Juliana. Eventually it was she who took care of him.

"Juliana came to visit us from time to time, but Father missed her terribly—she was all he had, so he would not let any of us keep her very long." Ada has a faraway look in her eyes, like she's going back in time. I feel like I'm going back right along with her.

"There was one winter we went home for Christmas. Juliana was around ten years old then. When we arrived we found only our father at home. Father was bedridden and had asked Juliana to go to buy some bread. It was so cold out, and Juliana went out with no shoes or stockings, only a little flour-sack dress. That was all she owned. We had bought her some winter clothes and socks for Christmas from some of the money we'd earned at the factory, but we didn't arrive in time. Apparently, on her way to the bakery, it began to snow. Juliana had to walk barefoot through the woods. Along the way she fainted. The snow came down and covered her up. When we finally found her, she was beneath a blanket of snow, nearly frozen to death. We carried her home and warmed her up by the fire. She has never liked the snow since.

"After that Father sent Juliana to stay with me. He told her to be good and stay until he could come for her. But he never came. I knew something was wrong, because Father never liked to send Juliana away. As I suspected, when my husband returned from checking on him, he gave us the sad news that our father had died." Ada reaches up and wipes a tear from her eye. "I've never stopped missing him."

I think I understand why Nonna says her father was a prince.

Ada looks tired. "Thank you for telling me about Nonna. I'd better let you get some sleep. I'm real happy I got to meet you." I give Ada a good-night hug.

"*Bonne nuit, ma cherie.*"

Must be French.

Ada catches the confused look on my face and smiles. "*Buona notte, amore mio,*" goodnight, sweetheart, she says, and kisses me on both cheeks.

We part ways to our bedrooms.

Nonna and I get to share a double bed in the tiny guestroom. I try to climb in without disturbing her, but the springs on the old brass bed wake her up. Nonna takes one of the pillows, goes around and climbs in at the opposite end of the bed. "Good night," she says.

"Nonna . . . what are you doing down there?"

"I snore. This way I won't keep you up. This is how we did things when we were married."

"*Sogni d'oro, Nonna.*" Sweet dreams. I lie here thinking of Nonna as a young girl, something I've never really done before—especially being my age, cold and hungry, without a mama or daddy. The only Nonna I've ever known has been my sweet, old, funny Nonna. Sweet to me, anyway, not to everyone. She always tells me I'm her favorite. I think it's because of my name. Mama says I bring out the best in Nonna like no one else can. Daddy brings out the worst in

Nonna—only because he married her baby and she was left alone again. Seeing her now as that brave young girl—walking through the snow to bring her father some bread—I'm so proud of my Nonna. *Prospettiva.* Perspective.

I drift off, knowing I have a heritage I am truly a part of. I knew I was Italian, but it's different when you really look like the people you belong to. Maybe that's why God made us in His image, so we would know we belong to each other.

La Bambina Santa Fede (Little Saint Faith)

A remote country road winds up the mountain like a snail shell, leading us to Conques. The small medieval village rises up out of the morning mist like a setting in a fairy tale. Tall steeples and slate-stone roofs give way to majestic churches and quaint mountain cottages. Old but cute. No, not cute, but charming. I know there's a better word for this ... something ancient ... and mysterious ... *Enchanting.* That is the word I'm looking for. This town is *enchanting.*

We pull up to the Château Sainte Foy, across the street from the aged yellow stone Sainte Foy Abbey. Rudi holds the car doors open for us ladies, letting out a big yawn. Probably due to all of our jabber.

"I'll check us into the hotel while you *mademoiselles* visit the abbey." He kisses Gina on the cheek and says he'll meet up with us after he takes a short nap.

Crossing the street to the abbey, Nonna and Ada are like Siamese twins joined at the hip, sandwiched between Gina and me. Now that I'm actually here, I'm kind of excited about our little Sainte Foy pilgrimage, but a little nervous, too. This is, after all, my first saint encounter. Entering the musky cathedral, we're greeted by a man with pure white hair and a white robe—looking much like a saint himself. He introduces himself to Gina as Sainte Foy's guardian. I never realized that saints have earthly guardians in the same way we have heavenly guardians.

When we're brought before the statue of Sainte Foy, I can understand why she needs a guardian. Sainte Foy is a three-foot-tall gold statue, encrusted with glimmering stones and jewels. The statue of Sainte Foy. The head seems oddly large for the small body it sits on. I am captivated. Who was this child? Behind me her guardian is telling the story to Gina in French, who is translating it to Italian for Nonna and me. Ada understands both versions.

I can hear Gina's voice in the background, but as the story of little Foy unfolds, her cold, hard statue slowly transforms into a twelve-year-old girl, running about these green hills, the same as I once ran around Indian Island …

"When she was very young, she had a nurse who secretly taught her about Jesus. Little Foy took bread to the poor people in her village and told them about her Jesus. But her parents were not believers and were very upset about her Christian faith. They insisted she worship the goddess Diana, as they did. Little Foy refused. She was brought before the proconsul Dacien at Agen on October sixth in the year 303. She said, 'My name is Faith, and I am a Christian.' She explained to him, 'His name is Adonai. Since I was a little child and first learned of Him, I have loved the Lord, Jesus Christ.'

"When Dacien ordered her to sacrifice to the goddess Diana, little Faith said, 'No,' in a great loud voice for all to hear. 'No, I will not.'

"That was the end for little Foy. As they marched her off, she could hear her mother crying and asked that her mother be told that it was with joy she was going to her Savior. Her mother's name was Sophie."

Sophie? That's my mama's name. I'm stunned this really happened to a little girl with a mother named Sophie. This is one of those spine-tingling moments when I suddenly realize this happened to someone not so different than me. Nonna gently takes hold of my hand. I don't know how long we stand together, grieving for this brave little saint. I only notice Gina's voice again when we are walking away. She says there is a book in the abbey, *Liber Miraculorum Sanctae Fidis,* Book of Miracles of Sainte Foy. "Sainte Foy's miracles include stories about animals that came back to life when Foy prayed to Jesus for them," she says.

Oh, little Foy, where were you when my Ruby drowned?

The others follow the guardian to see the book. Standing alone at the altar, I'm wondering if I will ever do anything brave for Jesus. The only one I've ever risked my life for was Ruby Jean, my hamster. It's not likely I'll be sainted for that.

⊱✦⊰

When you're in the company of people over the age of sixty, afternoons are reserved for nap time at the Château Sainte Foy. While the *mademoiselles* join Rudi in slumbering the hours away, I pull out my travel journal to write about my first saint encounter.

Conques, France, November 4, 1972
Sainte Foy: French
Saint Faith: English

Santa Fede: Italian

Santa Fe: Spanish—hey, Santa Fe, New Mexico!

Sanctae Fidis: Latin, and the title of her book of miracles.

To Saint or Not to Saint? ... That Is the Question

I've never felt a kindred spirit with Nonna's saints before.
They were always so far beyond me. But little Sainte Foy, I'm
kind of taken by. She was so courageous and brave, but she
was also once a real girl like me. This is the first time I've
realized that saints started out as ordinary people. The icons of
the saints with halos and crowns have always led me to believe
they were born holy. But I realize now they weren't. They were
born sinners just like the rest of us, and made the choice to live
and die for God. If the artists would paint the saints in their
street clothes, without the gowns and halos, more of us not-
so-holy folks could relate to them better. Not to say they don't
deserve to be honored, but if they could hold off until heaven
for the halo and crowns ...

I don't know ... maybe little Foy would rather just wait and
be honored by God up there in heaven anyway. I like having an
example to follow, but would feel better if she were presented
as an everyday kind of sinner who went the extra mile for Jesus.
Then people like me might feel we have a fighting chance to earn
something more than a Girl Scout badge in our lifetime.

Cousin Rudi is still snoring … in concert with Nonna. Sounds
like a good time to throw on my winter gear and explore this
enchanted little town. By the time I'm ready to roll, I've got myself

so bundled up I can barely walk, but I'm in no hurry since I don't know where I'm going.

Waddling my way through the lobby and out to the sidewalk, I consider my options. Stroll uphill, or stroll downhill. I choose downhill. That's downhill on a cobblestone street. Even though it's misty and dreary out, it's all kind of charming and enchanting at the same time. But, I have to say, this town is *way* old. I was just getting used to the idea of Italy being old, but this place makes Tuscany look young. I'm walking on cobblestones that were probably laid by cavemen. Seriously, stone ages, as in *stone everything*—stone houses, stone walls, stone roads, stone sidewalks. I'm almost expecting Fred Flintstone to come rolling around the corner in the Flintmobile. *Ya-ba-da-ba-doo*! Where do these ideas in my head come from anyway? Dunno.

Strolling through town, I stumble upon a tiny rock bookshop— rock walls on the outside, books on the inside. My heart starts to pound the second I step in from the cold to the warmth of the small reading room. I'm in my personal heaven once again, surrounded by books … wonderful old books. It dawns on me that they're all written in French. *Rats.* I can't read French. For now, I can look at the pictures in the kid's books. Some things in life are universal, and art is one of those things. Yessiree, a picture book is a picture book no matter where in the world you go.

Once the short, hunched-over shopkeeper realizes I don't speak or understand French, he stops limping around behind me and leaves me to myself to browse. It takes me a while to find some illustrations I recognize, but I finally come across some French fairy tales, including *Beauty and the Beast.* I love the art they've used in this and look at the pages over and over until I figure it's about time for the folks back at Chateau Sainte Foy to wake up. At least I hope it's time, because I am starving. "*Merci*," I announce to the little hunchback on my way out the door. "*Adieu*," farewell. The sum total of my French vocabulary.

Returning to our room, I'm relieved to find that naptime is officially over.

"What took you so long?" Nonna asks me. "We've been waiting all afternoon for you."

I've only been gone an hour.

We all traipse down to the hotel lobby for supper. I have no idea what I want, since I have no clue what anything says on the menu. I tell Gina I'd like whatever we had at their house last night, so she helps me with my order. "It isn't exactly what we had, but if you like things with a sweet sauce, you should like this." She tells the waitress what I want. *I wonder what I just ordered.*

Ada orders beef stew for herself and Nonna. She says Nonna loved beef stew when she was little and only got to have it on special occasions. Personally I have never seen Nonna eat beef stew before, but maybe she forgot that she loved it. The waitress brings us a steaming pot of tea, which really hits the spot after my chilly walk. Nonna puts a pinch of salt in her tea but drinks it anyway. She lets us all know that's the way they drink tea in Italy, and that Italians will often add a twist of lime to it. Welcome to Nonna's world.

When the waitress returns with our orders, I quickly scan the plates trying to guess which one is mine. *Crepes.* French crepes with butter and apricot sauce—*oh, yeesssss!*

While I'm happily indulging in my sweet, warm crepes, Nonna

is pouring sugar all over her beef stew. "Nonna," I whisper, what are you *doing*?"

"I wanted sweet sauce too, and you're the only one who got it."

She obviously forgot how much she loved beef stew. I dish one of my crepes onto my bread plate and slide it over to her. "Here, we'll share."

Nonna starts dishing her sugar stew concoction onto my plate— on top of my last crepe.

"… What are you doing?"

"You said we're sharing."

My white dog is telling me to see Nonna's good intentions.

My black dog is growling.

White dog reminds me to cherish my time with Nonna.

Black dog reminds me of the long train ride ahead.

⚭⚭⚭

The train pulls out from Nîmes at seven o'clock sharp, Monday morning. Fortunately Gina packed us a picnic lunch, so I won't have to endure public embarrassment in the dining car again. Nonna is busy rearranging her purse. I never realized what she kept in that big old bag until I had the chance to sit next to her on a long train ride.

I take out my travel journal.

Travel Journal Entry: November 6, 1972

Returning from Afar

Today we begin our journey back from France, and

leave behind the miraculous world of Sainte Foy. Even more miraculous was discovering I have true Italian roots. I'd like to come up with one poetic stanza to describe my pilgrimage with Nonna ...

Tucked in this town so quaint and steep
Lie hidden mysteries old and deep
I've roots and memories to keep ...

Just one more line . . .

"Move your big cast, it's in my way." Nonna elbows me and pulls out a box of paper clips from her purse. She turns each one over and faces them the *other* direction, then rearranges them back into the box—which she *tosses* back into her purse. She takes out some old S&H green stamps that she must have saved from back in the States—from about a hundred years ago. She licks each of them and sticks them to index cards. Next, out comes a hole punch, and she starts punching away at the stamp-covered index cards. *Punch ... punch ... punch ... punch ... punch ... punch ...* Little white and green circles are flying everywhere.

"Nonna?"

She looks over, while continuing to punch.

"Stop ... please."

She makes five more punches and puts it all away.

I go back to my journal. *Hmm, one line, one short line ...*

Rhythmic sifting sounds start up and begin to grate on my nerves. Looking over, I expect to find Nonna with a pair of maracas. She is shaking a large a plastic tube of red glitter. *SHAKA-shaka-shaka-SHAKA-shaka-shaka ...*

Where on earth did Nonna get her hands on red glitter?

When exasperated, plagiarize:

> Tucked in this town so quaint and steep
>
> Lie hidden mysteries old and deep
>
> I've roots and memories to keep ...
>
> ... And miles to go before I sleep
>
> And miles to go before I sleep ...

Robert Frost must have had a Nonna too. I close my journal. Abruptly.

Nonna's keeping rhythm to the *clickity-clack* of the train tracks with her glitter maraca. I reach for the tube before disaster ensues. I grab hold of one end, and Nonna pulls the other way ...

Welcome to the red blizzard on the Glitter Ball Express.

"Oh sweet stars of heaven," Nonna exclaims, "look what you've done!"

This would be really funny if it were happening to someone else. I'm doused in bright red glitter. Thank goodness Christmas is just around the bend. I can be a living holly tree. *Happy holidays!*

∽✺✹✺✹✺∽

The loudspeakers announce our arrival as we screech to a halt for a stopover in Nice. Estimated departure time: thirty minutes.

Personally I don't feel much like moving, but Nonna insists on seeing the train station. I should know better than to let her wander off the train without me, but there is really nowhere else she can go except inside the station.

"Nonna, you have only enough time to get off the train, take a quick look around, then come right back. Do you understand?"

"Of course I understand. I've been on more trains than you could shake a stick at."

While Nonna shuffles down the aisle toward the exit door, I picture her shaking sticks at trains. Glenda the Good Witch with her glitter wand. Why do I have this nagging fear that I may never see her again? I redirect my thoughts back to my poem. Maybe I'd better forget trying to come up with the perfect ending for the Sainte Foy pilgrimage. I've had a new thought. *What if I lose Nonna?*

Nonna … where is she? Watching nervously for her little gray head to poke back through the door of the car, I ponder the thought of her missing the train … *As the train pulls away from the station, Nonna is wandering around, happy and clueless as can be … as Peter, Paul, and Mary sing, "If you miss the train I'm on, you will know that I am gone, you can hear the whistle blow five hundred miles …"*

I can't risk it. Mama would never forgive me for losing her mother. I dash off the train and into the train station. I can't see Nonna anywhere. Frantic, I suddenly spot her standing in line out on the platform—about to board the train.

The *wrong* train.

"*Nonna!*"

Once we're seated—on the *right* train—I make an executive decision that this will *never* be mentioned—to anyone, anywhere. Not even in my journal—as history has proven that even teen diaries sometimes get worldwide recognition. Nor will I risk this incident going down in the Degulio family dynasty record book, as the day Angelina Juliana Degulio, age fourteen, almost lost Nonna on a train bound for Yugoslavia.

When we arrived safely back in Florence, Mama and Daddy are waiting out on the platform, all smiles. I am not smiling. *Someone* has been a little bit *testy* ever since I had to pull her out of line, and drag her back to the right train. I was the lucky one who got to endure all the glaring faces while Nonna screamed, "Someone help me!" at the top of her lungs. In the time it took for me to pull out her ticket and prove to the conductor that she really was supposed to be going to Italy, *not Yugoslavia*, she had the entire train station convinced that I had kidnapped her against her will.

"Welcome home!" The minute we step off the train, Mama greets us with a kiss on each of our sparkling red cheeks.

"How was the trip?" Daddy asks.

I look back at Daddy, cross-eyed, shaking glitter from my hair. "We had ourselves a dazzlin' good time, didn't we, Nonna?"

And miles to go before I sleep …

18

The Wonder of It All

Language Assignment: November 7, 1972
A Poetic Correlation of The Hound of Heaven
By Angelina Degulio

Hooves of Heaven

How can I explain ...
How can I express ...
This Love that crosses oceans
And hounds me east to west?

He took me from my island
Far across the sea
He took me from my Sailor dog
To a land called Tuscany

He brought me to a castle
A crumbling tower of stone
And there He left the Yankee
To bear it all alone

Lo, in my deepest darkness
Amidst my tears and strife
The mighty Hooves of Heaven
Brought me signs of life

Yea, the Hooves of Heaven
Came to me in the night
And whispered, "All is not so bad.
In fact it's all just right."

He gave to me a stallion
And nuns who love to ride
And books that give perspective
And family by my side

He chased me down the train tracks
Behind the French Express
On mighty Hooves of Heaven
He rode into Conques

Twas in the old stone Abbey
I saw the little Foy
Twas just a teeny tiny lass
Twas not a little boy

But oh, how brave, how bold!
Denouncing goddess Di
And for her King of Heaven
The sweet wee Foy did die

Then dawned on me, my Nonna
T'was once a brave lass too
Who ran and played and laughed and cried
As little lassies do

Oh, Noble Knight on horseback
Upon Your snow-white steed
You brought me gifts of wonder
Upon great hooves of speed

You took me from my island
Far across the sea
But on the Hooves of Heaven
We're taking Tuscany!

By the end of class I turn in my assignment and hope for the best. I figure most great poetry takes a commentary to explain the intent behind the poets' work. If Signorina Luzi doesn't understand a word of what I wrote, she can always request a commentary. I'll be happy to give her one.

On my way to lunch I encounter a small traffic jam in the hallway. Sure enough, wherever you find queen Annalisa, you'll find the rest of her subjects nearby. Beehive roadblock. This is probably my least favorite hallway scenario—walking alone toward the swarm, and it's too late to ditch and run, so I have to walk right through the middle to get to lunch. If that's not enough to ruin one's appetite, I don't know what is.

"Angelina!" A big arm comes flying around my shoulder. I turn, to find Dominic's friendly smile. "Where have you been?"

"France—I went to France for the weekend." Sounds pretty impressive—minus the bit about going with my grandmother on a saint pilgrimage.

"France? Man, I was looking for you at the pond and the ice ditch all weekend."

It's nice to know someone around here is happy to see me. Looks like the Hooves of Heaven sent Dominic to run interference for me in just the nick of time.

> He followed me to school
> Where halls of torture thrive
> If looks could kill, I should be dead
> So far, I'm still alive ...

Dominic walks me to lunch and wants to hear all about my trip to Conques. He plunks his schoolbooks down next to mine at the back table and goes to buy his lunch. I brought my usual salami-and-cheese sandwich. While Dominic is going through the lunch line, I feel a strong prompting to try and make amends with Annalisa. She's been on my mind lately, like an annoying song that won't go away ... to the tune of "Mona Lisa": "Annalisa, Annalisa, Anna-l-i-i-i-s-a ..." It has to be dealt with, now, if for no other reason than I'd hate to be driven insane over her name. If little Foy can forgive her offenders, so can I.

Not wanting an audience, I wait until Annalisa is heading over to the lunch line.

"Annalisa?"

She turns with little enthusiasm. "*Che cosa?*" What?

"I—I just want to say I'm sorry for the things I've done to offend you."

Annalisa looks over at the lunch line where Dominic is standing. "If you think your phony apology is going to stop me and Dominic from being together, you're wrong. I know how you think, Angelina. You don't want me and Dominic together in the lunch line, so you thought you could separate us by making up this dumb apology, didn't you?"

She turns on her high heels. With that winning Kentucky Derby smile of hers, she calls out, "Hey, Dominic ... I saved you a place at *our* table ..." *Yak, yak, yak.*

Oh, neigh-whinny-whinny. I do not get this girl at all. I believe this may be a classic case of what my psychology teacher refers to as projection—when you project your own intentions onto someone else's behavior. Some people make it really tough to feed the white dog.

Dominic meets me back at my table with his steaming bowl of minestrone soup and rolls. He quickly fills me in on all the excitement I missed at the Winter Olympic preliminaries while I was in Conques. Apparently my mother caught wind of this mini-Olympics idea and has blown it into a full-scale 1972 Winter Olympics. Not only did Mama take it upon herself to invite every family on *La Collina di Papaveri*, she enlisted all of the mothers to make fancy gold, silver, and bronze ribbons, as well as to bake cookies for the awards ceremony.

The boys couldn't be more excited. I'd heard all about the ice-ditch time trials from Benji and Dino. They were thrilled they both made the final cut for the tobogganless toboggan race. Apparently J. R. and Celeste are skating doubles for the skating pond event.

The official Poppy Hill Winter Olympics are being held after school today.

"I still think my previous long-distance jump on the ice ditch should qualify for the gold, even if I can't compete," I tell Dominic.

He ponders the thought a moment. "Officially you'd have to forfeit your spot by not showing up for the time trials over the weekend, but if you show up to compete today, I can probably sway the judges to make an exception."

"Um, excuse me, but thanks to the five pounds of plaster on my arm, I'd say my days as an Olympic hopeful are pretty much over. If they won't count my last run on the ice ditch as official, then it looks like I'm out of the games for both the singles ice-skating competition, and the tobogganless toboggan race."

"*Pazzo!*" Crazy! he tells me. "You are not going to let a silly little cast keep you out of the Olympics, are you? I won't let you do it. The Winter Olympics comes to Poppy Hill only once in a lifetime, Angelina."

Not if you know my mother. This will become a new Tuscan tradition for years to come. "Dominic, my mother will break my other arm if she finds out I'm competing with my cast on."

"Meet me at the skating pond after school. I have the perfect solution—one that even your mother will approve of."

This I've got to see.

When I show up at the skating pond, I'm quickly swept up into the excitement. The competitors are all out on the ice practicing for their chance at the gold. The opening ceremony for the skating competition will begin at four o'clock, with barely a glimmer of daylight still left. J. R. and Celeste are out on the ice practicing their doubles routine.

"*Buongiorno,* Angelina." Dominic is skating toward me, pushing a chair across the ice. "Have a seat, *signorina.*" He skids to a stop in front of me.

"Are you serious?" I am laughing too hard to stand up, so I take his advice and sit down.

He starts to push me around the ice in my skating chair. "I have the routine all figured out—you just hold on and enjoy the ride."

Four o'clock sharp, all the skating contestants are checked in and ready to go. The skating event will last until everyone who wants to compete has skated, then we'll all move up to the ice ditch for the tobogganless toboggan race. The boys already have burn barrels flaming away at both locations to signify the Olympic torch—as well as help to light up the events and keep us all from freezing to death.

Thanks to Mama the entire community begins to appear around the pond, including mothers with blankets, cookies, hot cocoa, and handmade ribbons for the winners. We have three couples and four singles competing for the gold in skating, and probably thirty spectators on the sidelines. Dominic waves to a big group of kids along the edge of the pond. Half a dozen hands wave back.

"Who are they?" I ask.

"My family," he answers.

Sure enough, six olive-skinned, black-haired kids who look exactly like their brother are here to cheer him on. Right on cue everyone stands and sings the Italian national anthem to begin the opening ceremonies of the 1972 Poppy Hill Winter Olympics. We have skaters representing Italy, America, and France. *God bless us all.*

As the cheering slowly dies down, I'm suddenly aware that my mother, the instigator of this whole shindig, is nowhere in sight. She assured us she would be arriving "with bells on" to honor those who lost their lives in the hostage tragedy at the Summer Olympics in Munich, Germany. She thought it only right to rally the entire community and dedicate our event to their memory. *So where is she?*

Moments later my eyes are drawn to a bright flash in the distance. Lo and behold, here comes Mama, marching down the hill. Apart from her red, white, and blue sequin crown, she's draped in a red, white, and blue blanket, waving a small American flag in one hand, and a lit sparkler in the other, belting out "The Star-Spangled Banner." She looks like the Statue of Liberty. *Go Yankees!*

⟨⟨∽⟩⟩

First up—singles skating. Bianca breaks the ice, so to speak, in a fancy French fur jacket of her mother's. She surprises me with a few nice spins that she must have learned within the past few days. Last time I saw her, she couldn't skate worth beans. Unfortunately the little kid who's up second has been skating in an ice arena since she was four years old and has the fancy skating outfit to prove it. Bianca hardly stands a chance next to little Anna Enrico.

By the time Dominic and I are up, J. R. and Celeste have already stolen the hearts of the judges with their romantic ending. After spinning her brains out, J. R. took Celeste in his arms and bent her over backwards until she nearly touched the ice. Moms always fall for that kind of stuff. I'm not exactly holding my breath for the gold as the one-armed ice skater. Maybe they'll have a special category for the six-legged skater.

Dominic takes me out on the ice, and begins pushing me in slow crazy-eight formations. Getting carried away, he puts a spin on my chair that is sure to make Mama shudder. The move that really scores big for us, though, is Dominic serenading me with an Italian love song about a swan—probably "The Ugly Duckling"—while skating around me.

Pushing his luck, Dominic ends our routine with a grand finale spin on my chair, intending to impress the judges. They're all smiling—until he loses his grip. Skidding across the pond on my Olympic throne, I hit the edge where the ice meets the earth and fly out of the chair. A graceful face splat in the snow adds a nice finishing touch to our performance. This pretty much botches our chances at the gold for this year.

Dominic is by my side in seconds, mortified. "I'm so sorry … are you okay?"

Although facedown I somehow managed to hold my arm out of harm's way. "I don't think I nailed that landing very well."

Dominic tells me that it was a perfect ten-point landing, but he may have a hard time convincing the judges. One in particular, my mother, is clearly not pleased at the moment. After the judges hash over the scores, Celeste and J. R. walk away waving the gold ribbon. Dominic and I take silver.

With ribbons flying we trudge up to the top of the ice ditch for the tobogganless toboggan races. The crowd gathers in a big huddle around the burn barrel to watch the games.

Disqualifying himself right off the bat, J. R. skids off course and loses too much time recovering for any hope at making the finals. He becomes the official stopwatch judge instead. Benji, Dino, Dominic, Dario, and a few other neighbor kids are still in the running. These speed trials are a tough one for the moms to watch. It's all they can do not to yell "Slow down!" at their kids, knowing that would totally defeat the purpose.

After nearly an hour of watching human torpedoes fly down the ice at neck-breaking speeds, Dominic and Dino are tied for first. They'll have to run a tiebreaker if their records hold. It's the strangest thing to have my own brother and my good friend up against each other. I honestly cannot decide whom to root for, so I'm cheering for both of them.

Benji's friend Christiana is the last competitor to go. She takes a running start and flies down the ditch headfirst. No one has tried that position yet. She's such a featherweight, she skims over the ice like a leaf on a breeze and flies across the finish line two seconds faster than Dino and Dominic's record. The crowd is stunned.

"A girl beat you, Dino!" Benji teases. Benji is beaming with pride for his little friend. The power of a cute girl over brotherly loyalty … tsk, tsk. Dino and Dominic take the setback in good spirits. Christiana takes the gold. Benji offers to carry her ribbon for her over to the burn barrel where we've all gathered for the closing ceremony. With a hot chocolate toast, we all salute the Poppy Hill Winter Olympics of 1972.

Journal Entry: November 7, 1972

A Wondrous Winter Night

Twas on a winter's night
Beneath a pitch black sky
The wondrous Hooves of Heaven
Breathed a peaceful sigh

19

Un Giorno Ventoso
(One Blustery Day)

Saturday morning, Daddy and the boys are up and at 'em. They're hoping to finish a roofing project on an old farmhouse before the forecasted storm rolls in. The Lacolucci family lives at the bottom of our hill and are in dire need of a new roof to get through the winter. They have six children under the age of ten and make their living selling fresh eggs and milk. Daddy's only charging them for materials to do the project. I think they're throwing some eggs in with the deal.

Mama and I have decided to stay indoors and bake up a storm of our own. A big batch of sugar cookies should help sustain us through the tempest. When I say *big batch*, I mean *colossal*. From the amount of dough we've mixed up, I'd say we're talking at least a hundred cookies.

Mama wants to make sure we have enough to freeze for our traditional American Thanksgiving. We have cookie cutters for everything from pumpkins to pilgrims. It won't surprise me if we have enough dough left over to pull out the Frosty and Santa cutters, too. That reminds me to tell Mama something. "I know what Benji wants for Christmas." He's not the only one who wants it, but it might work better if she thinks it's for Benji instead of me.

"What's that?"

"One of Ci-ci's puppies. Luigi is the runt, and Benji just loves him."

"Ha! Nice try. Angelina Juliana, you need another dog like you need a hole in the head." She gives me a lecture on why having dogs on two different continents doesn't work for people like me.

Mama gets busy cutting out pilgrims, while I mix up the frosting. Suddenly, a loud crash of thunder makes both of us jump. The sky opens up and the rain comes pouring down in sheets. "Oh, boy, there goes a day's work for the guys," Mama says. "Looks like they'll have to come home early and eat warm cookies instead."

Since we don't have anything in the way of Thanksgiving music, Mama throws on my favorite Andy Williams Christmas album. It's confusing to mix orange and yellow frosting with Christmas tunes, but it's so nice to hear songs we know the words to. At the top of our lungs, we belt out "Come on, we're goin' for a sleigh ride …" Then, for the ever-so-sentimental, I croon, "I'm dreaming of a white Christmas, just like the ones I used to know."

Mama takes the next line, "Where the tree tops glisten, and children listen …"

We're interrupted by the phone but keep right on singing. By the fifth ring Mama finally grabs it. "North Pole!" she says cheerfully, then stops. "Sonny? … *Benji?* … *Fell?* … I'm coming!" She is untying her apron before she even hangs up the phone.

"A. J.!" she screams, "Benji fell! Get my purse, get my purse!" She's running around, frantically looking for her keys.

"Here, Mama, here's your keys ..." We run out in the downpour and jump in the car. "Where are we going?"

"To the hospital—Daddy's already there with Benji." Mama swings the car around and speeds down the slick roads, then flies onto the *autostrada* heading toward Saint Augustine's Hospital.

⚮⚮⚮⚮⚮

Mama bursts through the emergency room doors, with me right on her heels. *"Dov' è mio figlio?"* Where's my son?

The startled reception lady nods toward the door of the restricted area, where a nurse motions to us. *"Seguimi,"* she says, follow me. She leads us through the double doors and down a long hallway to a small waiting area.

As soon as we see Daddy, Mama runs to him. "Where's my baby?"

Daddy grabs Mama and holds her back. "You can't go in there now, Soph," he says calmly, but his eyes betray him.

"Can't go in? I'm his mother!" She tries to break free from Daddy.

Daddy holds Mama even tighter. "Sophie, listen to me." He makes Mama sit on the couch beside him. I sit down beside J. R. and Dino, who look like they know something bad. I look back at Daddy.

"Benji's hurt ..." Daddy says. "He's with the doctors ... he isn't ... he's unconscious," he whispers.

Mama stammers, "Un-unconscious?" Then she screams, "Why can't I see him?"

"Honey, Benji ... fell from the roof."

"The *roof*?" Mama looks stunned.

"He hit his head. They're trying to stabilize him. After they get him stabilized, you can see him." Daddy doesn't sound very sure of himself.

A doctor comes out to talk to Daddy. "There's a lot of swelling around the brain that we need to bring down. We'll have to keep him sedated to do it. Once we can get the swelling down, we'll have a better idea of what's going on. For the time being, I can't let you see him."

"Not again," Mama sobs. "I can't do this again." She must be having a *déjà vu* of when I bashed my head at Pirate's Cove trying to save Ruby Jean. I think Mama has gone into shock. In a monotone she says, "J. R., call Adriana, tell her to come home. Call my sister, tell her to pick up Nonna and take her to their home. Have her call the church for prayer."

J. R. goes to the nurse's station to use the phone.

I don't know what to do. Nobody is telling me what to do. No one is saying it's going to be okay. I want someone to tell me Benji is going to be okay. I go over to the nurse's station. "*Signorina?*"

The nurse at the desk looks up.

"Can you help me find a phone number?"

"*Che nome ha?*" What's the name?

"*Le Sorelle di Francescano di Siena.*" The Franciscan Sisters of Siena.

The nurse looks through the phone book and dials a number, then hands the phone to me.

"*La reveranda madre, per favore.*" The reverend mother, please.

I hear the reverend mother's voice. "Angelina?"

"My brother ... Benji ..." I start bawling my head off. I tell her he fell. "Please pray ... tell the sisters to pray, tell Sister Aggie to pray ... he's at the hospital ... St. Augustine's ... he won't wake up...."

"Angelina, *Benji sarà giusto*," she says quietly. Benji will be okay. "We'll all pray. It's going to be okay."

"*Grazie, Madre ... grazie*," I sob. That's what I needed to hear. I hand the phone back to the nurse.

Time ticks by, rain pounds against the windows, the gray sky turns darker. The doctor comes back and says they're putting Benji on ice to help keep his swelling and temperature down. They're going to keep him under sedation, like inducing a coma so his body has a better chance to recover. He also suggests we go home for the night to get some rest and come back in the morning. Mama tells him he's crazy. She says she's not going anywhere as long as her son is here. She starts to sob about Benji being cold, and wants to go warm him up.

By midnight Mama tells the nurse that if they don't let her see her son she will break the door down. Mamas and their babies ... just like what Benji and I were talking about that day with Ci-ci and her puppy.

The doctor finally agrees to take Mama back to Benji, but she has to promise not to touch him. Daddy goes with her to make sure she keeps her promise. The rest of us fall asleep on the waiting room couches.

In the middle of the night I'm awakened by the sound of the emergency entrance doors. A chain of angels come filing through. I wonder if I'm in a dream. Then I recognize Sister Aggie. The nuns

have come. I hustle across the room and am enveloped into Sister
Aggie's black robe. "*Siamo venuti per pregare*," she whispers. We've
come to pray.

⸎

Throughout the night I'm in and out of sleep. It's hard to get comfortable on these old couches. Each time I awake, I hear the hushed
prayers of the nuns, and drift back asleep. At the crack of dawn
Adriana appears. She drove hours through the storm to get here.
Mama and Daddy are still back with Benji. Adriana curls up on the
couch beside me and falls asleep.

A loud buzzer goes off, jolting me awake. Nurses rush back
through the double doors with a sense of urgency about them.
My eyes try to adjust to all the commotion. Mama and Daddy
suddenly appear, looking scared and bewildered. People are racing around, phone calls are being made. Daddy asks Adriana to
take us kids home. Something has gone wrong and no one is saying what. I look to the nuns for assurance. Sister Aggie nods at
me, telling me with her eyes, *It's going to be okay.* But it doesn't
feel like it.

"C'mon, let's go home," Adriana says to me, "get your
brothers."

"No … I don't want to leave … I know something's wrong. I
want to know what's wrong."

Daddy hurries past me and I grab his jacket sleeve. "Daddy, what
is it … what's wrong with Benji?"

Daddy stops for a brief moment, long enough for me to catch

the grief in his eyes. "... You need to wait at home ... Mama and I need to deal with Benji ... we'll call."

⁂

I drag myself up to my tower, and fall on my bed sobbing. I feel like my snow globe just fell to the ground and shattered all over. The pieces go everywhere. I'm washed away in the flood, but none of it matters anymore. Nothing matters but my little brother. *God, I'm scared ... I'm so scared. Help me.*

Adriana comes in my room and sits on the bed beside me. She starts to rub my back. I roll over to face her. "Is Benji going to ... die?" I can barely even whisper the word.

"I don't know." She sighs. "I don't know ..." A tear falls from her cheek. "This reminds me so much of when you ..."

"When I almost drowned?"

"Yeah."

"Ruby did drown."

Adriana nods. "I know. I've always blamed myself for that."

"It was an accident ... I only wish Ruby didn't have to die." My tears come again. "I'm still waiting for God to show me the good in that. I don't see how anything good could come from having my hamster die."

"A. J.," Adriana says, "the good has already come."

I sit up and wipe my eyes to make sure I'm hearing her right.

"Remember what I was like with boys before that happened?"

"You mean ... how you let them kiss you and break your heart?"

"Exactly. If I was still going down that road when we moved

here ... I've seen girls in modeling who act just like I did then. It's not pretty when girls my age act that way. They end up getting used and hurt in this business. When you lost Ruby and nearly drowned, it was a real wake-up call for me. It changed me, A. J."

Come to think of it, I haven't seen Adriana date anyone since we moved here. She went dancing, but that's about it.

Adriana gives me a hug. "I'll always be sorry about your hamster, A. J., but know that Ruby didn't die in vain. God used her to help me. He's going to help Benji, too."

> And yea, the Hooves of Heaven
> Come to me in the night
> And whispers in my darkness
> And bring to me His Light

❧

I wake up a few hours later with a start. It must be the middle of the night. I go downstairs and can hear Daddy talking on the phone. He's home, but not Mama. I wait for him to hang up.

"Is ... Benji ... okay?"

He releases a heavy sigh. His eyes are red. "They found a bone chip from Benji's skull, which has caused the swelling to worsen. Daddy wipes his eyes. "They have to do surgery, but it's risky. We're trying to line up a surgeon, but there are ... complications."

"What kind of complications?"

Daddy looks at me like he's deciding if I can take the news. "We need a surgeon and we need blood."

"Doesn't the hospital have surgeons and blood?"

"There are no brain surgeons available and all the hospitals are short on blood."

"Can we give our blood?"

"Some of us can. You, Dino, and I are the only ones in the family with Benji's blood type."

We all learned our blood type from the umpteen trips to the Squawkomish emergency room our family has made over the years. Mama says we are the most accident-prone bunch of kids on the face of the planet … especially Benji.

Daddy takes a deep breath. "Grab your brother, we'd better go."

When we return to the hospital we're ushered into a room for the blood draw. Daddy looks at the nurse.

She nods, yes. "We found a new supply of blood."

"What?" Daddy asks, surprised. "How?"

The nurse opens the door to the hallway. "*Vieni qui.*" Come in.

We watch three nuns enter the room, take seats, and roll up their sleeves.

Outside, the rhythmic beat of helicopter blades pound through loud gusts of wind. Commotion starts up in the hallway outside of our door. People hustle past our door in all directions. As soon as the nurse is done drawing my blood, I stand up, dizzy, and stick my head out in the hall to see what's going on. A doctor dressed in surgical garb rushes through the emergency entrance, as wind and rain sweep in along with him. Two nurses meet him at the door and usher him down our hall. He whisks right past us like he knows where he's going and what he's here for. I'm glad someone seems to know what he's doing.

"*Grazie a Dio*." Praise God, Daddy whispers, as the surgeon passes by.

❦

We all have to wait out in the lobby while the surgery is taking place, even Mama and Daddy. It's comforting to see the sisters still praying for Benji. They're a comfort for my family, too—which is more than I can say about our relatives, who have been nowhere around though this whole ordeal. Mama even had to call Fabrizia to stay with Nonna, because she couldn't ever reach her sister. Anger rises up inside of me when I think of them. I realize there were little squabbles between our families, but this is Benji's life we're dealing with, not the color of a dumb villa. Where are they anyway? I have a feeling this is the weekend for the Dante Awards in Rome, where Cousin Stacy's being honored for her poetry.

It seems hours before the surgeon emerges from the operating room. He brings our whole family into a small room down the hall. There's nothing inside but two couches, a faint lamp, and a box of tissues. My heart stops beating. I sit down, dazed, and wait.

The surgeon wipes his brow and begins to speak in perfect English. "The surgery went well. I was able to remove the bone chip. I won't lie; this is the point where we all have to fight for Benji, and Benji will have to fight to make it. The swelling must come down, that's our only hope. Benji's a strong little boy, and I'm betting on him, but I need you to be aware of how critical this is."

When the surgeon walks out, we all sit in silence. Daddy wraps his arms around us and prays. Our tears fall like the rain beating on the window.

I stay behind after everyone else gets up and leaves. I have to talk to God alone. I must look a mess to Him right now. I'm beyond the little raggedy doll. I feel more like a torn and shredded doll that a dog got hold of and shook back and forth in its teeth until its stuffing came out.

"Jesus," I whisper, "please help Benji. Please let him live. He's my little brother." I think back to the morning Benji and I sat outside the horse stall together and listened to Nonna singing to the animals. I remember Benji's smile. It makes me cry some more. "If you just let him live, God, I promise, I will serve You the rest of my life like the sisters do. I'll be bold for you like Sainte Foy. Please don't let him die. *Please ...*"

❧❧❧

By evening the swelling hasn't gone down, but the doctor says that could be from the surgery. The good news is the bone chip is gone, and Benji has a much better chance to recover. Mama hasn't slept at all since the accident. Daddy decides we should all go home to try to sleep, and hope the morning brings good news. As we file out the door, Mama and Daddy thank each of the nuns for coming to pray, and for giving their blood. I hug Sister Aggie.

We pull into our driveway in the dark, run through the rain, and are met with the unexpected. All the lights are on in the kitchen, and every inch of counter space is covered with food: homemade casseroles, breads, meats and cheeses, and baked goods. There are bouquets of flowers and cards from names I can't even pronounce. Mama says most of these names are Greek.

Greek? Greek has become a bad word to me ever since our Greek relatives never showed up at the hospital. "How did all this food get here?"

"The only one with a key to our home is your Aunt Genevieve," Daddy says.

"My *sister*?" Mama says. "That's doubtful."

"Yeah, I'll bet she's still living it up in Rome with Stacy since she won that dumb Dante award," I add.

Daddy looks at Mama and me. He says we all need to get everyone together in the living room. There is something he needs to tell us.

We enter the living room and find a warm fire already burning. Once we're all seated, Daddy begins to talk, but he can't seem to get the words out—he just chokes up.

I'm scared he knows something about Benji that he hasn't told us yet. "Is it Benji, Daddy?"

He shakes his head. "It's … Nick," he says in a hoarse voice.

"Uncle Nick?" Adriana asks.

Daddy nods. He takes a deep breath and begins to explain. "When the doctors discovered Benji's swelling was getting worse, they told me if they didn't get the bone chip out, Benji would … he wouldn't make it." Daddy closes his eyes. "None of the doctors here were skilled enough for that type of brain surgery, and the hospital did not have the means to bring in a brain surgeon—especially one who needed to be flown in. I called Nick to tell him. He said … 'I got you covered, Sonny … I got you covered.'" Daddy chokes up again, wipes his eyes, and continues. "He arranged the whole thing … he knew a specialist who could do the work, a renowned brain surgeon, Dr. Kargianis. It was your Uncle Nick who …"

He never finishes his sentence.

All which I took from thee I did but take,
Not for thy harms,
But just that thou might'st seek it in My arms.
All which thy child's mistake
Fancies as lost, I have stored for thee at home:
Rise, clasp My hand, and come!"

Halt by me that footfall:
Is my gloom, after all,
Shade of His hand, outstretched caressingly?
"Ah, fondest, blindest, weakest,
I am He Whom thou seekest!
Thou dravest love from thee, who dravest Me.

20
The Home Fires

With the morning comes the sunrise, a clear blue sky, and the news that Benji's swelling has come down during the night. My brother is going to live. There is rejoicing in our home again. But not without some regret that we had thought so poorly of the people who had done the most to help save my brother.

When we arrive at the hospital we are all allowed back in Benji's room for the first time since the accident. He's sleeping soundly. Even to watch him sleep is enough for now. We are all gathered around his bed just looking at him. There's a gentle knock at the door, and Uncle Nick and Aunt Genevieve enter. Daddy gets up and embraces Uncle Nick with a big bear hug.

Mama and Aunt Genevieve are back to being sisters again. "Why didn't you come?" Mama asks.

"We did come as soon as we heard, Soph, but they wouldn't let us back there. You and Sonny were they only ones allowed back with Benji, and your kids were all asleep out here, so we went by to get Mother. Fabrizia was already there and said she was happy to stay with her. That freed us up to help in other ways."

Mama and I walk down to the lobby to see Stacy and Nicky, who still aren't allowed back in intensive care to see Benji. After greeting Stacy, I congratulate her on getting the Dante Award.

"Oh, thanks. I haven't really seen it yet. My teacher got it for me."

"What do you mean your teacher got it for you—didn't you go to Rome for the award ceremony?"

Stacy looks at me, puzzled. "Of course not—that was the same day Benji got hurt. Mom and I stayed home to organize all the meals. We had the entire Greek Orthodox Church cooking around the clock—the women at Saint Constantine were very willing to help."

"I delivered the food to your house and kept a fire going for you," Cousin Nicky says.

Mama and I look at each other. I know we are feeling the same way. Grateful but ashamed at the same time.

"Well," Mama says, "we certainly have a lot of wonderful food waiting for us, and a nice warm home to go to. Why don't we all go enjoy a nice meal together?"

On our way out of the lobby, I notice the nuns have gone home. I sense an emptiness in the hospital lobby without them. Their presence helped to fill this room with hope.

We arrive to our warm home, fire still burning, food everywhere, and, most of all, family. I feel very grateful for our Greek relatives and the people at their church. Flowers and cards fill the living room— some from people we've never even met. And there are telegrams sent all the way from our relatives in Greece.

As we gather around the table, Daddy asks a blessing over the meal and gives thanks for Benji's recovery. Mama drinks a toast to "Nick and Genevieve," and adds, "thank you … for my son."

Halfway through our meal, Nonna appears in the dining room.

"Well, you've decided to come back after all. Did the guilt of deserting your own mother finally get to you?"

"No one deserted you, Mother," Mama tells her. "Benji needed some medical care, and we didn't want to worry you. He's going to be fine and will be coming home soon."

"A likely story," Nonna says. "You tried to leave the country and got caught, didn't you? That's the only reason you came back. Don't think I don't know what that husband of yours is up to …"

"Mother, it has been a long weekend. Please sit down and have something to eat with us." Mama goes to get her a plate.

"Oh, very well, but don't expect me to forget this anytime soon.… Pass the potatoes."

Monday comes, and Mama lets me play hooky from school. She knows how little sleep I've had. And I know I'm in no position to take any more guff from Annalisa after what we've been through this weekend.

When J. R. arrives home from school, he calls me to the door. "Someone's here to see you."

Bianca is standing in the foyer with an armload of envelopes. "Hi, Angelina. I have some cards and letters from the kids for you to give your brother, and a few for you, too."

"Me? I'm not the one who got hurt."

"Maybe not, but some of the kids wanted to say hi and let you know they're thinking of you." Bianca heaps the whole pile of letters into my arms.

We push the couch in front of the fire and climb on, with the pile of letters between us. I notice an envelope with little pink hearts all over it for Benji. It's from Christiana. *Just friends, hmm?*

"So why weren't you at school today?" Bianca wants to know.

"Mama gave me the option of resting up for a day or going to school. Imagine how torn I was. Stay home and relax … or spend the day dodging people who hate me for no good reason."

"If you're talking about Annalisa, I'd say she definitely has a reason."

"What? Because I'm a Yankee?"

"It's pretty obvious Annalisa's insanely jealous of you."

"Jealous? Of *what*?"

Bianca rolls her eyes. "That you stole her boyfriend."

"Dominic?"

"Why do you think she always tries to embarrass you in front of him? To make you look stupid. Annalisa has liked Dominic forever—then you came along."

"Dominic is my *friend*. He's not my *boyfriend*!"

"Annalisa doesn't see it that way. He used to like her before you came along. Even if you are just friends, he obviously gives you more attention than he gives her."

Jealous. Of me? Whoa. This is much more bearable than thinking someone hates me just for the heck of it. "Bianca, thank you. I have been enlightened. You deserve a cookie for telling me that—and I just happen to have about a hundred of them in the freezer."

While we're busy biting the heads off of orange-frosted pilgrims, something doesn't settle right with me about Annalisa. "Bianca, it's got to be more than just jealousy over a boy. There's something more to it."

"Like what?"

"Well, remember when we were at Annalisa's Sweet Fourteen party, and she had everything a girl could possibly want? Decorations, ice statues, a princess cake, piles of gifts, friends, food ..."

"Yeah?"

"Well, even with all that, I remember feeling like something was missing. I couldn't put my finger on it. I especially felt it when Annalisa was opening her presents, and you know what I realized?"

"She didn't have a dog?" Bianca starts to laugh. She knows me too well.

"No, you nut. Her mom and dad were nowhere around—ever—for the entire party. No brothers or sisters either. The only people there besides her friends were the house servants."

"I didn't even think about that. I know her parents travel a lot for their wine business, but you'd think they'd be around for her birthday. I think her brothers and sisters are all grown too, and she's the only one left at home."

"Yeah. Sounds to me like maybe she was a P. S. baby—a late addition to the family. Know what I mean?"

"Yeah, she is a lot younger than the rest of their kids."

"And have you noticed how Annalisa always needs people around her?"

Bianca thinks about that for a minute. "You know, you're right. I never see her alone at school."

"She does whatever it takes to make sure she has her clique with her everywhere she goes."

"And she's always throwing herself at Dominic—which, she hasn't figured out, does *not* work," Bianca says.

"Yeah, my mama always told me guys don't like it when girls do that."

Bianca snaps her fingers like she's just solved the mystery of the decade. "That's another big reason Annalisa doesn't like you."

"What is?"

"Your mom."

"Mama?"

"Yeah. Think about it. Your mom is exactly what Annalisa needs but doesn't have. A mom who cares about what you're doing. Your mom is there for you, Angelina. She stands up for you—even against Annalisa."

I think back to Mama telling Annalisa off for trying to use me to get to Dominic and for calling me names. Mama gave her a trip to Pietro's pond over that. Wow. I can understand girls being jealous over a boy, but this is the first time I've heard of someone being jealous over somebody else's mama—especially a mama like mine. Will wonders never cease?

◈◈◈◈◈

Daddy comes home and hands me a letter. Danny wrote back.

> November 10, 1972
> Dear A. J.,
>   I received your letter, and want to thank you and the
> nuns for your prayers for Chuck. I've been spending a lot
> of time with him. He's actually a pretty interesting guy. He's
> starting to consider the possibility that God cares about
> him. Please keep praying.

My family is planning to spend Thanksgiving here. Grandpa's not up to traveling anymore. I'm looking forward to seeing everyone. As far as Jason, I don't know if he has a girlfriend right now. He doesn't talk about anything much, except farming. I guess I'll find out when he comes.

About Dorothy, I wanted to let you know that my youth group is praying for her. In light of the way Dorothy is treated by the other girls, especially Annalisa, it makes me wonder if maybe it's not more about jealousy than hatred. If you could pray for Annalisa, maybe God could help you see why she's so mean in the first place. You might pray that both Annalisa and Dorothy get what they deserve. Just a thought.

Sailor wanted to wish you and your family a happy Thanksgiving. I told him they don't celebrate that holiday in Italy, but he figured you'd be celebrating anyway.

So happy Thanksgiving,

Sailor and Danny

P.S. No, I don't have a girlfriend.
P.S.S. Who's Dominic?

I have to read those last two lines again—about five times. *No, I don't have a girlfriend. Who's Dominic?*

... Let's see, if I'm fourteen now, and Danny is seventeen.... when I'm fifteen, he'll be eighteen ... when I'm sixteen, he'll be nineteen, when I'm seventeen, he'll be twenty, and when I'm eighteen ... Danny will be ... twenty-one. Oh ... my ... gosh ... not much difference in age when you get up into those digits. *Molto interessante.* Very, very interesting!

I carefully fold the letter back up and tuck it into the front bib pocket of my overalls, then curl up by the fire, and drift off … *four more years … only four more years …*

When I awake, Mama is sitting across from me sorting through recipe files. "The Morgans are all planning to have Thanksgiving on the island," I tell her.

She looks up. "That's great. I'd sure love to see Stella and the family again. I do miss that island at times."

"Yeah, me, too."

Mama looks at me and smiles. She's only heard that every day since we moved here.

"Hey, what would happen if, say, a Catholic and a Baptist got married—would they become Catholics or Baptists?"

"They'd become Baptolics." She looks so proud of herself for being so clever. "Add that one to your book of A. J.-isms, compliments of me."

"Oh, Mama."

I tell Mama what Bianca said earlier about Annalisa—about her being jealous and not having much attention from her family and all. Mama stares into the fire for a long time thinking that over. "That's sad," she says. "Really sad."

⁂

By Tuesday Benji's swelling is nearly all the way down. Late afternoon they take him off all the monitors and say it shouldn't be long before he wakes up. So far I've only seen him when he's sleeping. When he finally opens his eyes, we're all gathered around his bed to welcome him back to the living. The doctor says they want to keep him here for a few more days, but if all goes well, he should be home by the end of the week.

I'm a little confused by this news. Back on the island I saw a guy with a serious head injury on *Marcus Welby, M.D.*—a TV doctor. The guy had to stay in the hospital for a month after surgery, in case his brain swelled back up. They said he wouldn't have time to get to the hospital if it swelled up at home. Now that Benji's surgeon has left, I'm not sure these people really know what they're doing. Following the doctor out to the hall, I try to get his attention. "Sir?"

He turns toward me.

"Are you sure Benji should be coming home so soon? I mean, what if his head swells back up and we can't get him back here fast enough? Shouldn't he stay here a little longer, just to be on the safe side?"

The doctor smiles at me like I'm just a cute little dumb kid. "We'll keep a close watch on him, don't worry. You're brother's a tough little guy. He gave us all a scare when we almost lost him, didn't he? But don't worry, he'll be fine. He's a fighter." The doctor turns and walks away.

Lost him? … Almost *lost* him?

I return to Benji's room to find Mama and Daddy in the middle of a warm embrace, swaying slowly from side to side. I want to ask them what the doctor meant about almost losing Benji, but I don't think this is a good time to ask. I have a feeling this is the first time Mama and Daddy have stopped holding their breath since this whole thing began. Right now they look like they're just holding on to each other for dear life. *Dear life* … I've never really thought of that phrase before. But come to think of it, life *is* dear.

21

Il Giorno del Ringraziamento (Thanksgiving)

Mama has her Thanksgiving feast all planned out and ready to roll for tomorrow. She's invited everyone who sent food, flowers, and cards to join us for the feast. I have been given the honor of rolling out the pasta dough while Nonna stuffs the ravioli squares with meat. This is Nonna's handed-down recipe, which she insists I carry on to future generations. It could take days to make up enough ravioli for so many people. Mama has declared it a Degulio tradition to have ravioli every year for Thanksgiving along with our turkey, just like we did back in America. She expects us to make six raviolis per person, which equals three hundred of these little squares.

So far, we have thirty.

Nonna may not remember who she is half the time, but she sure remembers how to make ravioli. She made the entire batch of meat filling without looking at the recipe. Mama samples it just to be safe. "*Bravissimo!*" she cheers. "You still have the touch."

Thank goodness for that. I'd hate to think of what we'd do with three hundred of these things if she messed up the recipe.

"There's no such thing as Thanksgiving in Italy," Nonna says.

"It's okay," Mama tells her. "We're going to show them what it's all about."

This should be interesting. "So, Mama, how are you planning to do that?"

"Well, I thought it might be fun to put on a little dramatization for the guests. You and J. R. can dress up like Pilgrims, and Dino can be an Indian …"

"Oh no." *I will not be caught dead wearing a Pilgrim costume in front of fifty houseguests.* "We are not in first grade anymore, and there is nothing you can do to get me to wear a Pilgrim costume—nothing."

❦

Thanksgiving Day, I greet each guest at the front door in my gray and black Pilgrim dress, complete with white apron and pilgrim bonnet. Dino escorts the guests to the dining room, dressed in his fringed suede pants, moccasins, and full feather headdress. Father Pilgrim, played by J. R., is in the kitchen, helping Daddy carve the turkey. All I can say is everybody has their price, and Mama is willing to pay it. Even Benji wanted in on the cut, but Mama said he was in no position to be wearing feathers on his sore little head. She thought about setting his bed up next to the dining room table so he could join us for the feast but decided that would be a little much. Instead he's going to come out and say hello for a few minutes, then will be sent back to his room with a plate of food.

First to arrive—the Sophronia family. "Happy Thanksgiving!" Along with Uncle Nick's traditional bear hug comes, "Let me guess … Florence Nightingale?"

"Um, close. I'm a Pilgrim."

"I know ... but I gotcha, didn't I?"

"Yeah, you sure did." Next I receive Aunt Gen's lipstick kisses and don't even bother to wipe them off. I even hug Cousin Nicky. If there is any such thing as a likable dweeb, Cousin Nicky takes the cake. Interesting how something as small as building a fire for someone can change your whole impression of a person.

Before long fifty of our closest friends and relatives show up on our doorstep. Some have even come from Greece on the train and will be staying either with Uncle Nick's family, or at the Ritz—wherever there's room.

Just when I think everyone in the free world is here, the doorbell rings again. "I'll get it," I yell and swing the door open.

"... A-Annalisa?" I'm speechless. I'm in a Pilgrim costume. With all of my *weird Greek relatives*, as she calls them.

"Annalisa!" Mama exclaims, suddenly beside me. "I'm so pleased you could join us. Please, come in." Mama nudges me to move my shocked little self out of the doorway. "I thought the Tartini family might like to enjoy an authentic American Thanksgiving," Mama says.

"My parents are in Paris right now, so it's just me, but thank you for inviting me."

Mama nudges me again, hinting that I might find myself some manners. "Great," I say, "I'm glad you came. Come on, I'll show you where we're sitting and introduce you." I offer Annalisa a seat right next to me and introduce her to some of the younger generation. Surprisingly Annalisa knows Greek and strikes up a conversation with Damon and Arturo. She appears much friendlier than when she's at school.

Kemo Sabe, the little moccasin brave, continues to escort the guests to the table. Mama announces it's time for the feast to begin and helps usher everyone toward the dining room. Once everyone is finally seated around our rectangular "Round Table," Daddy sends Kemo Sabe to fetch Benji. No one but our family has seen him since the accident.

As Benji enters the room in his flannel pajamas, a great cheer goes up from the crowd. "*Salute*, Benji, *salute!*"

Daddy puts his arm around Benji at the head of the table and bows his head to give thanks. "Lord, we thank You today for our family and friends who have made our lives so rich. We thank You especially for sparing our son's life. Thank You foremost for Your Son, whose life You did not spare, for our sakes. Be with us today as we give You our thanks. Amen."

"Thank You, Lord, for giving me hard-headed children," Mama adds. *Amen.*

All of the kids and teens have gravitated to our end of the table, thanks mostly to Annalisa, who is carrying on engaging conversations with everyone between ages ten to twenty—and Nonna. Nonna is dressed to the nines, wearing every necklace and bracelet she owns—and to top it all off, a hat with a feather in it. "I made the ravioli," she says, every three minutes.

Annalisa leans toward Nonna. "I like your hat," she says.

Nonna turns, giving Annalisa a suspicious eye.

"Who are *you*?"

"I'm Annalisa Tartini. I go to school with Angelina."

"My granddaughter, Angelina *Juliana*?"

Annalisa looks over at me and smiles. "Yes, Angelina Juliana."

"She's named after me, of course."

Oh boy, here we go.

"Angelina Juliana and I just went to France to visit Sainte Foy. She was beheaded, you know."

Thanks for that, Nonna.

"Really?"

Yes, really. I realize most people, including your family, say things like, "We've been to France to visit Paris." Not my family. We tell people we've been to France to visit beheaded saints ...

"I wish I had a grandmother I could do things with, but both of my grandmothers have passed away."

Nonna reaches over and sets her hand on top of Annalisa's. "You call me Nonna," she says.

"Nonna," Annalisa replies.

Everyone is busy passing ravioli, polenta, turkey, potatoes, gravy—the works. There is no language barrier when it comes to a feast—somehow, between smiles and gestures, we're all getting through it.

Somewhere between the turkey and the pumpkin pie, Mama decides she's going to get her money's worth out of Dino, J. R., and me. She calls the three of us into the kitchen and hands us our scripts. "Okay, now, I want you to go out there and show them how it all happened."

"I can't speak Greek. What if they don't know English?" Dino asks.

"Most of them do, and for those who don't, just use dramatic hand motions—between that and your costumes, they'll get the picture."

Normally I wouldn't be caught dead doing something like this in front of Annalisa, knowing the rumors she could spread, but at this point, what can I do? Besides, Annalisa is keeping the same company I am today and appears to be enjoying it.

Dino has the opening line. He runs out in front of the fireplace, peering through a paper towel roll—his makeshift telescope. "Ahoy, I see a ship in the harbor! It says *Mayflower* on the bow and it is full of white people wearing funny hats."

J. R. and I go out together. "Look!" I shout. "I see land—it must be America, the land of the free, where we can worship our God without being persecuted, put in prison camps, tortured, or beheaded."

"Hooray!" J. R. yells. "Hooray for America! I see a rock. Let's land there and name it Plymouth Rock, after the car manufacturer."

"Let us prepare a feast and invite the Indians, since it's all their food anyway, and we will give thanks to our God for bringing us here alive—most of us, anyway," I say. "No more stale bread and gruel. We will have roasted corn, and ravioli, and kill some turkeys and have stuffing and cranberry sauce with gravy; and for dessert, pumpkin pie and ice cream." *I should be sainted for having to humiliate myself like this.*

J. R., Dino, and I gather in a little circle and pretend to eat a meal together. Then we stand up, face the guests, hold hands, and belt out, "God bless America, land that I love ..."

When we finish, we all take a bow. The cheers go up, and the three of us smile, knowing how much we soaked Mama for to do this ridiculous skit.

When I return to the table, Annalisa takes a break from engaging the guests and looks at me. *Here it comes. She's going to tell me she took a photo of me doing that and will use it to ruin me.*

"Angelina, you are so lucky to have such a big family. My family is so spread out, I never get to see them all at one time. It was nice of you to invite me."

Okay, God, I'm sorry it took me so long to be nice. Actually I wasn't nice … it was my mother who was nice. Why couldn't I have been the noble one?

I glance around the table trying to picture this through Annalisa's eyes. All of these loud, obnoxious people—with joyful faces, warm smiles and laughter all around. The Lacolucci family and their six small kids have joined us as well.

Then there's my own family … whooping it up, full of relief, thankful to still have each other. The three of us kids in our goofy Pilgrim and Indian costumes. Adriana has outgrown us, and has graduated to the adult end of the table now. She's engaged in conversation with some of the Greek women who are trying to match her up with their sons. Mama, always the gracious hostess, making sure everyone is stuffing themselves silly. Daddy seems happiest just watching Mama. And Nonna … placing her feathered hat on Annalisa. *I love my Nonna.*

There really is something to be said for belonging to a big, loving family. In a sense Annalisa has a right to feel jealous. Family is not something you can come by on your own. It is a gift, a true gift from God. A gift that should never be taken for granted.

Taking all of this in, from where I'm sitting, I am thankful. After all of the shake-ups and heartaches life throws at us, there are moments when everything goes right, and for a split second, time stands still as in a perfect picture. This is one of those moments.

When the good-byes come, I prop myself at the front door like a
hospitable little pilgrim. "You sure made a great *Mayflower*," Uncle
Nick says and roars with laughter.

Aunt Gen squishes my face and leaves her Rigatoni Red lipstick
on my cheek. "Bye, dollface. Love you bunches."

*Okay, so some things will never change, but I can change how I see
things.*

Even Annalisa gives me a hug. "I'll see you at school," she says.
She turns around before climbing into the car that has been sent for
her. She looks great in Nonna's hat. "Thank you for sharing your
Thanksgiving with me, Angelina Juliana," she calls back, and laughs.
But it's a nice laugh. This time she's laughing *with* me. "Now I know
what Thanksgiving is all about," she adds.

Yeah, me, too.

As soon as the last of the guests head out the door, my brothers
and I corner Mama in the kitchen with our hands out. She lays the
equivalent of ten dollars in lira in each of our greedy little hands.
Then I produce my bonus papers:

CONTRACT TO AMERICA

I, Sophia Degulio, on Thanksgiving Day 1972, do solemnly
swear, in exchange for forcing my children to perform in a
ridiculous play, "The Pilgrims and Indians," in front of fifty
guests, to purchase for my daughter, Angelina Juliana Degulio, a
one-way airline ticket to SquawKomish, Idaho, upon or before,
but no later than, her eighteenth birthday, where she will return

for veterinary school—which I also agree to pay for. IN FULL.

This is a NON-NEGOTIABLE contract.

Signed: _____

Sophia Degulio

Did she really think I'd do all that for ten bucks?

I'm almost done clearing the dishes, except Nonna is still sitting at the enormous table alone, working away on her pie. There's a loud knock. Mama makes for the door and swings it open. It's Angelo. But he isn't alone. He's holding Little Luigi in his arms and hands him off to Mama.

"Oh, Angelo, I just know this will help Benji get well," Mama switches to Italian and asks him to come and have some pie.

Escorting Angelo into the dining room, I offer him a seat next to Nonna. Darned if she doesn't look over and wink at him.

I follow Mama back to Benji's room. "Are you really going to let him keep it?" I ask.

"Of course I am; that's why I asked Angelo to bring him over."

"That was *your* idea, Mama?" I'm shocked.

"Let's just say a mama always knows what's best for her babies, and this little runt is going to help my baby get well—you just watch."

Mama hands the little butterball to my brother. Benji lights up like sunshine on snow. "Little Luigi! He's … mine?"

I have never seen a happier face.

While I'm waiting my turn to hold Luigi, Mama bows out to check up on Angelo—we did, after all, leave him alone with Nonna. "A. J. will be happy to help you with the housebreaking task until you're up and about," Mama says.

Thanks, Mama. I knew I'd get the short end of this deal. Luigi is a real piece of work—in the creative sense. He is a shaggy ball of gray, white, brown, and tan, with enormous feet to grow into. I have a feeling he will look like one of those prehistorical hairy mammoths when he's full-grown. Watching Benji hug that pup, I wonder how on earth Mama ended up giving in. But that isn't all I'm wondering about.

"Hey, Benji, you know in the hospital when you were unconscious and the doctors said they … almost lost you, were you—I mean, where *were* you?"

A quizzical expression comes over him. "I was having a really good dream."

"A *dream*? About what?"

"I was back on Indian Island." He smiles.

Lucky. "What were you doing?"

"Fishing. Me and Dino were fishing out in the rowboat. I even caught a fish."

"Was I in your dream?"

He thinks for a minute, then laughs.

"What?"

"Well … Mama was getting mad at you for talking with your Southern accent. Adriana was mad 'cause you let Sailor shake water all over her. And J. R. was mad at you for throwing his fish back in the water."

Yeah, those were the good ol' days. "Was Danny there?"

Benji thinks. "Yeah. He was the only one not mad at you. He was just laughing."

"That sounds more like paradise than a dream." If I'd had that dream I would have thought I'd died and gone to heaven. It would almost be worth falling off a roof to have a dream like that.

I leave Benji alone with his hound *from* heaven and walk back through the dining room. Nonna and Angelo are eating pie together. I can only imagine what Nonna is telling him, but whatever it is, Angelo is smiling his toothless grin. I slip out the door to the courtyard.

Looking around at Nonna's statues, I'm wondering who all these saints really were when they were living. *I'll bet there are some stories here.* Mama comes out and asks if I can give her a hand straightening up the guesthouse. They're short on rooms over at Uncle Nick's and will be sending a few relatives back over to stay with us. I'm glad they're coming—I'm not ready for all of this to end.

After helping Mama make up the beds, I stand at the big picture window looking out over the Tuscan hills. "Mama," I say, "come over here and tell me something."

Mama makes her way over to the window and stands beside me. "Tell me what you see when you look out there."

Mama stares out the window for a moment. She puts an arm around my shoulder and sighs. "A. J.," she whispers, "I see family."

"Me, too, Mama." *Me, too.*

Finita

Epilogue
Two years later . . .

November 27, 1974

Dear Danny,

How's Sailor? Here's my school photo of me at sixteen. I can't believe I've been here for six years! I'm still planning to come to Indian Island when I turn eighteen, to attend veterinary school. Be sure and reserve Papoose for me to rent for the summer. Only two more years until I get to see Sailor again.

How are you? Are you a pastor yet? Besides being a vet, I'm kind of thinking of being a nun. Then I could help starving animals and people. I wrote Sister Abigail about it. She said I could probably do both.

Write back, please.

Yours truly,

A. J.

❦

In December of 1974, Grandma Angelina comes to visit us for Christmas. When she arrives, she hands me a gift and a Christmas card, but won't say who it's from. And she tells me not to drop it. Whisking it carefully up to my tower, I set it gently on my bed while I open the card.

A photo of Sailor falls out. He's playing in the snow in front of our cabin. On the back it says:

MERRY CHRISTMAS!
Love, Sailor

I unfold the letter:

December 13, 1974
Dear A. J.,

Sailor really liked your school photo. You sure don't look ten years old anymore. Sailor is very glad you're coming back. He wants you to be sure to call me as soon as you get here. Things are going well for me. I'm now the youth pastor at Squawkomish Baptist.

I was walking through Saddlemyer's Dime Store when I saw this. For some reason it make me think of you. Merry Christmas, A. J.

Hurry home.

Yours,
Sailor & Danny

P.S. About the nun idea—have you ever thought about being a youth leader? They're always looking for help at the Baptist church.

Inside the box is a snow globe. A winter scene with a church, a boy, a girl, and a dog standing in the snow by a nativity. Snow swirls gently down, then lays completely still ... all is calm ... all is bright.

... a little more ...

When a delightful concert comes to an end,

the orchestra might offer an encore.

When a fine meal comes to an end,

it's always nice to savor a bit of dessert.

When a great story comes to an end,

we think you may want to linger.

And so, we offer ...

AfterWords—just a little something more after you

have finished a David C. Cook novel.

We invite you to stay awhile in the story.

Thanks for reading!

Turn the page for ...

Return to Indian Island

(Excerpt from *Heading Home*)

Indian Island, Idaho, July 1976

The rowboat smashes into the dock with a thud. A startled mallard plunges into the lake and paddles quickly away.

"I'm home!" I yell at the top of my lungs. I've waited eight long years to hear myself say those two words again. Stepping onto the shores of Indian Island is like stepping back in time. Hidden among the trees in the Pitchy Pine Forest sits little Papoose, our lost cabin, waiting for its family to return. Voices and laughter still echo from its walls: Mama, Daddy, Adriana, J. R., Dino, and Benji. The faint squeak of a hamster wheel drifts from the shed like a sad melody, carrying the memory of Ruby Jean.

Running toward the cabin, the words ring over and over in my head, *I'm home! I'm home!* I whisper it this time, just to hear myself say it again. I let myself in, relishing the thought that no one else knows I'm here. I'd debated over clanging the bell on the main shore, knowing the mini-tug would come for me, but I wanted my reunion to happen right here, on my old beloved island.

I'm relieved to find everything in Papoose the same as when we left, as though no one has taken our place. My eyes dart to the phone number of Big Chief, still tacked to the wall above the phone. I've played this moment in my mind so many times.

Lord, help me to pull this off. Dialing the number, my hands begin to shake. The old familiar ring blares in my ear ...

"Hello?"

It's Danny. That same Southern voice that made my heart skip a beat the first time I ever heard it is making it pound now. "Well, howdy on ya!" I bellow, in the best Southern drawl I can muster— not easy, after spending eight years in Italy.

There's a long pause. "Howdy yourself. May I ask who's callin'?"

"You can ask all ya want, but I ain't gonna tell ya. I'm frankly more in'erested in that log cabin you've got over yonder from your place a piece. Any chance it might be up for rent this summer?"

There is no way Danny would even think of being stuck on an island with some kook. He'd rather leave Papoose empty than have to deal with a nutty neighbor.

"Who's this?" He sounds more curious than annoyed.

"Well, who in the Sam Hill do ya think it is?"

"Um, I really don't know, but in answer to your first question, I don't rent that cabin out. I have a family I keep it reserved for whenever she ... whenever *they* come back."

I can't stand it any longer. "Well, Danny boy, it just breaks my li'l heart that you don't recognize a true Southern belle when you hear one." *That'll get his wheels turning.*

"... No way ... *A. J.? Is that you?*"

"*Bingo!* Race you to Juniper Beach—and bring my dog!" I slam down the receiver and dart out the screen door so fast it nearly flies off its hinges.

I'm whippin' down that old Pitchy Pine Trail faster than a baby jackrabbit. The first thing I see when I reach Juniper Beach is my big old dog.

"Sailor!" I cry, with tears streaming down my face. Sailor comes barreling down the beach, twice as fat and half as fast as when we parted. He pounces on me so hard I nearly fall over. I bury my face in his fur and sob like the day I found him on death row. When I look up, I see Danny walking toward me real slow, as though he doesn't want to intrude on my reunion with Sailor.

As I wipe my tears, my eyes come to focus on the face I've so longed to see—besides Sailor's. *Oh ... my ... gosh.* This is *not* the Danny I remember. Before me stands a towering six-foot-somethin' sandy-blond, sun-bronzed cowboy—a perfect cross between the Duke and Little Joe Cartwright. When we're within arm's reach of each other, we both just stop. Eight years is a long time—from saying good-bye as kids to saying hello as adults.

"Hey, A. J.," Danny says, real tender.

No one has *ever* said my name the way Danny says my name ... with the most beautiful Southern accent I've ever heard in my entire life. I stand still, just staring at him ... and I have only one thing to say. "Can you ride a horse?"

Danny looks taken back and amused at the same time. "Did you just ask me if I can ride a horse?"

(Daddy once told me, "A. J., when you find your cowboy, make sure he can actually ride a horse. Any man can put on the hat and the boots and call himself a cowboy, but only a real man can actually ride the horse.")

"Um ... never mind," I answer. "But can you?"

"Ride a horse?"

I nod. "Uh-huh."

Now he's grinning, like he just realized I must be the same quirky kid he knew before. Not bothering to ask why, he just answers the question. "Yeah, A. J., I can ride a horse."

"Oh. Okay."

"Is that good?

"Yeah. That's good." *That's real good.*

Now Danny's looking at me with those blue, blue eyes that always made me feel like he could see right into the depths of my soul. Is this really my childhood friend? Our nearly four-year age difference that once posed such a gap between us seems strangely insignificant now.

Danny sticks his hands in his pockets. His quizzical expression suggests that maybe he's thinking the same thing.

Yep, I'm the same freckle-faced kid, with the fake Southern accent, who could squirt half the lake between my two front teeth. At least I've grown into my teeth now and speak Italian instead of Southern.

So here we are face to face, after all these years, in a standoff, wondering how we're going to fill this awkward moment …

References

The Diary of Anne Frank by Anne Frank (New York: Bantam, 1997).

The Hound of Heaven by Francis Thompson (New York: Dodd, Mead and Company, 1937).

Information on Sainte Foy:

The Book of Sainte Foy by Pamela Sheingorn (Philadelphia: University of Pennsylvania Press, 1995).

Little Saint by Hannah Green (New York: Modern Library, 2001).

Information on hiding Jewish children during World War II:

A Thread of Grace by Mary Doria Russell (New York: Ballantine Books, 2005).

"WW2 People's War: An Archive of World War Two Memories," http://www.bbc.co.uk/ww2peopleswar/, accessed Nov. 26, 2008.

The Stories Behind the Story: Writers Were Once Quirky Little Kids Too...

As a fiction author one question I probably get asked most frequently is: "How does your mind come up with this stuff anyway?"

Do you really want to know? Okay, here it is . . .

I write what I know.

I've found that in writing fiction, what seems to work best for me is to write what I know—along with a big dose of *what if.* In doing so, I feel somewhat knowledgeable about what I'm writing but have the freedom to add some interesting twists and turns, along with a little nonsense. The other reason is probably more accurate—my own life, for the most part, has been exceedingly more comical and off the wall than anything I could possibly dream up on my own—so why not take advantage of it? Were there an official category for Stories Sort of Based on a True Story, *Taking Tuscany* would certainly qualify. Here are some facts about my life that have contributed to help make up the story you have just read. Personally, when I read a fictional story, I often wish or hope that some of what I'm reading is true ... especially if I like the story. I guess I'd like to think that some of the good stuff really did happen to someone. I hope you, too, will enjoy finding out that some of the good stuff in *Taking Tuscany* really did happen ... to some degree ... somewhere ... to someone.

ഐൟൟൟ

Let's begin with the notion that A. J. has gone from being a ten-year-old child (in *Saving Sailor*) who lived in the small town of Squawkomish her entire life, to moving halfway around the world to a foreign country. *Taking Tuscany* picks up a few years into this adventure, where A. J. is now thirteen. Just as she was adjusting to an Italian girls' school, she was pulled out two weeks before the end of the school year and put in a new coed school. All of this took place during a very impressionable time in her life.

Enter real life. In 1972, the same year that A. J. was thirteen, coincidently, so was I. I had lived my entire life on the west side of a small lake in Washington state, and my parents decided to move our family of seven across the lake to the east side. Not exactly halfway around the world, but with the drama that comes with being thirteen, it may as well have been. It had taken me thirteen years to establish my popularity status, my lunchroom status, where I sat on the school bus … and suddenly there I was, a nobody, down there at eye level with the rat at the bottom of the totem pole, starting all over again.

I thought being cool consisted of owning a pair of Big Mac overalls or baggy navy jeans and a sailor top. These east-side girls were weird—they had matching three-piece outfits from Nordstrom's—brand new, no less. And they even fit! They couldn't even begin to appreciate the amount of Clorox it took to make new navy jeans look ages old (by soaking them overnight in a tub of bleach)! What was considered cool on the west side of the lake wasn't even on the radar on the east side.

Add to this an abstract, philosophical A. J.-type mind. As a creative little poet and devout Catholic girl, I had an insatiable curiosity for the deeper mysteries of life. I loved, *loved* books—read everything I could get my hands on about heroic and noble people. They intrigued me to no end and I wanted to be one of them. I had lofty moments where I daydreamed of joining the convent or living a life of charity like Mother Teresa. (This continued throughout my life—until I met a really cute guy and married him instead.) At one point some of the new-age teachings of the seventies began to creep into our school. I often engaged my "Search for Identity" teacher in discussions about living the life of an enlightened loner—you know, in a cave, like Siddhartha—to try and figure out my sole purpose of being, or whether my true essence was more yin or yang.

The majority of the east-side girls, however, were more interested in which matching outfit they would wear to school the next day, what car they would get for their sixteenth birthday, or when cheerleader tryouts began. Rather than conform to their shallow material way of life, I spent many solitary hours in my modest bedroom with my mattress on the floor, writing poems of teenage wisdom while listening to the latest Crosby, Stills, Nash & Young album. Favorite song: "Don't Let it Bring You Down." Did I mention this bedroom of mine was inside a five-bedroom waterfront home on Evergreen Point Drive in Medina ... about a mile from where Bill Gates recently built his current home? I'm sure Siddhartha would relate.

So there I was, the teen guru with no followers. And I got lonely. Real lonely. I refused to give in to the superficial game of life going on around me, so I just pulled inside of my melancholy little mind and wrote more poems and rode my huge palomino draft horse, Mooney—who could understand me better than anyone else. My dad had an inkling of what was going on inside his troubled child and gave me the books *I'm Okay, You're Okay,* and *How to Be Your Own Best Friend.* And for a while I was okay and my own best friend. I asked him a few years ago what was going through his mind about me during that time. "You were pretty scary," he replied with a smile.

At one point in *Taking Tuscany,* A. J. alludes to thinking she's possibly possessed by the devil, and asks Sister Aggie about it. As far as thinking I was possessed with the devil goes … I'm sorry to say, but I have to admit that it's true, true, true. I did manage to make one very good friend who was equally as intellectual and "deep" as I was. Karen had a horse named Lucky and together we rode and *philosopholized* (an A. J.-ism) about all of the shallow, empty dweebs among us who had no clue what life was really about. We made up for all of them. Sometimes I thought so hard and so deep I drove myself completely nuts. I asked Karen's mom once what was wrong with me. Why was I so different? Why could I not stop pondering infinity, eternity, and the all the unanswerable mysteries of life that drove me to the brink off insanity? She told me there was a name for my deep thinking. It was called *meditating.* So there I was meditating my way through life at age thirteen, scared to death my mind was going to wander so far out there it would never come back. Leave it to Karen's sixteen-year-old brother to set me straight. "I know what's wrong with you," he offered, free of charge. "You're possessed."

This was not said as a joke. And the movie *The Exorcist* had just come out in the theaters. The entire mention of it freaked the living daylights out of me.

"Why do you think I'm possessed?" I asked.

"Look at you—it's in your eyes."

Great—that explained a lot. Now I felt sick to my stomach every day at school and scared out of my mind. I kept going to the nurse's office saying I didn't feel right. I guess one wouldn't … if she were … possessed.

The school nurse had a little chat with me and finally got it out of me. "I think I'm possessed by the devil."

She was a big black woman who couldn't conceal her huge grin. "Child, you are not possessed. I think maybe you feel a little guilty about something." She asked me about my family life and learned that I was the middle child, a right brainer, emotionally and hormonally out of whack, and a tad on the dramatic side. In other words: the black sheep of the family. That was why I felt bad, she said. "Go home and talk to your mom."

Right. Couldn't do it—for at least a week—until I overheard the school nurse say that she would call my parents if I kept missing class.

So I sat my mom down one afternoon and enlightened her. I told her the whole ugly truth. "Mom, I think I'm possessed by the devil and probably need to talk to the priest. I lie awake all night and drive myself crazy, thinking about things that have no answers, like, how can infinity go on forever and ever and ever … ?"

My mother stared at me … and *laughed.* "I've been telling you you're crazy for years!" She said I was not possessed, and she had a surefire cure. "When those kind of thoughts start up, just think of something a little less complicated—like baking cookies." She said there are just some mysteries God is not going to let us in on until we get to heaven, and things like infinity were one of them.

And that is where we left it. But it did help. I felt delivered—after all, if your own mom doesn't think you're possessed, you probably aren't. I do have volumes of cookie recipes memorized, if anyone's interested.

⟨⟨⟨⟨⟨⟨⟨⟨⟨

Winter was my favorite time of year when it snowed. As far as the hundred-foot ice ditch goes … true! We spent our childhood winters sliding down the world's best and longest frozen ice stream—with the two cutest boys in the school. We'd hit speeds in the double digits. The only drawback was instead of draining off into a field, the ice stream crossed a busy street at the bottom of the hill, so we had to have someone give us an "All clear!" shout before we launched ourselves—then we'd pray it was still all clear by the time we reached the bottom! There were only a few close calls over the years. We also ice-skated under the moonlight on our friend's pond at Silver Bow Farm, with a burn barrel ablaze to keep our hands warm.

About those chutes and ladders … Yes, we really did lower my little brother down the three-story laundry chute on a rope while mom and dad were out to dinner. He was the runt of our family and we still call him "the Ween" to this day. He's a good sport. And we also had a very large housekeeper named Tammy who locked us out of the kitchen while she mopped the floor and ate all of our food.

The character of Annalisa was based largely on a childhood enemy of mine who *always* liked whatever boy liked me, and made my life miserable because of it. And, as a matter of fact, she really did look like a horse. Adding her character to my story is only poetic justice. One of life's finer moments. Especially when she went sailing across the room as a troll doll!

Moving on to the steamy romance scenes: as in, A. J.'s Spin-the-Chianti-Bottle fiasco at Annalisa's birthday party. I have to confess that I have never played spin the bottle … However, I once found myself in an equally traumatic predicament, with an equally valiant escape effort. While other girls my age were going to parties and playing spin the bottle, I was usually at home curled up with a good book, like, Beverly Cleary's *Fifteen*, still holding out for true love. At one point a boy asked me to *go steady* with him (translation: He walked me home from school each day). On our way home one afternoon, we were invited to go along with three other "couples" to a sticker fort, which, they neglected to tell us, had recently been turned into a *kissing* fort. I should have known better—these girls had all been around the block a few times. I had never kissed a boy in my life. For some odd reason, I agreed to go along. I'm not sure what I thought we were going to do there.

Once we were all situated in a circle on the dirt floor in the sticker fort, it didn't take long to figure out that we weren't there to play cards. Two by two, the other couples started locking lips. Eventually all eyes turned to us—the only pair *not* kissing. Talk about peer pressure! Like A. J., I decided that this sticker fort was not the place, nor was this the guy I wanted to make "first kiss" history with. In the books I'd read, the girl always got butterflies in her stomach when it came to her first kiss. Me … I was getting more nauseous by the minute.

Rather than pucker up, I suddenly jumped up, blurted out something brilliant, like, "I have to go do my homework," and fled like Cinderella at the strike of midnight, leaving my abandoned little prince behind.

Have I ever regretted that dramatic exit? Never. A true lady always knows when it's time to go. She will also wait for her *true* prince to come along. That is one thing in life a girl should never compromise on.

Everything in *Taking Tuscany* about loving animals, having a critter cemetery, rescuing dogs from pounds, hiding hamsters from parents (after asking friends to give them to me for my birthday), sobbing my eyes out over sad animal and people stories, wanting to be a veterinarian ... and a writer ... all true. And I'm still hoping to lead the animals through paradise one day in my little white robe ... Lord willing.

I'm happy to report that *somehow* both A. J. and I survived the tumultuous teens. By the time I finished my journey with Siddhartha, he was pretty much finished with me, too. When I stopped to look around, Jesus was the one who hadn't given up on me, and was, *thankfully,* still out looking for me when I realized I was lost and wanted to go home. A Good Shepherd is like that—always keeping an eye out for that one lone straggler.

As for the theme of the story: *The family is everything* ... absolutely true. At the end of the day: Family matters, life is short, eternity is long, heaven is good, and God is love. That is the message.

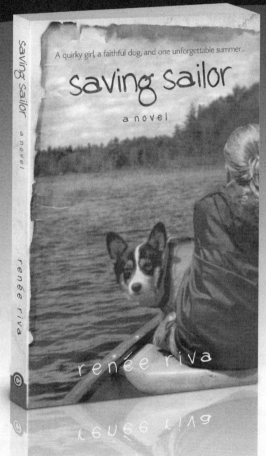

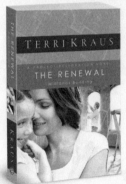